To
Angelina

Realm
of the
Goddess

SABINA KHAN

Enjoy !

Sabina Khan

Library and Archives Canada Cataloguing in Publication

Khan, Sabina, 1968-,
author Realm of the goddess / Sabina Khan.

Issued in print and electronic formats.
ISBN 978-0-9939176-1-5 (pbk.).-- ISBN 978-0-9939176-0-8 (pdf)
I. Title.
PS8621.H353R33 2014 C813'.6 C2014-907147-7
C2014-907148-5

Technical Credits:
Editing: Allister Thompson, Toronto, Ontario, www.altereditorialservices.com
Proofreading: Jennifer McKnight, Toronto, Ontario
Cover designed by Skylar Faith, truenotdreams.weebly.com

To Sonya, Sanaa and Jaanu
Every day you inspire me to be better

ACKNOWLEDGMENTS

It takes a village to write a book. There are many people I would like to thank: Ed Griffin, whose constant encouragement, patience and willingness to read those first awful chapters made me believe that someone other than my family would actually like to read this; my friends whose excitement and support kept me going even when I wanted to give up and last, but not least, the beta readers who gave me incredibly insightful feedback. But most of all I would like to thank my husband Ron, my most ardent supporter and maker of the best mango salsa. He stood by me through the tantrums and the triumphs and I am so grateful to have him in my corner.

ONE

THE DEMON'S EYES were wide open, staring up at me in surprise as blood dripped from my sword and pooled at my feet around his severed head. I looked over to where the rest of his corpse lay, arms outstretched, the right hand still clutching the curved scimitar with which he had planned to finish me off.

Well, who's laughing now? Never underestimate a pissed-off girl with a sword.

I surveyed the battleground on which I stood. Corpses littered the field, demons and mortals alike. In the distance I could see the flames, their smoke turning the air into a thick haze that carried the stench of burning flesh. There was still fighting and I could hear the sounds of battle coming from beyond the hills in the north. I turned around just in time to see another demon heading toward me, clutching a long dagger in his right hand. When he was close enough I caught my reflection in his shield in the split second before he raised his weapon.

I woke up gasping. With my lungs on fire, I opened my eyes. The room spun uncontrollably. My sheets were damp with sweat and for several minutes I just concentrated on breathing, sucking in air, then slowly letting it out. By the time my room came to a standstill, I could breathe normally again. I ripped off the thick comforter, throwing it on the floor. Then I lay back down and stared at the ceiling.

What the hell just happened?

My eyes burned so I closed them for a second. Big mistake. Images from my nightmare seared the insides of my eyelids. I opened them as wide as I could.

Great. Now I'll never get back to sleep.

I reached for my cell phone on the window ledge by my bed. Two o'clock in the morning. Who would be up?

I texted a short message. *Ben, are you up?*

No reply. I put the cell phone back on the ledge. I was too afraid to close my eyes now. But even with my eyes open, I couldn't get those images out of my head. All that blood. And that creature, whatever it was. And why did it feel like a rerun? I couldn't remember when, but I'd had this nightmare before. I shook my head. I was being silly. What I needed was to get back to sleep and to lay off the chips and salsa before bed. I forced my eyes shut. There, that was better. I could see nothing but the redness on the insides of my eyelids. Maybe now I could go back to sleep. I tossed and turned for a while but finally fell asleep.

My alarm woke me at 7:00 a.m. Half-asleep, I stumbled to the washroom. I looked at my reflection in the mirror and winced. My normally smooth brown skin was blotchy today. There were dark circles under my eyes and I looked like I'd spent the night crying. My curly black hair stuck out in all directions, making me look like the troll dolls I'd collected when I was younger. With a groan, I pulled it back into a tight ponytail and began to get ready. A half hour and a lot of under-eye concealer later I was dressed and downstairs, hoping to sneak by my mother, who had probably been awake since the ungodly hour of 5 a.m. She always tried to sneak in a half hour of yoga, a habit instilled in her during her childhood in India. Unfortunately, I had not inherited this trait and she never seemed to get that I was not a breakfast person. For the past three days she'd been trying to make me taste some godawful mushy oatmeal concoction from her latest diet. I had to be careful today. I tiptoed as fast as I could into the den to get my bag. Grabbing my jacket, I snuck to the door. Too late. She'd heard me.

"Callie, do you want some breakfast? I made the oatmeal again. Do you want some?"

Do I want some? Hmm, let's see. I would rather stab myself in the eye with a pencil.

"No, Mom. I have to go early today, I have a test."

I ran out the door, slamming it shut just in time to drown out whatever she was saying. The Seattle sky was predictably overcast as I walked quickly up the street, turning onto the little road that led to the high school. The parking lot was still fairly empty. I made my way to the lockers, put my stuff in and went to my first class. I could barely stay awake, and Ms. Brennemann, my English teacher, wasn't making it any easier. She droned on and on, until, thankfully, the bell rang and it was time for my spare. I walked to the library on the second floor, found a quiet corner to begin reviewing for my History test. It wasn't working. The words blurred on the page and at some point my eyes must have closed. Then the images flashed again, as vivid as though I was actually standing there. In the middle of the battlefield. With blood on my hands. And that smell. My eyes snapped open and I was still in the library. I looked around to see if anyone had noticed me zoning out, but there was only a couple furiously making out behind the sci-fi section. I had to get some fresh air.

I packed up my books and went outside. Seattle was gorgeous in April. The cherry trees were in full bloom and the clouds from this morning had been replaced by sunny skies. Thankfully, no one was there as I took in a few big gulps of air, trying to clear my head. When the bell rang, I headed back inside to my history class, sitting down in my usual spot. The teacher, Mr. Burke, started handing out the test, and when I got mine I turned it over and got started. But the words were swimming on top of the page and I couldn't get them to stay still. My head was pounding and my eyes burned. This was not good. Then something that had been stuck at the edges of my mind popped up. I remembered something about the nightmare. I knew when and where I'd seen those images before.

Ten years before, my parents and I had lived in Kolkata, City of Joy — only I didn't remember a whole lot of joy, just heat. Intense heat and an unbearable stench. It was everywhere, rising from the open sewers in waves and permeating the air so that it stayed with you wherever you went. And all the people. I was used to big crowds and intense heat, but this was ridiculous. You could barely move, and then only at a snail's pace. That was bad, because your first instinct was to get out of the crowds and into a secluded spot, preferably in the shade.

But here on the banks of the Hooghly River in Kolkata in the middle of summer there was no escape. We were visiting the temple of the Goddess Kali, one of the oldest, most revered places of worship in the city.

That morning we tried to get an early start to avoid the crowds that were expected later in the day, but judging by the number of people there already, I didn't know how there could be any more. As we slowly made our way to the temple grounds, the crowd started to thin. I could see many people heading off toward the courtyard while a few entered the main temple that housed the famous statue. Mom had told me that she and Dad had to get special permits to enter the restricted areas on the inside. Apparently some of the worshippers did not come for the Goddess but rather to try to steal the valuable gold ornaments she wore and the ancient artifacts she held in each of her six arms.

"Wow," I said breathlessly as we approached the main temple. "This is amazing." The two-thousand-year-old structure stood majestically, its nine spires rising up to meet the sky. The intricate carvings on the outside ran all the way to the top.

Dad put his arm around my shoulder. "Callie, we'll need about an hour with the head priest to go over our research, but you can look around, okay? Just don't leave the main building. We don't want you getting lost."

I rolled my eyes. "I'll be fine, Dad. Just don't take too long. You promised we would go to the mall after."

Just then the head priest came out to meet us. He was dressed in a cream-colored *dhoti* and a saffron shawl, typical attire for a man of his position. In the middle of his forehead was a vermillion circle surrounded by three white vertical lines and a Y-shape. I knew that the Y-shape meant he was a devotee of the Goddess Kali and Lord Shiva, her consort.

"Ah, Mr. and Mrs. Hansen. You have arrived at last. I trust your journey was pleasant." He greeted us warmly and deftly maneuvered his rather large frame down the stone steps that led down from the temple. He joined his hands in a *namaste*, the traditional Indian greeting, and bowed slightly. After we had all exchanged pleasantries, he led us back up the stairs toward the main temple.

As we entered the inner sanctum, I was struck by how large it was inside. The high ceilings and curved walls gave it a cave-like appearance, while the low, discreet lighting kept the temple cool and dark. After my parents had left with the priest, I looked around first to decide where I was going to start. The main statue stood in the center of the inner temple, while several smaller ones were scattered around the periphery. Each had its own alcove and was cordoned off with thick ropes, no doubt to deter sticky fingers. I decided to leave the Kali statue until the very end and made my way over to some of the smaller ones. I came to a stop in front of a statue of Lord Shiva the Destroyer. There he was in his famous dancing pose as Lord of Dance. I liked this particular version of him, dancing on top of the demon of ignorance. I moved on to the next few statues.

There was one of the Goddess Parvati, Shiva's wife, as well as other minor gods and goddesses of the Hindu pantheon. Finally I came to a stop in front of the statue of Kali. I'd saved the best for last. It was awesome. She was usually depicted as dark and a little frightening, but here she was, bronze and quite beautiful — if you liked strong, powerful and kick-ass women, that is. She was supposed to elicit terror in the evil-hearted, but to me she was the coolest goddess of them all. She was dressed in a beautiful sari made from red silk with gold threads woven in an intricate pattern. Her eyes were black and fierce. Around her neck she wore a necklace of skulls. They belonged to all the demons she had killed. With each of her six arms she carried a weapon. With her three left arms she carried a bow with arrows, a discus and a mace. With the right she carried a thunderbolt, a trident and her sword. Legend had it that all these weapons were given to her by the gods who created her so that she could vanquish the demon king, Mahisha. The gods had each given her their powers so that she was virtually indestructible. My parents, who were both anthropologists, talked about this sort of stuff all the time, so I was quite well versed in Hindu mythology. I stared at the goddess. She looked right back at me, her piercing eyes unwavering. I shook myself mentally, laughing at my silly imagination.

As my gaze wandered down, I noticed something. Centered on the base of the statue was a rectangular engraved metal plate with the words DO NOT TOUCH. I really wanted to touch the goddess. I looked around furtively to make sure no one was watching then gingerly reached out to touch the cool stone surface of the statue. Instantly a painful jolt shot up my arm. I jerked it back and glared angrily at the warning. *Shouldn't it be more specific? Like DO NOT TOUCH UNLESS YOU WANT TO BE ELECTROCUTED.* My arm was still tingling from the shock and I decided it was time to find my parents. As I made my way toward the back rooms, I saw them coming out with the priest, still talking animatedly. I walked up to them.

"There you are, good timing," said Dad, putting his arm around my shoulders. "So, did you have fun looking around?"

"Yeah, loads. How about you guys? Got all the information you wanted?" I looked at my mom, who was trying to stuff a thick stack of papers into her huge bag.

"Yes, Mr. Bhandal has been most helpful. We got a lot more than we expected. Thank you once again, Mr. Bhandal, it's been a pleasure." Mom folded her hands in a *namaste*, as did the priest, and we made our way out of the inner sanctum into the blazing heat of the courtyard. Outside was the usual assortment of beggars and *sadhu*s, the holy men who gave blessings and sometimes told your future. I really wanted to get to the mall, so I was walking quickly down the steps when I almost tripped over an old man sitting on the ground right by the bottom of the steps. Fortunately, I caught myself before I ended up in his lap. I muttered something unintelligible, trying to get around him.

"Don't be so hasty, my child," he said in a raspy voice. "Enjoy the beauty and serenity of this sanctuary." I looked down at him. He was really old, his leathery skin tanned a deep brown from the sun. Little wisps of hair grew from random spots on his otherwise bald head. Although he was looking straight at me, I could see that his eyes were sort of opaque. I realized he was blind and I felt really sorry for being annoyed a moment ago. The poor man probably didn't know how close he was to the steps.

My dad, who had walked ahead, now turned back and came to where I was standing.

"Callie, what are you doing? Let's go."

"Dad," I whispered, "I almost tripped over him. He's blind. Can you give him some money?"

My dad began to fish in his pocket, but then the old man spoke.

"It is not wealth that I seek. I wish to tell your daughter about her destiny."

"It's okay, Baba. Take the money. You don't have to tell her fortune."

"Oh, but I must," the old man replied. "I have been waiting for this moment for many years."

"What does he mean, Dad?" The old man's eyes looked straight at me and I was feeling a little creeped out.

"He probably doesn't want us to think that he's a beggar. Just let him tell your fortune and then we can go."

The old man smiled at me, revealing toothless gums. "Come closer, my child."

I shuffled forward reluctantly and bent down a little as he reached out with his right hand. He placed it on my forehead and began chanting under his breath. Suddenly his body jerked a little and his eyes opened wide. He stared at me as if he had seen a ghost. By this time I'd had enough and I stepped away. His hand fell back on his lap. My dad put his arm around my shoulders and we were turning away when the old man spoke again.

"Your daughter has many difficulties ahead of her," he said.

"Yes, just like every other person," my dad muttered under his breath, clearly not very impressed.

"Do not turn away from your destiny, my child. You cannot fight it."

We began to walk away when he called out once more.

"Take this talisman. It will keep you safe."

I couldn't help myself. I turned around to see what he was talking about. A pendant hanging from a braided black cord dangled from his hand. Against my better judgement I walked back to him and took a closer look. It was a little skull made from mother-of-pearl. I had to touch it, and when I did it felt cool and smooth. I loved skulls. Skull earrings, necklaces, anything. I really liked this pendant.

"Take it, my child. It will keep you safe." I took it from his hands and turned back to look at my dad.

"Can I keep it, Dad?"

"Oh, alright, if you really like it." He turned to the old man. "How much is it?" he asked, fishing in his pocket again.

"It is priceless. There is not enough wealth in the world to buy this pendant, but it belongs to you, my child. You must take it," the old man said. I knew he was trying to sound mysterious and was probably hoping that we would give him a generous amount.

My father shook his head, took a few twenty rupee notes out of his pocket and pressed it into the *sadhu*'s hand. As we were walking away I could feel his eyes following me for a long time. I knew he was blind, but it felt like he could still see. A strange feeling stayed with me all day. That night I had a hard time falling asleep. When I eventually did, I had a nightmare. I was on a battlefield, killing demons with my sword.

TWO

THE SOUND OF the school bell shook me out of my reverie. I was still sitting at my desk in history class, and my test was in front of me. It was blank. I hadn't answered any of it and time was up. I stood up abruptly, knocking over my chair in the process. It crashed loudly to the floor, and of course every pair of eyes in the room turned to me. I could feel the blood rushing to my face. Mr. Burke came over to me, his face a question mark.

"Callie, are you okay?" Then he looked down at the test in my hand. "You didn't answer any of it."

"I'm...I don't feel so good, Mr. Burke. Is there any way I can write the test later?"

Mr. Burke looked at me for a moment before replying, "Yes, of course, Callie. But maybe you should go see the school nurse."

I nodded and picked up my things. I needed to get home and just sleep. I went up to the second floor to get the rest of my books from my locker. I would have to do some catching up this evening. Hopefully Ben could fill me in on whatever I was missing today. The bell rang for lunch just as I reached the lockers, and students were streaming out into the hallway. I was still worrying about my history test, so I was really startled when I felt my locker door hit something hard and then I heard someone swearing. Confused, I looked down and found myself gazing into the brownest eyes I had ever seen. They belonged to the face of a boy I didn't recognize. He still had one hand inside the locker and didn't look too pleased with me. I felt a rush of guilt as his other hand flew to his head and he grimaced.

"I'm so sorry...I didn't see you there. Are you alright?" He pulled his hand out of the locker while he gingerly touched his forehead with the other. It was bleeding. Great. Now I felt awful.

"I think I'll live," he said, one corner of his mouth tilting up in a most appealing way. He looked at his fingers, which had a smudge of blood on them. I pulled a pack of Kleenex from my locker and offered it to him.

"I'm so sorry..." I said again, clearly unable to say anything more coherent. He was really tall, I observed while he dabbed at his forehead with a wad of tissues. "Do you think you should go see the nurse?" He was still bleeding.

"Nah...I'll be fine, it's just a little cut." Of their own volition, my eyes wandered down from his face and I noticed the ends of what looked like a tattoo peeking out from under the neckline of his blue T-shirt. They were some sort of swirly lines, the black ink standing out prominently on his brown skin. I couldn't help wondering what the rest of the tattoo looked like.

"By the way, I'm Shiv," he said, crumpling up the now bloody ball of tissues. It looked like the bleeding had stopped.

"I'm Callie. I don't remember seeing you here before." I knew most of the kids in our grade. It wasn't a very big school, and a lot of us had gone to the same elementary school.

"We just moved here a week ago. So I'm still finding my way around." He looked at me with a mischievous glint in his eyes. "I'm going to get my books out of the locker now," he said, bending down but keeping his eyes on me. "So don't say I didn't give you a fair warning."

God, his eyes were delicious. I felt like I was drowning in a pool of hot chocolate. *Get a hold of yourself, Callie.* I didn't normally swoon over boys, but I had to admit there was something about Shiv. And it wasn't his exotic looks, the dark, smoldering eyes or even the black hair that curled enticingly at the base of his neck. After all, thanks to my mom's Indian side of the family, there had always been plenty of eligible boys paraded in front of me since I'd turned sixteen.

But none of them had interested me even the slightest bit. Most of them seemed to me like momma's boys, incapable of finding a girlfriend on their own. Plus I had always been too focused on school to pay attention to them. Thankfully, my parents treated all interest from the Indian aunties as nothing more than Bollywood-style entertainment. But there was something about this guy that had me all hot and bothered.

I shook myself mentally. What I needed was to pull myself together. Shiv was looking at me expectantly and I realized he was waiting for a witty retort. Unfortunately, I had none so I just gave him a watery smile and blurted out the first thing that came to my mind. "Why don't I show you around? I mean, it's the least I can do, considering that I wounded you."

Really, Callie? I said to myself. *That's the best you can do?*

His eyes brightened and he smiled again. Something warm and fuzzy bubbled deep inside me. Well, maybe this wasn't such a bad idea. I would show him around, he would say or do something asinine and I would get over the instant crush that I seemed to have developed in the last fifteen minutes. End of story.

He got his books out of the locker, slammed it shut with a resounding clang and stood up. We walked together toward the plaza where all the 'cool' kids hung out during lunch. I was strangely curious to see how the Bitch Squad would react to him. That was my personal name for Dahlia Evans and her groupies. I didn't even know all their names, but they hung around Dahlia all the time like bees swarming around their queen. More like Queen Bitch.

As I walked toward the plaza and saw Dahlia and her entourage, I just wanted to see her face when I walked in with Shiv. I checked him out surreptitiously, trying to see him the way Dahlia might. She would see a tall, gorgeous hunk with dark tattoos on his neck and arms. I realized now that there were more swirly lines showing from beneath the sleeves of his hoodie. Once again, I found myself wondering what they looked like.

Dahlia looked up when she saw me approach. I wish I had a video camera to record the way her mouth shifted from its usual disdainful droop whenever she saw me to a slightly open look of disbelief when she noticed Shiv standing next to me. I couldn't help myself. I moved the slightest bit closer to Shiv as we walked right past them to where Ben was sitting with his basketball buddies. Ben was my best friend, had been ever since that day in grade two when he had stood up to Dahlia for me. Dahlia and I had history; I'd hated her since elementary school, ever since she took my lunch box, in which my mom had packed my favorite chutney sandwiches. I loved the potato slices, layered with spicy tamarind and cilantro paste, topped with the salty Amul cheese slices, my favorite cheese from my years in Kolkata.

It was hard at first, after we moved. I had to leave behind all my friends, my cousins and all the things I knew and loved. But I had made friends quickly and adjusted well. But Dahlia, who was used to being the center of attention, didn't appreciate the newbie from India with the weird lunches. So she took my sandwich and held it up for everyone to see. She called it a puke sandwich, squeezing it until the green sauce dripped on the floor. I didn't know what to do, especially when everyone turned to stare and talk about puke. That's when Ben had stood up and walked over to Dahlia. He took the sandwich from her and bit into it. Then he proclaimed that it was the yummiest he'd ever eaten. That was ten years ago. Ben and I had been inseparable ever since. He practically lived at our house, having developed a taste for my mother's spicy Indian cooking. And he always looked out for me.

"Hey guys," I said now, walking up to them. "This is Shiv. He just moved here." The guys all shook hands, mumbling introductions. I could see Ben sizing him up. He was always very protective of me, especially when it came to other guys. Everyone would always tease us about our close relationship, but I never saw Ben in that way. He was my best friend, and nothing was worth jeopardizing the closeness we shared. But I couldn't deny that I enjoyed watching other guys squirm under his intense glare when they first met him. I watched Shiv now and I couldn't help feeling impressed. Ben could be intimidating to those that didn't know what a softie he really was. At six foot two and with a muscular build, he was quite the imposing figure. But

Shiv returned his gaze with an equally unwavering look. He was asking Ben about the basketball team and I noticed that the other guys were warming up to him. But I could read Ben's face well enough to know he wasn't going to make things easy. I decided to rescue Shiv before things became awkward. Just then the bell rang conveniently, signaling the end of the lunch period.

"Guys," I said, "sorry to break this up, but I promised Shiv I would show him where the chemistry class is."

We took off down the hallway toward my next class. I felt a small thrill knowing that I would spend the next period with Shiv in chemistry and that Dahlia would be there too. I knew it was petty, but I deserved to watch her squirm a little. I was enjoying the anticipation on her face when we walked in, so I didn't notice Mr. Burke standing outside his history class until I nearly bumped into him. He was glaring at me.

"Miss Hansen, I'm surprised you are still here." He looked at Shiv and something in his face changed. It was barely discernible, but I caught it nonetheless. "And who is this?"

Shiv put out his hand immediately. "Shiv Kapoor. I just moved here. It's my first day. Callie offered to show me around."

"Did she now?" Mr. Burke said, looking unimpressed. He turned his gaze back to me. "I take it that you're feeling much better now? Then you must be well enough to come to my office after last period." *Great. Now he'll never let me take that test again. Just what I need.*

"Yes. Mr. Burke. I'll be there." I could feel my face getting warm, and I really wanted to just go into class. Mr. Burke gave me one last look of disdain before turning around and heading into his own classroom.

"I hope you're not in trouble because of me," Shiv said as we walked in.

"Don't worry about it. It's fine," I said, walking over to my usual seat. I looked at the empty seat next to me. It didn't look like the kid who usually sat next to me was coming today, which was no surprise since he had only shown up a few times since the beginning of the semester. I gestured to Shiv that he could sit next to me. I had just taken out my chemistry textbook when the clattering of high heels signaled the arrival of Dahlia and her entourage. I wondered how they were still in this class since all four of them seemed to share a brain.

Dahlia walked past me, slowing down just long enough to take a good look at Shiv. Her gaze lingered at the base of his throat, where the dark blue swirls of his tattoo were visible. I watched her mouth go from a sexy pout to an awkward grimace when she realized that Shiv gave her nothing more than a fleeting glance and then turned back to me. Twice in one day. That must have been a record for her. I had a strong urge to let out a hoot of laughter, but I managed to control myself. During the entire period Dahlia and her friends whispered to each other and shot darts at me with their eyes. Shiv was blissfully oblivious to the turmoil he was causing. No doubt the Bitch Squad couldn't figure out why on earth he would want to sit with me. I had never enjoyed chemistry more.

Afterward, I showed Shiv to his next classroom and then didn't see him for the rest of the day. I was preoccupied with why Mr. Burke wanted to see me as I walked down the stairs to his office on the lower level. He was on the phone when I knocked, so he gestured for me to sit down. I looked around while I waited. His office held an eclectic array of décor from all over the world. There were tiny statuettes of gods and goddesses from different cultures lining the shelves on one wall. A stone tablet engraved with what looked like Sanskrit words perched on a metal base on a little table next to his big desk. I wouldn't have pegged him for a mythology buff, but then again, I only saw him in history class. He finished up his conversation and hung up.

"So, Miss Hansen. You said you were feeling unwell earlier today, so I agreed to give you another chance to write the test."

"Yes, and I really appreciate it. I was going to go home, but then I started feeling a bit better and decided to stay," I said.

Mr. Burke looked at me skeptically for a moment.

"Miss Hansen, I feel that your work hasn't been up to your usual standard. I read your last essay and frankly I was not impressed. It lacked focus, and you rambled on quite a bit. I know you have your sights set on a good university, so I will give you a chance to pull up your grade."

I gaped at him in disbelief. I always got good grades and worked really hard for them. I had no idea what he was talking about. I did not ramble.

"I will let you do some extra credit work," he was saying, ignoring my shocked expression. "You will come to my office every day after school and work on the assignments I give you. Is that clear?"

I nodded, not trusting myself to speak. As I got up to leave, I was bristling with resentment. I would have to cut back on my after-school tutoring hours. I'd been saving for a car for summer, and now Mr. Burke was messing everything up. I stomped all the way home, glad that my parents weren't back yet. I just needed to be alone to figure out how I would deal with Mr. Burke and my plummeting history grade. I ate some crackers and hummus then got ready for work.

The tutoring center was a ten-minute drive from my house and when I got there the place was already humming with kids of all ages. I walked up to the reception desk to sign in and say hi to Carla, the owner. Then I went to my usual room to spend the next three hours helping my students with their math homework. On the way home I stopped for a latte because I knew I would have to stay up late doing my homework. By the time I got home it was getting dark and my parents' car was in the driveway. I was lucky they shared a ride to work at the university and I could use the extra car. But that would change in the fall when my dad started his new job and my mom would have to use her own car. Now it looked as if I would have to get used to riding the bus everywhere. When I walked in I found them chatting excitedly. It sounded like she was making dinner plans for the weekend.

"Callie," she said, her voice several octaves higher than usual. "I'm so glad you're home. You'll never guess who I met."

I could guess. She'd met another Indian family and had invited them to dinner. And they had a son who was around my age and, oh my, it was all so exciting.

"I met the nicest couple at the store today...you know that new Indian store around the corner from Starbucks? I was just buying some mangoes and cilantro...I thought Dad could make mango salsa for dinner...what was I saying...oh yes, the couple that I met, they just moved here from California a week ago. But they're actually from Kolkata. So of course I said that they simply had to come over for dinner, and they said this Saturday would be good."

My head was reeling. My mother tended to go off on several tangents during a single conversation. It was hard not to get entangled in her excitement about the new couple, the new store and my dad's mango salsa. I looked at her affectionately. She was a lot to handle after a long day, but there was something very infectious about her enthusiasm for...well, just about anything. She was like that about the course in Eastern mythologies she taught at the University of Washington. There was always a waiting list for the course, and whenever she had students over for her monthly Mythology Club dinners, I could tell that they were enthralled by everything she said. There was something about her, her skin the color of a mocha latte, her long, black hair, usually knotted up in a stylish bun at the base of her neck, and her dark eyes, always intense as if they could see right through a person. But I'd always felt it was her accent that gave her an air of mystery. Her education in one of Kolkata's most prestigious schools had left her with a refined accent when she spoke in English, and my grandparents' love of Bengali literature made her equally enchanting when she spoke in her mother tongue.

I watched her now, getting dinner ready while my dad was making his delicious mango salsa. I liked to watch them together. There was something about the way they moved together, like two parts of a well-oiled machine. Their movements were almost choreographed, as if one could read the other's mind, knowing what their next move would be. They worked perfectly in unison, maneuvering around the kitchen, never bumping into one another as they went about emptying and refilling the dishwasher, getting ingredients out of the refrigerator, putting dishes away. In less than half an hour dinner was ready and we were sitting in our respective recliners. We weren't really a family that ate at the table. When we had first moved to Seattle my mom had gone back to school for her doctorate, and dinners were usually something from the freezer that could be heated up in the oven and eaten in the family room while my mom worked on her thesis. But somehow she'd always made time for me, asking me who my new friends were, inviting them over for cookies and ice cream and throwing the best Halloween parties ever. Over the years eating in the family room had become our thing. That and watching *American Idol*. My mom and I loved the show, and my dad had long ago given up trying to get us to watch football instead.

Now as we ate my mom continued gushing about the new Indian family. In the back of my mind I already knew this must be Shiv's family, and of course I was right. A few minutes later she casually brought up the fact that this new couple happened to have a son and wondered if I had seen him at my school yet.

"Actually, Mom, I hit him in the head with my locker door at lunchtime today," I said nonchalantly, as if violence was just a regular part of my daily routine. I waited a few seconds for this to sink in. And then it all started. My dad just grinned as he calmly ate his chips and salsa while my mom unleashed a torrent of horror at having a clumsy daughter. She calmed down only after I told her he was very nice to me afterwards and that I had made up for it by showing him around. Somewhat mollified, she began to plan what kinds of Indian sweets we could bring them as a welcome gift, which, of course, I would walk over to their house later that evening. I hadn't been planning to tell her about the whole Burke situation, but I couldn't think of a better way to distract her. So I threw myself under the bus.

"Mom, Dad...there's a problem at school," I started. I could literally see their ears perk up. When it came to school, my parents were über-involved.

"What kind of problem, Callie?" my dad said. "Is everything on track with your university applications?" He was very keen for me to attend his alma mater, UW, where he taught anthropology.

"Yes, that's all fine. But Mr. Burke is giving me a hard time. He says my mark is dropping and that I have to stay after school to do extra credit work."

I was hoping they would feel as indignant as I did, but I had no such luck.

"Well, if that's what needs to be done, then just do it," said my dad, ever the voice of reason. My mom looked a little miffed, but I could tell from her lack of argument that she basically agreed.

"I'll have to cut back on my tutoring hours and also my volunteering," I mentioned, hoping that they would realize just how much this would cramp my style. I volunteered at the local retirement home, and I hoped my mother would find it unacceptable that the sweet old ladies there should be deprived of my awesome company. Also, I wouldn't have time to watch *Vampire Diaries*, which I religiously recorded so I could watch at night. Of course, I didn't say that out loud. It wouldn't do anything to help my case.

I was not disappointed. My mother took the bait and said, "Why don't I go and meet with him next week to see if he can't let you bring the work home?" She turned to my dad. "Paul, you're off early on Wednesdays, why don't you come with me?" Dad mumbled something about catching the game on his only evening off, but my mom had selective hearing when it suited her. Either way, I was happy. Hopefully Mr. Burke would get off my back.

"Thanks, Mom, you're the best. I have to work on my essay now, and I have tons of math homework too," I said as I jumped out of my chair, gave both my parents a hug and bounded up the stairs before my mom remembered the sweets.

The next day was pretty uneventful. Shiv and I talked about our parents meeting and rolled our eyes as we commiserated on how embarrassing they could be. Ben came and started talking to me at length about an English essay he was having a hard time with. I found this very suspicious since he wasn't taking English this semester. He ignored the pointed looks I was giving him to hint that I would like to be alone with Shiv. Finally he left, giving me a chance to get some more information out of Shiv.

"So, Shiv, how long did you live in California?" I asked, hoping it would lead to some subtle follow-up questions. Unfortunately, subtlety was not my strong suit.

"We just stayed there for six months," he said. "My dad was supposed to be in charge of a project there, but it didn't work out the way he'd hoped." Just then the bell rang for the next period. We both had chemistry, so we walked down the hall together to our class.

"What about you? What made your family move here from Kolkata?" So much for my follow-up questions. I gave him the same rehearsed answer I'd been giving whenever someone asked me that.

"My dad got a teaching position here and my mom wanted to go back to school. Plus my dad grew up here, and after spending so many years in India, they thought it was time for a change." For some reason I felt guilty about lying to him. But then what would I have said? That I started to have these insanely graphic nightmares and was beginning to lose it, so my parents got scared and relocated us? I could just picture seeing the back of his head as he ran away if he ever found out. Luckily, we had reached the class and chemistry kept us busy for the next hour.

That Saturday, Shiv and his parents came to our house for dinner. My mom had been like a whirlwind all day, cooking up a storm. My dad and I spent the day driving back and forth from the store because she kept forgetting one thing or the other. After the third trip he planted himself on the kitchen stool and said he would help her with whatever she needed to get things ready for that evening, but he refused to go to the store one more time.

My mom was making all my favorite dishes. There was succulent shrimp swimming in fragrant coconut milk, grilled spicy eggplant, basmati rice studded with peas and carrots and a cooling yoghurt and cucumber salad. Then of course there was the sweet yellow rice that my mom only made on special occasions. I loved the pretty edible silver paper she used as a garnish. And it was accompanied by the traditional Indian rice pudding I could never keep my hands off.

They arrived around seven. Shiv grinned at me conspiratorially behind our parents' backs. I was glad they had come. Even though I had only met Shiv a few days ago, it felt like we'd known one another much longer. I was very comfortable around him, which was good because I was pretty sure that I was developing a major crush. I looked around for him at school whenever we didn't have classes together. Usually I talked to Ben about my crushes, but the last few days, whenever I met up with Ben in our usual place, Shiv would join us and I got the distinct feeling that Ben did not like him. Plus I'd been busy with my extra after school work, so I hadn't had any time to spend alone with Ben. Either way, I figured he would just get over it. I had misgivings about many of the girls that Ben had dated in the past, and I always managed to keep my most negative thoughts to myself. Things had a way of working themselves out where Ben was concerned.

I looked at Shiv now, sitting in our living room with his parents. He looked a lot like his dad, Dev. The same dark skin, curly hair and intense brown eyes. His mother, Nina, was a total contrast. She was petite, with delicate features and black hair that hung down her back in a long braid. It was a nice evening. Our parents got along really well and Shiv and I talked about our years in Kolkata. It turned out we had acquaintances in common, but Shiv had been there more recently, so he updated me on some of them. Nina asked to use the washroom, and after I showed her where it was, I went upstairs to grab some old pictures of my school friends in Kolkata. As I was coming back down the stairs I could hear voices floating up. I didn't pay much attention until I heard my name. I stopped on the third step and listened, not sure what I was eavesdropping on.

"She has to find out sometime," Nina was saying. Then I heard Dev's reply and it chilled me to the bone.

"She might not make it, Nina. You know what happened to the other girls."

I must have shifted my weight from one foot to the other because the stair I was on squeaked and Nina's head shot out from around the corner.

"Oh, there you are, dear," she said, showing no signs that anything strange was going on. "We were wondering where you'd gone off to."

"Umm...I was just getting this to show Shiv," I said, holding out the album and trying hard not to let any panic show on my face.

"Oh, let me see," Nina said, taking the album out of my hand. "Are these photos from your school in Kolkata?" She turned to Dev, who was watching me with a strange expression. "Dev, look...maybe Shiv will know some of the kids in here. Such a small world." I didn't know how much longer I could stay calm. I just wanted them to leave so I could tell my parents what I'd overheard. I went to the kitchen, where my mom was getting the dessert tray ready.

"Mom...I need to —" I began, but my mom cut me off.

"Oh good, Callie, you're here," she said without looking up from the dish of rice pudding she was garnishing with raisins and pistachios. "Come help me with the *chai*."

When I didn't respond, she looked up. Whatever I was feeling must have been on my face, because the next minute she was by my side.

"Callie, honey, what's wrong? You look so pale? Are you feeling alright?"

She looked so worried that I decided not to say anything for the moment. I didn't want her to start asking too many questions. I didn't want her to find out about my nightmares either. When I first started having them in Kolkata, my parents had been very stressed about me. I didn't want them to go through all that again. I hoped that maybe all this was happening because it was a stressful time waiting to hear back about scholarships and university admissions. I was sure the nightmares would go away once I knew what I would be doing after high school. So I lied now and put on a brave face. I would talk to Shiv later and see if I could find out what his parents were talking about.

"I'm fine, Mom," I said, smiling and giving her a hug. "I just have a headache, that's all." I started putting the teacups my mom had inherited from my grandmother on the silver tray that was part of the set. As a little girl I used to love having pretend tea parties with my cousins, and my grandmother would always let me use her fancy tea set. When my mom protested that I might break something, my grandmother would always tell her that the teacups weren't as important as seeing her granddaughter enjoy herself. I loved my sweet grandmother and I made sure to be extra careful with the cups. I never did break a single one, and when we left Kolkata, she insisted we take it with us. My mom didn't use it very often, but when she did it always brought back sweet memories of my grandmother, in her white sari and the little gray bun at the nape of her neck. She would tell me stories of gods and goddesses, and when I first started having nightmares, she told me that maybe I was a little goddess myself and that the dreams were just memories of my past lives.

When we walked back into the living room, my

dad was telling them the story about how he'd met my mom, as a graduate research assistant in Kolkata. Nothing looked amiss. Shiv's parents seemed to be having a great time. Shiv looked up as I walked in with the tray and got up to help me. I started to think that maybe I had imagined the whole thing. I was sleep-deprived, after all.

The rest of the evening went by fast, and then it was time for Shiv and his family to leave. I helped my parents clean up and then we all went to bed exhausted.

The next few days passed with the usual monotony of school, homework and chores. Finals were fast approaching and the teachers were piling on the work. I had to stay after school from the beginning of the week. The first day Mr. Burke sat there, and I felt as if he was watching me the whole time. It creeped me out a little, but there was really nothing I could do. Then it was Wednesday and my parents had an appointment to talk to Mr. Burke. I was beginning to regret that decision and hoped it wouldn't make things even weirder for me. My parents had asked me to meet them by Mr. Burke's office, so I waited for them after school. When they arrived we all went into his office. I could see that they were as impressed by the décor as I had been. After the usual pleasantries were over, my mom got right to the point.

"Mr. Burke, Callie tells us she is not doing too well in your class."

"That's right. Mrs. Hansen, her grade has dropped

a lot. I have offered to let her do some work for extra credit."

My dad spoke up this time. "Mr. Burke, we're just a bit surprised because she was sitting at 95 percent just a couple of weeks ago. How could her grade have dropped so much in such a short time?"

Mr. Burke took off his glasses and leaned forward. "Mr. Hansen," he said, his face a stony mask. "Have you asked your daughter why she might be doing so badly? I find her unfocused in class, and her last two essays have not been up to my standard." He was pointing a finger at my dad, jabbing it in his direction, punctuating his sentences.

I had never seen Mr. Burke like this. There was something distinctly hostile and menacing about his expression and tone. I glanced at my parents and realized that they were staring at Mr. Burke's hand, which was still in midair. I looked too and saw a tattoo on the inside of his right wrist. I couldn't be sure but it looked like the head of a bull or something with horns. My parents were still staring, their faces ashen, as if they had seen a ghost. I expected them both to be quite upset with the things that Mr. Burke was saying about me. I definitely hadn't expected this. I had never known my parents to be so intimidated. They got up hurriedly and ushered me out of the office, up the stairs and out into the parking lot. I tried to stop them but they were adamant, not saying a word until we got home. As soon as we got inside I turned on them.

"Mom, Dad, what was that? Why did we run out of there like that? Mr. Burke is going to think you guys are so weird." I was really upset and I wanted an explanation.

"Callie, listen," my dad said. "We don't want you to stay after school anymore."

"What do you mean? I have to stay. How am I supposed to finish all the extra-credit work he's giving me?" My voice had risen a couple of octaves and I was beginning to really lose my cool.

"Callie, just listen to us," my mom pleaded. "We don't want you around that Mr. Burke any more than you have to be. So come home right after school."

"You always have a problem with people, Mom. Why can't you for once just let me deal with my own problems? God, you two really need to get a life." With that I stormed off. I ran up the stairs to my room and slammed the door. I was furious. I didn't know exactly why Mr. Burke suddenly had it in for me, but I was willing to deal with a little extra work if it meant I would keep my grade in the class. The deadline for sending in final grades was coming up really soon and I had no time to waste. I fumed for a while longer, but finally fell asleep.

Sleep didn't bring any rest for me, though, since I was plagued by the same nightmare. The same demons and frightful creatures on a bloody battlefield. The next morning I woke up bleary-eyed and with a massive headache. I was glad that my parents left for work really early on Thursdays because I was in no mood to deal with them this morning. I got ready and walked to school, just as the five-minute warning bell rang. I had math first and then history. Mr. Burke wasn't any grumpier than usual and I hoped he'd met his fair share of over-protective parents and wouldn't hold yesterday's events against me. But then in the middle of the period the pounding in my head got so bad that I was overcome by nausea. Mr. Burke was giving us time to work on our research essays, so I went up to him and asked if I could be excused.

"Again, Miss. Hansen? This seems to be turning into a habit." By this point I was just trying not to throw up all over him, so I didn't reply. He looked at me intently.

"Is there something you'd like to tell me, Miss Hansen? Something that might be bothering you?" There it was. That weird, menacing tone, as if he knew something and just wanted me to admit it. A fresh wave of nausea rose and the pounding in my head became unbearable. Mr. Burke pulled a cell phone out of his coat pocket and pressed the screen. I had no idea what he expected me to do, but I wasn't going to wait around to find out. I mumbled an apology and ran out of the room, down the hall to the washrooms. I made it just in time. After the heaving stopped and there nothing left to throw up, I went to the sink and splashed cold water on my face. Then I put a wet paper towel on the back of my neck. The coolness felt so good that I sat down on the floor with my back against the wall to rest for a minute. I needed to get home and sleep it off.

I got up, went to the office and told them I was sick and was going home. I grabbed my books from my locker. At the exit, I pushed open the heavy double doors and went outside. The fresh air revived me a little as I went around the corner and headed toward the staff parking lot. It was sunny today for a change and I took off my jacket as I walked through the parking lot toward the little street that would take me to my house a couple of blocks away. I was deep in thought about my history class as I crossed the street and started walking down the hill that led to my house. I was just a couple of houses away when the screech of car tires ripped through the air. Startled, I turned my head just in time to see a dark blue SUV racing down the street. It was heading straight toward me.

I was about to jump out of the way when a dark shape came flying at me and knocked me to the ground. Stunned, I tried to get up but buckled as a sharp pain shot through my ankle. I looked to see if the car was still there but only caught a glimpse of it as it disappeared around the cul-de-sac. Then I noticed Shiv standing there.

"Shiv, how did you...? Did you see that?" I spluttered, pulling out my cell phone then realizing I hadn't noticed the licence plate. "Shiv, did you see the licence plate?"

"No, I'm sorry, Callie, all I saw was that car

coming toward you, and I had to save you." Shiv's voice was shaking a little, and he was looking up and down the street as if he thought the car might come back. "Let's get you into the house. I have to make sure that you're okay." He tried to help me up and I winced when I put weight on my right ankle. I sucked in a breath and tried again. It still hurt a lot but I felt I would be able to walk the rest of the way home.

Shiv put an arm around me. "Try to use my arm for support, and don't put too much pressure on that ankle," he said as we slowly started making our way down the street. When we crossed my front yard to the steps, I noticed the front door was ajar. There was no car in the driveway. Confused, I forgot the pain in my ankle as I shrugged off Shiv's arm and went up the stairs. I was almost at the door when Shiv grabbed my arm none too gently and pulled me back.

"What are you doing?" I said, pulling my arm from his grasp.

"I don't think you should go in there," Shiv whispered. "Why is the door open? I don't think your parents are home."

"Well. That's what I am going to find out," I said testily. An uneasy feeling was starting to bloom in my gut.

"Maybe I should go in first?" Shiv said, moving to stand in front of me.

Why, are you a ninja? I thought. *Be nice, Callie...he's just trying to help.*

"Sure, okay, whatever. Just be careful." I didn't want anything to happen to him, because he was trying to help me out. I let him walk in ahead of me, waited a second until he turned the corner into the living room and then followed him in. Since he was checking out the downstairs, I decided to go upstairs. On the way I grabbed a golf club from my dad's bag next to the hallway closet. Wielding it expertly like Kate Beckett from my favourite TV show, *Castle*, I walked stealthily up the stairs to my room, which was on the right at the end of the hallway. I poked my head in first, then went in and checked behind the door and inside my messy closet. As if anyone could find space to hide there. I was positive a burglar would rather get caught than try to untangle himself from the wormhole of clothes and shoes that was my closet.

Satisfied there was no one lurking in my room, I tiptoed gingerly across the landing to my parents' bedroom at the other end of the hallway. The door was half open and I could hear a buzzing coming from inside. That was strange. I walked in expecting to see some bugs that had come in through the bathroom window that my mom always forgot to close before she left the house. What I saw instead made me freeze on the spot. Someone was standing at my mom's armoire. The doors were open and this person was in the process of stealing something from it.

I reached my hand into my pocket for my cell phone, and at that exact moment the thief stepped away from the armoire and saw me. And I saw him. Only it wasn't a man. Or a woman. I didn't know exactly what it was, but my brain couldn't process what I was seeing in front of me. It was a creature of some sort, with the torso and legs of a man. But it was the head that made a cold fear grip my insides like a vise. I realized where the buzzing was coming from. The creature's head was sort of oblong and it was covered in what I could only describe as giant stingers like those on a wasp. They moved in a snake-like motion around its face, emitting a buzz. I wanted to scream, but my throat couldn't make the sound. The creature seemed as stunned as I was, but it recovered a lot faster. It moved toward me with alarming speed and my only thought as it closed in on me was that Shiv was still downstairs and the creature would get him. Then something flew through the air from behind me and hit the creature right in the middle of its torso. The monster exploded, sending hundreds of stingers flying through the air and some into me. When the blinding pain hit I fell backwards. But instead of landing on the hard floor as I'd expected, I felt someone's arms catching me from behind. I turned my gaze upward and saw Shiv's face. His deep brown eyes were the last thing I saw before blackness overtook me.

THREE

I WAS DREAMING. I stood on a battlefield again. The sword I held glinted in the sunlight. I looked down and saw that something was engraved along the entire length of the blade. It was in a language I did not recognize.

Then blackness again.

The sound of voices floated into my ears.

"…can't protect her from it any longer." The voice sounded familiar, but my brain could not string together any coherent thoughts. Then other voices, unclear as they faded away.

The light changed. It was bright, but then the pitch black took over.

The stinging brought me back. I tried to open my eyelids, but the light hurt. I closed them again.

"I was able to remove most of the stingers. Some of them were embedded deep in the skin. They will come out eventually." I didn't recognize this voice, but it brought back a deluge of memories. My parents' bedroom, that creature...then the pain, like a thousand needles puncturing my skin at once...and Shiv. I could feel my eyes getting heavier and then...nothing.

When I came to I was cold. I opened my eyes slowly; even the little sliver of light coming through the tiny parting in the curtains sent barbs of pain through my eyes. I sat up, careful not to move too fast, and winced as my head protested nonetheless. I turned my head slowly to get my bearings. As far as I could tell I was in someone's bedroom, a girl's room. I knew this from the abundance of purple everywhere. There was a white dresser with a big mirror against one wall. A small white desk sat in the corner, with a purple chair tucked underneath. Lilac curtains framed a large bay window. My brain was foggy. I closed my eyes and sighed from the relief of shutting out the light. How long had I been out? Images flashed in my mind. Shiv's face floated into my inner vision. A creature...attacking. Then there was a deluge of memories and everything came flooding back. My parents' bedroom, the attack, the creature exploding and then the pain that had wiped out everything else. Other bits and pieces of memory made their way back until they fit together like the pieces of a puzzle. Someone had saved me...Shiv. I remembered now. I looked into his eyes before I blacked out. He must have brought me here.

I stood up and immediately regretted that decision as the walls began to dance around me. I closed my eyes for a moment then opened them again. To my relief, the walls stood absolutely still. I took a small step, then another, hesitating before each movement, and walked gingerly to the door. I opened it, stuck my head out, stepped into a hallway and looked in both directions. There were wall sconces lining each side. Ornate frames held pictures of people I didn't know, but they all looked Indian. I assumed Shiv had brought me to his house. Down the hallway to my right I could see the top of a staircase, so I began to walk that way. When I reached it, I looked over the banister and saw that the staircase wound around a huge pillar in the middle of a large foyer. Voices floated up and I went down the steps, following the sound. It led me to a set of double doors just off the foyer. I stopped in front of them, not knowing if I should go in. I could still hear muted voices, so I was startled when the doors suddenly opened and Shiv stood in front of me.

"Callie...what are you doing down here? You should be in bed." He was obviously concerned and looked back to where I could see his parents walking toward us.

Nina stepped around Shiv and took my hands in both of hers.

"Callie, my dear, how are you feeling? You had us worried," she said, not unkindly.

"I'm a little dizzy, to be quite honest. Do you mind if I sit down?" I realized that the little walk from the bedroom had left me a bit winded and unsteady on my feet.

"Of course, come in and sit by the window here," Nina said, taking my arm and guiding me to an armchair. I must have squinted, because Dev walked over and adjusted the blinds so the sunlight wasn't streaming into the room anymore. I sat down while the others gathered around me. We were in some sort of library, judging by the dark bookshelves that lined all four walls. It was an enormous room with a fireplace in one corner and a large desk in front of it. It all looked antique; the furniture had elaborate carvings on the legs and sides.

"What happened exactly?" I asked, looking up at them.

"How much do you remember, Callie?" Shiv asked.

"Well...I remember going home early from school and then...that car...it was going to hit me. And then...someone was in my parents' bedroom. Not someone..." I looked up at Shiv. "What was that thing? Was it real?"

Shiv was looking down at my arms, so I followed his gaze. I gasped involuntarily. My arms looked as if they had been attacked by a thousand thumbtacks. The holes punctuated both my arms like little periods. So — I hadn't imagined the bizarre attack.

I looked at him incredulously. "What was that thing? What did it do to me?"

The three of them exchanged looks. I knew it couldn't be anything good.

Dev spoke first. "Callie, *beti*," he began and my heart lurched a little. He was using the term of endearment for a daughter, which meant something awful had happened. "There is no easy way to tell you," he continued, sitting down on the armchair next to me and putting his hand on my right shoulder. "You were attacked by a demon."

It took my brain a second to register the words. A demon. Okay. I drew in a slow breath, a really slow one, and held it, giving myself time to figure out just how to react to this. I looked at Shiv and Nina, trying to read their faces, but they did not look surprised at all. I had to say something.

"Are you sure? A demon?" I asked weakly, not wanting to insult this nice man. But I did think he was insane. Maybe that was why he had to leave California.

"Callie," Shiv said, looking at me as if I was the crazy one. "I know it's really hard to hear, but there's something you need to know." Yes. I needed to know the number of their psychiatrist. Hopefully they were getting a family discount. I knew I needed to get out of there. My parents were probably frantic with worry. Where were they anyway? Shouldn't they be looking for me?

"You know what," I began, "I'm so grateful that

you've taken care of me." I turned to Shiv. "Shiv, I owe you big-time for getting me out of the way of that crazy driver. If there's anything I can do for you..." I stood up. "I really should be going now. Thanks again."

"Callie, you can't go back to your house. It's not safe," Dev said. He took my arm again and gently but firmly directed me back into the chair.

"I'm sure it'll be fine," I said. "My parents will be home by now and they'll take care of it."

"Callie...your parents...they're gone." Nina looked at me and the look in her eyes told me that something had gone terribly wrong. I was in denial, but I knew something strange had happened at my house. Suddenly, a wave of nausea hit me hard and I took a deep breath. My head was spinning and I felt the room fading away. I could not pass out again. I willed myself to focus and stay conscious, but I lost the battle and once again everything went black.

When I came to, I could hear Shiv's voice.

"The venom is still lingering, Dad," he said. "She has to take it easy. Doctor Gupta said he took out as many stingers as he could, but the poison was already in her system."

"I know, son, but she has to learn the truth," Dev said. I opened my eyes carefully. I was still in the armchair. I must have only passed out for a few moments. I tried to sit up, but my head felt heavy and my arms were beginning to throb.

"Why did you say that my parents were gone?" I

said, sitting up straight and looking directly at Nina.

"Callie...they were taken. That's why you can't go back to your house. It's not safe." I felt panic rise, but I had to stay in control this time. Something very weird was going on.

"Who took them?" I asked, my voice sharper than I intended. "And why haven't you called the police?"

"The police cannot help in this matter, Callie," Shiv said. "Look, I know it's all very confusing to you right now, but if you let us explain, it will make sense."

My gut told me that I should listen to what they had to say. Plus it wasn't as if I had the strength right now to jump, run home and find out what was going on. I only had to look at my arms to know that something had attacked me and that Shiv had saved me from being killed. I decided I was going to trust my instincts and let them say their piece.

"Okay," I said, looking around at the three of them. "Tell me what's going on."

Dev spoke first. "Callie, how much do you know about Hindu mythology?"

"A lot, actually, thanks to my parents. But what does that have to do with anything?"

"Everything, actually," Shiv said. But he let his dad continue.

"You know about Kali, yes?"

Yes, I knew about Kali. I'd only been named after her. Of course, my parents had picked a Westernized version of the name, but Kali had been the inspiration.

They had both wanted a daughter who was strong-willed and fearless. I didn't know how well that worked out, since I was deathly afraid of spiders and deep water.

I nodded.

"There was a time when humanity was overwhelmed by the reign of the Asuras, the demons. The people felt abandoned by the gods and appealed to them to save them from the horrors that they were being subjected to. Mahisha was the king of the Asuras. He could not be defeated...by man or by the gods, many of whom responded to humanity's cries for help." I had learned this myth on my grandmother's lap as a little girl. I could still recall with startling clarity the faraway look on her face as she would regale me with her favorite tales of gods and goddesses. I knew what had happened next. The lesser gods, frustrated by their failures, went to the great Trinity, Indra, Brahma and Shiva and appealed to them for help in destroying Mahisha. The gods grew angry when they heard of the evil doings of Mahisha and from their wrath Kali was created, the ultimate goddess, Destroyer of Evil. My grandmother used to tilt my face up by the chin, look into my eyes and tell me that she knew one day I would go out into the world and destroy evil too, just like Kali. Now I wondered if there was any point to what Shiv and his parents were saying.

"Why are you telling me about these stories? I heard them all as a child. What does any of this have to do with my parents?" Normally I would never use this tone with adults, but now was not the time for politeness. If they were right and something had happened to my parents, I needed to find out quickly. And my patience was wearing thin. Plus I was afraid I might pass out again at any time.

"These are not just childhood stories, Callie," Nina said. "They are real events and everything that you heard was true. Mahisha was real, Kali was real...*is* real." Nina's face was flushed and she began to pace as she continued. "When you heard about the great battle between Kali and Mahisha, you heard that in the end Kali destroyed him. Even though he was a shape-shifter, right?"

I nodded and tried to recall details my grandmother had told me. According to her, Mahisha escaped every attempt at capture by changing from a bull to a lion and even into a man. But finally Kali managed to cut off his head while he was in bull form.

"Well, that's not exactly what happened," Nina said. I looked at her in confusion.

"What did happen exactly?" I asked.

"Kali was betrayed. It was a plot to destroy her before she could destroy Mahisha."

"But I thought she was created to be indestructible," I said. I remembered she was given gifts by each of the gods of the Trinity from whose wrath she was created. Indra gave her a thunderbolt, Shiva a bow and arrows, and Brahma a sword.

"That's right, but no one knows what happened exactly," Nina said. "There are those who believe that the Trinity feared that she might become too powerful and might try to overthrow them, so..."

All this was making my head spin. And I still didn't know what was going on.

"Why are we talking about this?" I asked. "We should be making sure that my parents are okay." I looked at Shiv pleadingly.

"That's just it, Callie. We know who took your parents...at least we have a pretty good idea who is behind all this," Shiv said.

"Then why —" I started, but Shiv interrupted me.

"Your parents were taken by demons. You were attacked by a demon. We are pretty sure that it was one of Mahisha's demons." He looked at his father triumphantly, as if to say *See, that wasn't so hard to blurt out, was it?*

I was numb. Nina sat down next to me again.

"Callie, the thing is...Mahisha was never killed. He was very nearly destroyed, but he was very powerful, and although it has taken him centuries, he is regaining his strength. In the meantime he has been gathering an army of loyal followers who have been slowly spreading corruption and evil. There are many who believe that he is rising again, and when he does, there is only one who can destroy him."

"Okay, I guess that must be Kali then. But she's not here, is she?" Frustration was making me snarky and I was getting tired of all this. Some of my strength was also coming back and I was ready to leave. I stood up. "I'm going to my house, and if my parents aren't there, I will call the police," I said with more conviction than I felt.

"Callie, don't leave. You have to trust us...trust me," Shiv pleaded. "There is a reason why this is happening. And it has to do with you."

I just stood there waiting for him to continue. I really had nothing more to say to him.

He must have sensed I was wavering, because he rushed his next words.

"Kali is reborn whenever evil threatens to overpower good. With the threat of Mahisha looming, we knew that she would be reincarnated soon. That's what led us to you."

FOUR

SHIV LOOKED AT his parents. So did I. I was completely taken aback.

"What do you mean...led you to me. Who are you people?" I felt I should make a run for it, but there was something in their faces that made me want to stay and see how this played out. They were looking at me as if...as if they were seeing something...I didn't know what.

"We are Rakshakari," said Dev. "Protectors of the Goddess. A council was formed five thousand years ago to protect Kali when she failed to destroy Mahisha and a conspiracy was suspected. We are descendants of the original Rakshakari. We are guided to the Goddess whenever and wherever she is reborn. And we were drawn to this place...to you."

"Why me?" An image flashed in my mind from my nightmares. A wild-eyed girl with a sword, blood and sweat staining her face. Could it be...no, it wasn't possible. These people were insane and I should get as far away as possible from here. But...my nightmares...that creature.

"Callie, have you ever dreamed about something really strange?" Nina asked, looking at me intently. It made me uneasy. Had my parents mentioned something to them? We never talked about it, but...why was Nina asking me? How could she possibly know? They were looking at me expectantly.

"What do you mean, strange?" I wasn't going to tell them anything until I was a hundred percent sure they were not crazy.

"Kali has been reborn a few times over the last five thousand years," Nina replied. "Evil doesn't really take a vacation." Her feeble attempt at levity did not amuse me.

"Each time Kali was reborn as a human avatar, the subject experienced violent nightmares and started exhibiting signs of severe mental stress," Dev said. "Not every girl was strong enough."

"What happened to those girls?" There was a slight quiver in my voice, which I hoped no one noticed. When I'd started having the nightmares I had almost suffered a nervous breakdown. My parents had taken me to a therapist and my grandmother had taken me to see a *sadhu*, a holy man in some remote village, but in the end my parents had to uproot their lives and move thousands of miles away to start over. All because of me. But the nightmares had stopped until after my seventeenth birthday. And now these people were insinuating that I might be some sort of reincarnation of Kali. They hadn't actually said it yet, but I could see it in their faces. Especially Nina, who was looking at me with a sort of fanatic light in her eyes. Shiv was answering my question, so I turned to him.

"You have to realize that the reincarnations happened centuries ago. Those girls didn't have access to any information or anybody to help them, really. It was more difficult for the Rakshakari to locate them. Some of them succumbed to mental despair. Some were burned as witches. Some didn't make it, even though the Rakshakari got to them. Not all of them had the psychological strength to withstand such a manifestation."

"Okay, so let's say, hypothetically, if someone had these nightmares, but they stopped after a while and then started again abruptly, what would that mean?" I knew I was being naïve thinking that they wouldn't see right through me, but I wasn't ready to admit or accept anything yet.

"Well, Callie, it would mean that the time has come for the Goddess to manifest in you completely," Dev replied. "It also means that the threat is closer than we thought."

"And my parents?" I asked, a pang of guilt

shooting through my chest at the realization that this was not a myth, and there was no denying that they had been taken. Something deep inside me knew, had always known, maybe, that I was different. But never in my wildest fantasies had I ever imagined this. My grandmother's face flashed before me suddenly in my desperation. She would have known what to do.

"Your parents will be alright, Callie." Dev came over and put an arm around my shoulders. "They would never dare to hurt them. They have only kidnapped them to draw you out."

I fell back onto the armchair, deflated. Everything was out of control. Every instinct in me was telling me that this was real, that there was no denying it anymore. But I had no idea what I was going to do, what I was *supposed* to do. How was I going to save my parents?

"So what do I do next?" I asked.

Shiv sat down beside me and took my hand. He looked into my eyes and for a moment he was silent. "Look Callie," he finally said. "You are not alone in this." He looked up at his parents, who were nodding.

"Yes, Callie, we are all with you," said Nina, sitting down on the other side of me. "This is what we have been waiting for...what we were born to do. We are sworn to protect the Goddess and we will defend you with our lives." She was freaking me out with her fervor, that crazy glint in her eyes again. But I did feel slightly less panicked.

"Can we go back to my house?" I looked at them

pleadingly. "I need to see if there's anything...a clue...something that can help us find my parents."

"Yes, I think you and Shiv should go. Callie, you should also pack some of your stuff while you're there. You'll be staying with us from now on," said Dev. "Nina and I will go to the Council and catch up the rest of the members."

He didn't really ask me if I was fine with his decision, and I bristled slightly at that. But then again, I knew that keeping me safe was his first priority now that my parents were gone. He wasn't just going to let a young girl stay on her own, goddess or not.

He turned to Shiv. "Be careful, son," he said quietly. "Callie, are you sure you're up for this?"

I stood up. I felt dizzy for a moment, but then it was gone. "Yes, I am. Let's do this."

Shiv led me from the library down the hall to the front door. A silver BMW was parked in the driveway. I raised my eyebrows slightly at him as he opened the door to the passenger side. I got in and he drove us down the street to my house. Even though it would have been just as easy to walk, I was relieved that at least we'd have a way to get away fast if things got hairy. We didn't talk until we reached the front door. As we approached it I noticed a transformation in Shiv. Gone was the laid-back, smiling guy I had grown to like...a lot. He was replaced by an intense, focused bodyguard who moved with a stealth I had only seen in spy movies. He pulled out a dagger from the back of his waistband. It was short, with a curved blade, but it was the handle that caught my eye. It looked like it was made of bronze and there were etchings of some sort running all the way up and down and around the sides of it.

Shiv motioned for me to stay behind him and then went absolutely still, his head cocked slightly to one side, listening. He checked the door handle, jiggling it lightly. It was loose, probably from when the demons had broken in before. He ran his fingers along the doorframe, checking the wood. I hadn't noticed before but there were marks on one side that looked like someone had dragged their fingernails across. An image flashed before me of my mom being forced out by the demons. She would have fought them with all the strength she possessed. I shook my head to get the picture out of my mind. Then I headed into the house, following close behind Shiv, who had just gone in. He did a sweep of the downstairs first, going methodically from part of the floor to another, always watching for anything that might be a threat. I stayed close by his side, quite fascinated by how thoroughly he checked everything.

When he was satisfied, we headed upstairs. Nothing seemed out of place — except for the fact that my parents weren't here and I didn't know when I would see them again. I pushed down the lump that had been stuck in my throat ever since I'd realized my parents were gone. There was no time to wallow in my emotions right now. We checked the rest of the lower floor in silence then went upstairs to my bedroom. I remembered too late that my room was a mess and that Shiv was going to see it. Hopefully he'd think that whoever took my parents made the mess. There was nothing there, so we made our way to my parents' bedroom. As soon as we walked in, the stench hit me. It smelled like sweat and feet and rotting eggs all at once. I cringed and looked at Shiv.

"That would be dead demon smell," he said with a crooked grin. "It can get really nasty, you know." I didn't know. It wasn't as if hanging around demons was what I did for fun. This was all so surreal. I felt as if I was watching myself go through all this. The stench was making me gag and I could only hold my breath for so long. I opened the sliding door, stepped out onto the little balcony and took big gulps of the fresh, demon-free air. The balcony overlooked a green belt that led into a golf course. I had loved hanging out here with a glass of milk and a plate of cookies while my mom got dressed up for one of the many Indian social functions that took place throughout the year. I would watch her drape a *sari* around her, put on matching glass bangles and stick a little sparkly *bindi* on her forehead. Now I looked in and saw their room in disarray, the comforter on the floor, a large gash through it. There was a dark stain on the cream-colored rug at the foot of the bed. That was where the demon had been standing when Shiv killed it. I felt anger well up at the thought that someone had just walked in and taken my parents. All because they wanted to get at me. I walked back in, determined to find something to tell me where they might be. Shiv was standing over the stain on the rug.

"I don't think that's coming out," he said, shrugging apologetically.

"Hey, you saved my life, Shiv. I'm sure my parents will get over the rug," I said, flashing him a smile. It was true. When they were back, they would not care about it. They would gush about how Shiv was such a hero and that he was so handsome, etc. And I would roll my eyes and tell them to stop trying to get me married off. And everything would be normal again.

I sighed, wishing I could turn back time. But that wasn't going to happen and I had to find something. I started at one end of the room and looked at everything methodically. The picture frames were still in their places on the wall. My mom's collection of sequined purses hung from their hooks under my baby pictures. I looked at the dresser. Everything was where it should be. I was standing in front of the armoire now, and something clicked in my memory. This was where the demon was standing when I walked in on him. He'd been looking for something in there. I stuck my head in and took a deep whiff. The scent of my mom's favorite jasmine perfume still lingered, although the demon stench was mingled quite strongly with it. Her jewelry drawer was half open. I pulled it open all the way and scanned the contents. There were velvet boxes of gold jewelry that my mom had collected over the years. Nothing strange here.

Then something caught my eye. There was something stuck in the back of the drawer. Something shiny. I reached in and pulled it out. It was my skull pendant. My mom had bought me a gold chain to hang it on. I'd worn it for a few months and then taken it off one day and forgotten all about it. Until now. I was surprised that she had kept it all these years. But then again, that's what mom did. She was a hoarder. She never threw anything out, especially if it was something I had worn or liked. I held it in my palm, turning it over, wondering if it meant anything. The *sadhu* who had given it to me all those years ago had said something about my destiny and how I shouldn't turn away from it. At the time I'd just thought he was a crazy old man. But now, given the recent turn of events, I wondered if there was some deeper meaning to his words. I was pondering what that might be when I noticed my palm was getting warm. I looked down at the pendant. Was it my imagination or was the skull glowing?

"Shiv, come here," I called out over my shoulder. He was by my side in an instant. "Look...the pendant." I held out my hand.

"It's glowing," he said, taking my hand. "Is your hand okay?" I nodded. I switched the pendant to my other hand and moved away from the window. Yes, it was definitely glowing, and now this hand felt warmer too.

"What do you think it means?" I whispered.

"I don't know," he whispered back. "Why are we whispering?"

I shrugged.

"Where did you get the pendant?" he asked, speaking normally again.

"An old *sadhu* gave it to me outside the Kali temple in Kolkata when I was seven. Now that I think about it, he was quite weird."

"Hmmm, well let's take it back with us," Shiv said. "My parents will know if it has any special powers. It's definitely associated with Kali because of the skull, but they'll know for sure."

We looked around some more, but after a while I knew there was nothing more I could find here. I went back to my room and packed an overnight bag with some of my clothes. Then I went to my bathroom to get my toiletries. When I was getting my toothbrush I stopped to look at myself in the mirror. I looked as if I'd been attacked by a raccoon. There were scratches on my face and the stingers from the demon had left nasty-looking puncture wounds all over my neck. I decided to jump in the shower and get cleaned up while I was here. The hot steam felt so good and I realized that every part of my body was sore. I stayed until I remembered that Shiv was just outside and dried off and got dressed in a hurry. It felt good to be clean again. I realized I might not be able to come back for some time, and as I went back down I looked at the pictures that lined the walls. I had to hold back tears when I thought of my parents. I could hear Shiv calling for me, probably beginning to panic. I found him in the kitchen about to go out the back door.

"Sorry, I just had to take a shower," I said, smiling apologetically.

"I was wondering what was taking so long," he said, his eyes lingering a little on me before he looked away. Before I could analyze why I felt warm inside all of a sudden, he was walking toward the front door. I followed him out, locked the door and got in his car.

"Do you think he'll hurt them?" I said, looking down at the skull pendant in my hand.

He replied without taking his eyes off the road. "You can't think like that, Callie. He won't harm them. We just have to focus on finding them." He took his right hand off the steering wheel and put it over mine. It was a gentle touch meant to reassure, but it filled me with a warmth that was familiar and new at the same time. Back at his house we showed the pendant to his parents. Dev didn't seem surprised to see it. We were in the library, and he went to one of the bookshelves and pulled out an old volume wrapped in a dark blue velvet casing. He thumbed through the pages until he found what he was looking for.

"Here it is. It talks about the skull pendant. It says here that it was given to Kali as one of the gifts from the gods who created her. The skull symbolizes her ability to detect evil, to see right through to what a person really is." He turned to me and his eyes looked almost feverish with eagerness. "May I hold it please, Callie?"

I was still holding it and put it on his open palm. Nothing happened.

"It was glowing before when we were in my parents' bedroom," I said, looking at Shiv for confirmation. He nodded.

"Yes, you said it felt warm." He looked at his dad.

"Do you feel anything?"

"No," Dev replied. "But it was a gift to Callie. She would be the only one to have a connection to it." He turned to me.

"Callie, you said that a *sadhu* outside the Kali temple gave it to you. Hmm, I wonder..."

He didn't complete his thought, because Nina interrupted him.

"Callie, I know this is all a lot to handle for anyone. You need to rest tonight. Tomorrow things will look better." She touched my face gently. "I promise that we will not rest until your parents are back with you." And with that they both left, leaving me behind with Shiv. I felt exhausted, as if all the energy had drained out of me and left behind an empty shell.

"I think I'll take your parents' advice and get some rest," I said.

"Let's get some food in you first," Shiv said, cupping my elbow and guiding me gently out of the library. We turned right by the stairs, walked down another hallway and entered the kitchen. It was huge, with oak cabinets, marble countertops, a huge island and the obligatory spice kitchen of Indian households. Shiv deposited me on a stool by the island and went to the refrigerator. He pulled out butter, a jar of tamarind and coriander chutney and a packet of Amul cheese. He gave me a conspiratorial wink and went over to the breadbox on the counter to get a loaf of bread. I couldn't help smiling. Chutney sandwiches were my favorite. A few slices of salty Amul cheese, a dab of tangy tamarind and coriander chutney and two slices of buttered bread. It was a party in your mouth.

"So...am I good or am I good?" Shiv said, grinning as he expertly cut the sandwiches into triangles and slid one of the plates over to me. He took a big bite out of his, looking very pleased with himself.

"Yes, Shiv," I said, unable to suppress a smile. "You're very good. How did you know that these are my favorite?"

"I didn't," he replied. "They're mine."

I was afraid I would start liking him a little too much for my own good. If good food was a way into a person's heart, chutney sandwiches were definitely a way into mine. It was funny how comfortable I felt around Shiv, considering we'd just met recently. I couldn't put my finger on it, but it was as if I'd known him for a long time. I wondered if he felt it too. He caught me looking at him and I felt myself blush. I got up abruptly and took my plate over to the sink. I rinsed it out, dried it and put it back in the cabinet.

"I think I'll go to sleep now. Thanks for the sandwich." I started walking out of the kitchen.

Shiv quickly got up, put his plate in the sink too and came after me. "Let me walk you back," he said. We walked upstairs in silence. When we reached the door to the room I'd be staying in, I hesitated. "Shiv...thank you."

He was leaning in to open the door for me and despite myself I felt my body respond to his closeness. I closed my eyes for a second. I saw my parents' faces flash before me and that was enough to bring me back to reality. Nothing else mattered now...not until I found them and they were safe. He kept his gaze locked on mine and I could see in his eyes that he was struggling too. Or at least part of me hoped he was. It all lasted only a millisecond and then he turned around and went down the hallway to a room just a few doors away from mine. I sighed and went in. As soon as I saw the bed in the corner, exhaustion swept over me like a tidal wave. I barely made it across the room before I collapsed and fell into a deep sleep.

I dreamed about my father. He was trying to say something, his mouth moving, forming words, but I couldn't make out what they were. I tried to get closer to him, but I couldn't move. My body was frozen in place. I tried to concentrate, to focus on his lips. "Callie..." I could finally hear him, but his voice sounded far away, as if it was coming from a great distance. "We're alright...cannot hurt us..." Then silence again. Still his lips continued to move. Once again I focused on his lips. "...the sword." He began to fade away.

In my dream I cried out. "Dad...don't go!" His image became clearer. I could see him again. He looked gaunt and I could see bruises on his face. But he was alive. "Dad...is Mom...is she…?" Even in my dream I couldn't say the words. But I didn't have to. Suddenly my dad's voice came to me as clear as his face was in front of me.

"Callie, honey...there's not a lot of time. Your mom and I will be safe. Don't worry about us. You've got to be strong. You have to find the sword. It will destroy him." His voice strained and I could see the effect on his face too. He was weakening right in front of me.

"But...Dad..." It was too late. He had faded away. There was nothing left but the darkness.

FIVE

MY EYES FLEW open. It was still dark, but a thin shaft of moonlight pierced through the gap between the curtains, illuminating the room with an eerie glow. I knew that it had been a dream, but it felt so real. It was as if my dad had been in the room with me. I also knew that wasn't possible, no matter how much I wanted it to be. I sat up slowly, still aching from the venom in the demon's stingers. There was no way I was going to be able to get back to sleep. I looked at the clock on the nightstand to my right. It was two o'clock. I looked around and noticed my cell phone on a white desk by the window. Normally it was an extension of me, but I had completely forgotten about it during the bizarre events of the last couple of days. Someone must have taken it out of my pocket when Shiv brought me here. I checked to see how many missed calls I had. Ben had called. Twenty times. And there were texts, so many of them. I felt a pang of guilt thinking about him. He must be frantic with worry. I texted a quick reply. I knew he'd probably be asleep, but at least he'd get them in the morning.

Sorry, Ben. I'm ok. Family emergency. I'll text you again soon.

I didn't know what else to say. I couldn't exactly tell him what was really going on. He'd think I was insane. I would make it up to him later. A little ping told me there was a reply. Surprised that he was still up, I looked at the message.

I was so worried. Is there anything I can do? Where are you? I went by your house, but nobody was home.

I didn't want him going to my house. I couldn't be sure that there wasn't still someone watching. What if they hurt Ben?

I'm staying with relatives. Things are a bit crazy right now. I'll call you as soon as I can, I promise.

Hopefully that would be okay for now.

I put the phone back on the table and looked around. I was too wired to sleep so I decided to look around. I wondered whose room this was. As far as I could tell Shiv didn't have a sister. But this was definitely a girl's room. There was a bookshelf against the wall near the foot of the bed. I looked at the titles, thinking that maybe some light reading would help me go to sleep. I pulled out a couple of the books. *The Temperamental Sage.* What the hell? *Gods, Goddesses and their Familiars.* Whoever this girl was, she had some weird reading interests. I picked a different section of the shelf and pulled out another book. *The Kali Conspiracy: An Analysis of the Council of Rakshakari* by Rupa Banerjee. That looked promising. It wouldn't help me go to sleep, but it could shed some light on my current predicament.

A loud crash came from somewhere outside and I ran to the window to see what it was. It was already dark outside, but by the light of the streetlamp I could make out the cherry trees that lined both sides of the walkway leading from Shiv's house to the back of our school. There were cars parked along both sides of the road. I didn't see anything unusual. It was probably a cat or a raccoon knocking over a garbage bin. I took the book and sat down on the bed. I opened the front cover. On the inside of the cover was an inscription. *To Priya, you make me proud every day. Love Ma.* I wondered who she was.

I turned the pages until I came to the first chapter. "A Background on the Origin of Kali." I already knew how Kali had been created. A yawn escaped my mouth. I needed to get some sleep, but my throat was parched. Also, my arms were beginning to throb. I decided to go downstairs to get some water and something for the pain.

I left the room as quietly as possible. The last thing

I wanted was for Shiv or his parents to panic, thinking there was an intruder in their house. I tiptoed down the stairs, went into the kitchen and turned on the light. I opened cabinet doors until I found one that held glasses. I picked a tall one and filled it with some ice water from the dispenser on the fridge. I drank the whole glass and refilled it before I started looking for some painkillers. It felt a bit weird opening drawers in someone else's house, but the pain was getting worse and I didn't want to wake anyone up. I finally found a drawer that held an assortment of over-the-counter medications. I rooted around until I found a bottle of ibuprofen. I took two and finished my second glass of water. I debated whether to go back up and try to sleep or to look around. Maybe I could find a computer somewhere and check up on what was happening.

Feeling a little bit like a cat burglar, I walked as quietly as I could to the library. The sliding doors were open. I stepped inside, found the light switch and flipped it. Then I closed the doors behind me. I looked around. It was bigger than I remembered, the shelves extending all the way along the walls. Scattered throughout were small sitting areas with armchairs, recliners and the occasional ottoman, all surrounding antique-looking tables. I guessed they must spend a lot of time in here. There had to be a computer somewhere. I couldn't see one, though. I would just have to wait until morning and ask Shiv. I walked over to one of the bookcases and looked at the thick volumes that sat fitted tightly together. They were well-worn texts, the *Upanishads*, books about the Trinity, and a lot of books on demonology. My eyes were beginning to feel heavy and I turned around to leave. I walked to the door, slid it open and walked right into someone. I had already turned off the light so it took me a moment to realize that it was just Shiv. He nudged me back into the library but didn't turn the light back on.

"What are you doing here?" he whispered, sliding the door closed.

"I couldn't sleep. I'm sorry, did I wake you?" I hoped his parents wouldn't come down as well.

"No, I thought I heard something so I came down to check."

I nodded and then there was an awkward pause. He stood between me and the door and I noticed that he wasn't wearing a shirt, just some sweatpants. His skin glistened in the moonlight that sifted through the blinds. I could see the rest of his tattoos now, and they were just as I had imagined. Two serpents were coiled around his neck and wound their way down the front of his chest. There they ended just where dark curls of hair tapered down over his belly and into the waistband of his sweatpants. I caught myself just as my eyes continued to wander down. I felt blood rush to my cheeks and I couldn't bring myself to look at him. He cleared his throat, and when I did look at him, I could see the amusement glinting in his eyes and in the twitch of his mouth.

"I, umm, was just going back to bed," I mumbled, squeezing past him, careful not to touch him. I was a little embarrassed at my physical reaction and I certainly did not want him to get even an inkling of what I was feeling. He barely suppressed a chuckle, following close behind.

"Since we're both up, do you want me to show you something?" he asked, grabbing my elbow so that I had to stop.

"Sure...what is it?" I was going to play it cool. I didn't want to give him the satisfaction of knowing that he had any sort of effect on me.

"It's this way," he said, turning down the hallway in the opposite direction of the kitchen. I followed him until he stopped in front of a door. When he opened it I saw a set of stairs that seemed to lead down to the basement. We went down quietly until we reached the bottom. I gasped. In front of us was an immense room, more like the inside of a gym. On the walls hung various types of weapons, swords, shields and helmets. I had never seen so many different kinds of swords. I felt like I was forgetting something, but I didn't know what.

"This is where we train," Shiv said, his eyes gleaming. "We have one of the best collections of ancient weapons here. Some of them are thousands of years old and have been used by the greatest warriors."

I believed him. I didn't know much about weapons, but even I could tell that this was an impressive collection.

"So what do you mean exactly by training?" Looking at Shiv in his current shirtless state, I could tell he was in great shape. That much was obvious from his bulging biceps and the way his shoulders looked like they could knock someone sideways. And the way the muscles on his chest rippled...I forced myself to look at something else, anything else. My eyes were drawn to a strange-looking weapon that looked like a sword, but the blade looked like it would be flexible, like a whip. I walked over to where it hung, a little out of my reach. I stood up on the tips of my toes to grab the handle, but I was just too short. Shiv had walked up beside me and reached across me. He grabbed the weapon off the wall effortlessly. When he brought it down his arm brushed my side and the effect was electric. I couldn't be sure if it was the sword he was holding or his body that had this effect on me, but it was all I could do not to touch him. I had to fight the urge to run my hands over his chest and trace his tattoos wherever they went. I looked at him, but he had the same knowing smile. He clearly was not having the same reaction to me. I exerted an impressive amount of self-control and took a step back. I reached out and took the sword from him. The hilt felt cool in my hands. It wasn't too heavy, and I swung it around a little. The top part of the blade was solid, but it parted a little further down into two flexible whip-like ribbons.

"It's called an *urumi*," Shiv said, watching me. He

put his hand on top of mine and guided my movements, smoothly, until I felt the rhythm. The blades undulated gently as I moved my wrist beneath Shiv's hand. He stood very close and I could feel his breath in my ear as he spoke.

"It's used mostly by the people of Kerala. Thousands of years ago it was used in battle, but now it's used in *kalaripayattu*, a type of martial art."

I had visited Kerala in the south of India when I was younger. I remembered the lush green tea estates and the beautiful mountain resorts we had visited. Each region in India had its own culture, cuisine and language. So it didn't surprise me to find out that they must have their own art of warfare as well. I handed the *urumi* back to Shiv and moved away, trying not to let on the effect his proximity had on me.

Suddenly I remembered something from the dream. My dad had said something about a sword. One that would destroy Mahisha. But that had just been a dream, a result of my desperate desire to find my parents. I vaguely remembered my grandmother telling me about a sword that only Kali could wield, which could destroy evil. I tried to remember the rest of the dream. My dad had said something about the two of them being safe, that Mahisha couldn't hurt them. That didn't make any sense. It was all in my head, but on some level I felt as though it had been real, as if my dad had been trying to communicate with me. I noticed that Shiv had stopped talking and was watching me with some amusement.

"I'm sorry, Shiv. It's just that...I had this strange dream. My dad was trying to tell me something and I don't know what to think." My shoulders fell and I felt exhausted once again.

"What did he tell you?"

"Just that they were safe and that I shouldn't worry about them. He also said that I have to find a sword that will destroy Mahisha." I looked up at him, my eyes willing him to say that it wasn't just a dream.

"Maybe your dad is trying to communicate with you," Shiv said. "It's not unheard of you know, at least not in our world."

"But how is that even possible? My dad's a professor, how would he even know how to do that?" A part of me couldn't help wondering, though.

"Look, Callie...I'm not sure how your dad fits into all of this, but I don't think we should dismiss anything, no matter how far-fetched it might seem." I nodded slowly. I really needed to find a computer. A bit of research might answer a lot of questions.

"Shiv, is there a computer I could use? I really need to let my friends know that I haven't been kidnapped and murdered. Ben already left like twenty messages." Shiv raised an eyebrow.

"Sure, you can use my laptop. It's in my room. I would ask you to come there and use it, but if my mom finds us in there together, she'll freak. Trust me, guardian or not, she's still very old-fashioned." I smiled as if I totally agreed that it was ridiculous, but secretly I was relieved. I didn't really trust myself right now. If the last few hours were any indication, my brain and my body were not exactly on the same page at the moment.

We walked up the stairs together and then Shiv went into his room while I waited outside mine. He was back in a flash and handed me his laptop. I thanked him and went in, relieved to be on my own at last. I wanted to find some information before I talked to Shiv's parents about my dream. I didn't like being the only one in the room who had no clue about what was going on. I sat down on the bed and put the laptop in front of me. Opening the browser, I typed in "Kali's sword" and hit search. A whole lot of results came up. I clicked on one that seemed to be informative and began to read. Most of what the article said was already familiar to me from my grandmother's stories. I went back to the results page and clicked on another link. Still nothing new. I went through several links and had almost given up when something caught my eye. Priestesses of Kali. I'd never heard of that before. I continued to read.

The Priestesses of Kali are part of a clandestine group of female devotees of the Goddess Kali. There is evidence to support that they have been around for thousands of years. Rumors of their powers have circulated for millennia. It is believed that the original priestesses were entrusted by Kali herself to safeguard her sword in the event of her failure to destroy

Mahisha. Archeologists have tried for centuries, without success, to find where the Sword of Kali may have been hidden.

The article went on to talk about possible locations of the sword, ranging from the jungles of Kolkata to caves buried in the snow-capped mountains of Mongolia. There were some who believed it had traveled to Greece during the invasion of India by Alexander the Great. I closed the webpage after a while. I would have to talk to Shiv's parents in the morning and see if they knew anything more about the sword and its possible location. I couldn't believe I was sitting here and contemplating the chances of getting my hand on a five-thousand-year-old sword that had once belonged to the Goddess of Destruction herself. Life was funny that way.

I turned my attention to something else that had been nagging at me: the fact that my dad had come to me in my dream and actually talked to me was strange. And I knew all about strange dreams. But this was different. He had tried to communicate with me and it had seemed so real, not like any other dream I'd had before. It was as if he'd known I'd be frantic with worry about them and he needed to tell me what to do next. I sat up straight and typed "dream manipulation" in the search box. A bunch of results came up. *How to Control your Dreams. Download an App for Dream Manipulation.* So it was true. There really was an app for everything. I cleared the search box and typed in

"Dream Manipulators, Hindu mythology." Not a lot of results came up, but once again one of them caught my eye. Oneiric manipulation. I clicked on the link.

Oneiric manipulators possess the power to enter someone's dream and take control. They can influence thoughts and actions, even during waking hours, by planting the seed of an idea or thought in their minds. They are also able to communicate with a person but at great cost to themselves. A successful communication requires the manipulator to drain his own strength. As a result he is weakened and cannot repeat this activity until energy has been replenished.

I stared at the screen for a while. Could my dad have such an ability? It was amazing how the realm of what was possible had expanded exponentially for me in the last couple of days. This seemed as good an explanation as any. How else would my dad know exactly what I was thinking and be able to tell me how to proceed? With a sigh I picked up the laptop and put it on the desk. I needed to get some sleep, even if it was only for a few hours. The clock on the nightstand said it was 3:30 a.m. I fell back on the bed and was asleep within minutes.

I awoke the next morning feeling optimistic. The dream about my father had given me hope. Firstly, I was now convinced that my father had in fact been communicating with me and I felt a sense of relief knowing that my parents were alive and relatively unharmed, at least for the moment. Secondly, I felt that Shiv's parents might have more information about the sword my father had mentioned. Once I knew its last known location, I might have a shot at rescuing my parents after all. This motivated me enough to get me ready and downstairs with a positive attitude, which must have shown on my face, because Nina noticed it right away. They were all sitting at the breakfast table in the kitchen. The big bay window looked out on a sunny yard.

"Callie, you look rested," she said cheerfully. "I'm glad you're feeling better."

Over a breakfast of eggs, toast and fresh fruit, I told them about my dream. They didn't seem too surprised. Dev was already nodding as I finished.

"It's not unheard of that some Rakshakari have powers of oneiric manipulation," he said.

"But my father is not a guardian," I said, a strange realization blossoming in my stomach. "He's a professor," I finished weakly.

"Callie, I can assure you that ordinary humans do not possess such powers. However, there are Rakshakari who have forsaken the call and chosen to live normal lives. Their powers diminish but are never truly lost."

I said nothing for a while. I tried to think back and remember if there were any clues, any signs I had missed. It was strange trying to look at my life and realize that there might have been so much I didn't know, so many things about my parents that they had kept from me. I thought about snatches of conversations from when I was younger, too young to understand their significance. I'd walk in on them and they would abruptly stop talking. I had probably been too self-absorbed to think anything of it at the time, but now I desperately wished I had paid more attention. Maybe I would have learned something that could have helped me now. I must have sighed or something, because Dev looked at me sympathetically.

"Callie, *beti*, you mustn't blame yourself. None of this is your fault."

Nina nodded in agreement as she buttered a piece of toast. "Callie," she said, "if your parents kept any of this from you, it was only to protect you. I'm sure they had their reasons."

I knew they were trying to make me feel better, but I couldn't help the tiny worm of resentment that was making its way into my mind. I was seventeen years old, for goodness sake, not a child. I could have handled whatever dark secrets they were hiding. They should have had more faith in me. Now here I was, completely in the dark, having to rely on strangers whom I felt forced to trust.

I bit into a piece of toast that Nina had put on my plate next to the scrambled eggs. I didn't want to be rude, so I just nodded politely.

"Shiv," Nina said, taking a sip of her coffee, "why don't you show Callie around and then this afternoon we are going to meet with Vikram."

I looked around the table. "Who's Vikram?"

"He's the head of the Council for the West Coast," Dev replied. "We went to see him yesterday to apprise him of the situation, and he is eager to meet you."

"Wait...you mean there are more of you?" I said. I regretted it as soon as I said it, because Nina raised her eyebrows slightly before replying.

"Yes, Callie, there are more of us. In fact, we have centers all around the world. We train our Rakshakari and warriors there. They are also taught all about the history of the Council."

She shot Shiv a glance. "Shiv, perhaps while you are showing Callie around, why don't you fill her in a little bit? That way she'll be prepared before we meet with Vikram."

She excused herself and left the kitchen. Dev finished his coffee and left too, leaving me alone with Shiv.

"Did I offend your mother in some way?" I asked as soon as we were alone.

Shiv, who had been uncharacteristically quiet throughout breakfast, just shrugged. "Don't worry about her," he said, putting down his glass of orange juice. "She just feels responsible for you, and maybe the rest of the Council isn't too happy with how things were handled with you and your parents."

"Handled?" I said, annoyance tinging my voice. "What exactly is that supposed to mean? If they knew that something like that would happen, why didn't they say something?"

Shiv looked at me and there was something in his eyes that I couldn't define.

"Why don't we go to the library and I can fill you in on what I can about the Council," he said, getting up without waiting for an answer and taking his plate and mug to the sink. I noticed that he had conveniently chosen not to respond to my previous comment. I decided not to push it. I got up and cleared some of the breakfast dishes as well.

We went to the library and settled in the seating area by the windows. Shiv was holding a thick bound volume of some kind, which he now gave to me.

I took it and placed it on my lap. The cover was soft, some sort of cloth, dark brown with the title in gold, embossed letters.

Rakshakari.

And underneath that in smaller letters:

History and Organization of the Council.

"So," Shiv said, nodding his head toward the book, "this has all the information you need about the Rakshakari. Everything you want to know about who's who and how it all got started."

"Could you maybe tell me the important bits?" I asked, thinking I didn't really need to know every single detail. There would be time for all that later, after I'd found my parents.

Shiv smiled and nodded. "I suppose I could do that.

So let's see...where to begin...I think I'll start by telling you about the organization. So we have the Elders, they are sort of the head of the Rakshakaris. They live in seclusion on Mount Kailash."

I nodded. I had heard about Mount Kailash from my grandmother. It was located remotely somewhere in Tibet and in Hinduism it was known as the home of Lord Shiva. My grandmother had described it as a place of great power and peace, the source of three great rivers in Asia, but most of all that it was older than any civilizations we knew about. I forced my attention back to Shiv.

"At first the Rakshakari Council only had branches in India, but over the last hundred years or so they have spread all over the world."

"It makes sense, I guess," I said, thinking out loud. "People from India live in all parts of the world now."

"There are training centers as well, so the new initiates can learn combat techniques. So in North America we have one center here in Seattle, one in Houston and one in New York. Vikram is the head of the Seattle center; you'll meet him tomorrow. He's quite the character, but I'm not going to tell you anything. You'll have to wait and see."

"And what do the Elders do?"

"They are the supreme authority on anything and everything to do with the Rakshakari," Shiv replied.

"But if they're in seclusion so far away, how do they even know what's going on?" I was imagining a group of old monk-like men sitting on a mountaintop and meditating.

"I've never seen one, but I've heard that they are really old, like hundreds of years old, and that they've developed special powers from all their years of isolation and deep meditation. Some even say that they are avatars of the Trinity."

The trinity included Brahma the creator, Vishnu the maintainer or preserver and Shiva the destroyer or transformer. The idea that these Elders were avatars of the three gods was a fascinating idea but not necessarily one that I bought into. There was still a large part of me, my cynical side, that didn't accept any of this. But then there was the other side of me, the voice of reason that said it couldn't be a coincidence I'd always had those dreams and that Shiv and his family knew all about them. That, plus the fact that at the moment they could provide me with some sort of help in finding my parents. Without them I had no clue where to begin. And then there was the fact that my father had come to me in my dream. That was what compelled me to believe that I was right in trusting Shiv and his family. Now I pulled my attention back to what he was saying.

"So tomorrow, when we go to the center, you will meet all the other Rakshakari who work or live there."

"They live at the center?" I asked.

"Yes, some of them have no family. Many of them come to us from orphanages."

"I thought that Rakshakaris were all descendants of

the same bloodlines."

"Yes, that's true," Shiv replied, "but many in India are orphaned as infants because their parents die in battle. And if there is no one left in that family, then they get placed in orphanages by a neighbor or someone."

A heaviness weighed down my heart at the thought of these poor children who would never know their parents. "But then how do they end up as Rakshakari?"

"Rakshakari are all born with a mark," Shiv said, turning around and pulling the right sleeve of his shirt down to expose his shoulder. I moved closer to get a better look. There it was, his birthmark, a dark bluish one, shaped a little like an eye. It was almost indistinguishable among his many other serpent tattoos. I sat back down and looked at him.

"So what is it exactly?" I asked. "It looks sort of like an evil eye." I'd seen symbols like this in books and movies, but usually they were actual tattoos, not birthmarks.

"Actually, that's exactly what it is," Shiv said. "It's a symbol for protection against evil. And that's what Rakshakari are born to do."

I was still fascinated with the whole orphan thing.

"So you're saying that somehow these orphans find their way to other Rakshakari?"

"Some are drawn to us when they're older and their powers start to manifest. Others are found by Council members."

"You mean that they actually go around to orphanages and look for them?"

"Yes, think about it," Shiv replied. "India has so many poor people, and orphanages are full of unwanted children. The Rakshakari do a lot of social work, including working with orphans, trying to get them placed in good homes. When they come across ones who have the mark, they bring them to the centers and give them a better life. One with purpose and security."

"But what about a family?" I couldn't bear to think that these children grew up without the love of parents and siblings.

"Callie, if the Rakshakari didn't take them, they would end up being turned out into the streets when they turn sixteen. The orphanages are full and there's no room for them once they get to that age. Plus, if they don't get initiated they end up with all kinds of psychological problems."

"What do you mean, psychological problems?"

"Well, we are different, all Rakshakari are. It's in our blood. And if we aren't doing what we're supposed to, things go wrong. Some Rakshakari have powers. And if they aren't taught to control them they can mess with their minds."

This was getting more and more interesting by the minute. So now they had powers too. But then I remembered that just this morning Dev had mentioned my dad having a power, oneiric manipulation.

"So you all have powers? What's yours then?"

"Not all of us," he replied. "Some do and they can develop at any stage in life. But the ones who get it as children have it the worst."

It made sense. I could relate with those kids on some level. When I'd first started having my nightmares, I thought I was going crazy. It wasn't as if I could just talk about it to anyone. So at first I suffered in silence until my parents and teachers began to notice little changes in me. I became withdrawn, avoided sleep and ended up passing out in class one day. When I told my family, their reactions seemed odd to me at the time. My grandmother immediately told my parents to take me to a holy man. It was strange, but my usually modern parents agreed immediately. At the time I'd thought they were doing it just to appease my grandmother, but now I had to wonder if they hadn't suspected something back then. Of course, the holy man had just muttered some things and nothing had changed. I continued to have the nightmares, and after a few unsuccessful sessions with a therapist they decided to move to Seattle. I guess at the time they must have thought they might be able to escape whatever was happening to me by running away. Now, when I thought about the orphans I felt glad that at least the Rakshakari were there to help them. I had to wonder, though, how many others were never found and what fates awaited them. I shook myself mentally. I had to get out of this funk. My focus had to be on my parents right now; that was all that mattered.

"Okay, so what else do I need to know before I meet everyone this afternoon?" I wanted to be prepared.

"Well, Vikram will insist that you start combat training immediately," Shiv said.

"Combat training..." I said. "That should be interesting." This Vikram fellow had no idea what he was getting himself into. I was a swimmer, so I was in good shape, but I was known to be quite clumsy. How that was going to translate into combat maneuvers, I wasn't sure, but I guess I would find out soon enough. Shiv stood up and looked at me.

"Callie, look, it's going to be a bit overwhelming meeting everyone and I don't want you getting stressed out or anything." He looked worried, and I was glad that I had him to lean on. I didn't want him to think I was getting all mushy, so I put on an expression that said I was totally fine with all the craziness going on around me.

"Don't worry, Shiv," I said nonchalantly. "I'll be fine. But I would like to borrow your laptop to do some research." He nodded as we walked out of the library and up the stairs. I spent the rest of the morning looking up oneiric manipulation. I was still shocked to realize that my father had this whole secret identity that I knew nothing about. Stirrings of resentment started up in my gut, so I was glad that my cell phone made the familiar bleep sound for a text notification. I picked it up off the bed and looked at the screen. It was from Ben. Damn it. I had forgotten to get back to him. I knew that he would be worried, really worried by now. My last text would have kept him going for a little bit, but we had never gone too long without getting in touch with one another before. I had to see him and give him some sort of explanation. I made an impulsive decision.

Can you meet me at the park in 15 minutes?

He responded, *Sure. Usual spot.*

I hesitated only for a second before deciding I wasn't going to tell Shiv where I was going. I needed to see Ben alone. I snuck quietly down the stairs and out the door and made my way to the park. Our usual spot was by the swings. We had played there as kids, and when we got older it just became the place we hung out whenever one of us needed to talk. I had no idea what I was going to tell Ben. If I told him the truth he would think I was insane. But there was a part of me that wanted to tell him so badly. I wanted someone from my real life to know what I was going through, someone with whom I had a history and who knew my family.

He was already there by the time I turned the corner of my street. From here I could see the whole area. There was a water park and it was empty today. During the summers it was packed with people, kids mostly who just wanted relief from the heat and parents who sat on blankets spread out on the grass. Today there were a handful of kids and parents scattered throughout the park, but there was nobody by the swings. Except for Ben.

SIX

HE WAS ALREADY sitting on one of the four swings, waiting for me. I sprinted over to him and sat down on the swing to his right. He looked at me for a moment before speaking.

"Callie, what's going on? You said you had a family emergency, but then I went to your house this morning and no one was there."

A feeling of dread shot through me. That was exactly what I'd been trying to avoid: Ben going to my house and being attacked by something waiting for me.

"I'm sorry Ben...things have been crazy for the last few days." I tried to think of a plausible reason and came up with the lamest one possible. "One of my aunts in Kolkata died, so my parents had to fly over there. I'm staying with some family friends."

I hoped he would let it go at that, but I should have known better. After all, it was Ben. He was nothing if not persistent.

"Why didn't you stay with us?" he asked, sounding a little insulted.

"I wanted to, but you know how my mom is. She was all worried about appearances and all that crap." I felt I was being convincing, and deep inside I felt awful about lying to my best friend like this, but I couldn't risk involving him in my mess.

"I'm sorry about your aunt. Were you close to her?"

This was not going well. I had to change the topic somehow.

"Kind of," I replied. "But I might have to fly there too, so I won't be able to stay in touch for a while."

"Callie...I know we haven't been spending that much time together recently, but..."

He began to fidget with the zipper of his hoodie. I had never known Ben to fidget. It just wasn't who he was. He was confident and funny and a great listener.

"Ben...whatever it is...you know you can tell me. I'm sorry I haven't been around."

"No...it's okay, you had your stuff to deal with. I just need to tell you something and I know this isn't the best time, but..."

He never got a chance to finish because just then Shiv came bounding around the corner. He stopped for a second and looked around until he saw us by the swings. Then he ran over to us.

"There you are...I've been looking all over the house for you," he said, barely out of breath. He nodded at Ben. I did not want to see the look on Ben's face, but I knew I would have to.

"Umm, I was going to tell you that I've been staying at Shiv's parents' place..." I said, knowing what Ben must be thinking. So much for how my mom felt about appearances.

Ben didn't say anything at first, but then he slowly got off the swing. "That's great...umm ...I have to get back..." he mumbled, giving us a weird little wave as he turned and walked back toward his cul-de-sac. I couldn't have felt worse if I tried. I had lied to my best friend and Ben deserved better.

"I'm sorry, Callie, I feel like I interrupted something, but my parents are looking for you and they're not too happy that you ran off without telling anybody."

"I'm sorry. I had to talk to Ben. I just disappeared and he didn't know what happened to me. I owed him some kind of explanation."

"So what did you tell him?" Shiv's expression was controlled, but I was sure he was worried I had told Ben something about the real situation.

I was beginning to feel a little annoyed, so my tone was sharper than I intended. "Don't worry, I didn't tell him the truth. Your secret is safe."

He gave me kind of a half-smile. "You know it's

your secret now too, don't you?" he said softly. I hated that he was right, but I wasn't going to give him the satisfaction of admitting that.

"Let's just get back," I said as I turned and started walking back toward his place. When we got there his parents were already setting the table for lunch. There was basmati rice with peas and carrots, shrimp sautéed with spinach, curried lentils and a yoghurt salad with tomatoes and cucumber. I realized I was hungry, but first I had to give them some sort of explanation.

"Callie, we were quite worried when Shiv said you weren't in the house," Nina began, her voice calm and composed but stern.

"I'm sorry, I should have told you that I was going out," I said as sincerely as I could. "My best friend Ben was worried about me and I knew he would go to my house looking for me."

"We understand, Callie," Dev said, offering me the dish of rice. "We just need to make sure that you're safe at all times. I'm sure you can appreciate that." I had finished helping myself to the rice and passed the dish on to Shiv.

"Look, Callie, we understand that you may be used to coming and going on your own, but things will have to change from now on," Nina said. I decided I definitely did not like her and there were a few things I could have said to her, but my parents had raised me better than that. Maybe I was being sensitive, but I didn't like her implication that my parents didn't care when I came and went. But I knew this was not the time to get into all that so I swallowed my resentment with the shrimp.

"I'm sorry, I didn't mean to worry you. I'll remember to let someone know next time."

The rest of the meal was eaten in somewhat awkward silence, but then it was time to go to the center. I was quite intrigued to meet this Vikram and to see what the other Rakshakari were like. Mostly I was hoping they could help me find my parents.

It was a long drive from their house to the center. About an hour later Dev pulled up outside a large compound surrounded by a wrought iron fence. A security guard opened the huge double gates to let the car pull in and Dev drove up a long, winding driveway and stopped under an awning in front of the main entrance. It was all very grand. A large staircase led up to the front doors. Two large lion statues flanked the entrance. We got out of the car and walked up the steps. Before we made it to the front door, it was flung wide open and a man stepped out. He was Indian and seemed older than Dev, his black hair peppered liberally with gray. But his luxuriant moustache was his defining feature. It reminded me of the villains in the Bollywood movies that my mom loved to watch. I almost expected him to start twirling it between his fingers. Thankfully, he did nothing of the sort, but I still couldn't stop staring at it as we reached the top of the stairs. He looked at me intently for a few moments. Then he gave a slight bow and smiled.

"Welcome to the Rakshakari Center, Callie. We are honored to have you here." And with that he turned around and led us inside. The interior of the mansion was even grander than I had expected. We stood on marble floors in the foyer. Statues of various Hindu deities stood in corners around us. Embroidered hangings adorned the walls. The scent of incense lingered in the air. To my right a curtain of marigolds separated the foyer from something on the other side. Vikram noticed me looking at it.

"That is our temple room," he said. "Come and have a look."

I looked at the others, but Dev nodded at me. "You go ahead, Callie. Nina and I have business to attend to."

"And I am going to the training room," Shiv said. "We'll catch up to you later."

And with that they were all gone, leaving me with Vikram.

"Guess it's just me then," I said. Vikram didn't say anything but just walked over to the flower curtain. He parted it and we went in. I stood for a moment to take everything in. The room was large, painted a golden yellow, which gave the feeling of being outdoors on a sunny day when in reality it was a typical cloudy Seattle day. There were more flowers everywhere, mostly marigolds, strung in garlands that hung from the statues of Durga, Kali, Saraswati and Lakshmi. I noticed that there were not many statues of gods. There were a few people praying in an alcove in a corner. Others were tending to the various offerings placed in front of the deities. Sweets, bowls of milk and more flowers. They were taking away the old ones and replacing them with fresh offerings. Soft music played in the background, creating a very tranquil atmosphere.

"So, what do you think, Callie?" Vikram asked.

"It's so serene and beautiful," I said. "Are these all students?" I looked at the people milling about, most of them young like myself.

"Yes, these are all initiates," Vikram said. "They come to us from various parts of the country and train here. We have some of the best teachers in the world here," he added.

"What about school? I mean, they all seem so young, aren't they in the school system?"

"No, everything they need to learn is taught here at the Academy. In addition to regular school subjects they also learn combat techniques and the intricacies of Hindu mythology."

I nodded, not really knowing what else to say. Luckily, Vikram continued.

"Why don't I show you around the Academy? It's quite large since we have residential halls and the school buildings. This is the main house. I live here, but it's also our headquarters. We have Rakshakari visiting from abroad quite frequently, as well as conferences."

He turned around and led me out of the temple room, back into the spacious foyer. I followed him out the front door, around the corner of the building. From here I could see what he meant by this being a large compound. It was enormous. There were three multi-storied buildings forming a semi-circle about fifty feet on the right of the main house. To the left I could see a tennis court, a swimming pool and another large enclosed space where some students were sparring with swords. Beyond all that, stretching out as far as I could see, were trees, tall pines that towered over the buildings and created a rich green backdrop. *Not a bad place to live and go to school,* I thought. The sun was beginning to set and I took a deep breath of the cool, pine-scented air before following Vikram, who had already begun making his way toward one of the buildings.

"This is our all-female dormitory," Vikram said, holding the glass double doors open for me. It took a few seconds for my eyes to adjust to the dim lighting. We were in a lobby. In one corner was a flat-screen television with a seating area, which was empty at the moment. In another corner there was a set of square tables with stools around them. On each table was a small square wooden game board. I walked over to take a closer look and gasped. They were Carrom boards. When I lived in Kolkata, my cousins and I would play Carrom all day long during summer vacation. It consisted of small circular disks arranged in a circle in the center of the board. The players would have to use a larger disk, called a striker, and a flick of the finger to hit the disks and send them to one of the pockets on the four corners of the board. I hadn't seen one of these in years. I must have had a smile on my face because Vikram came over.

"Memories of childhood?" he asked, his voice gentle. I nodded.

"I haven't played for years. I'm sure I've lost my touch."

He pointed toward the hallway and gestured for me to follow. "The ground floor is mostly for activities. The first two floors are for senior students and the remaining four are for all the rest."

"How many students live here then?" I asked, smiling at a couple of girls who had just come out of the elevator. They looked at me curiously but smiled back nonetheless before heading out the door.

"About one hundred and fifty in the girls' dormitory and another one hundred in the boys'. Remember that our Academy serves the entire West Coast."

"What about the third building?"

"That's for staff, trainers and other administrators. What I really wanted you to see was our combat training room. I was hoping you might pick a weapon."

I looked at him in confusion. "A weapon...?"

"Didn't Dev and Nina tell you? We feel that you should stay here and prepare."

"Prepare...for what, exactly?" I began to feel a little irritated. I did not appreciate being kept in the dark like this. I had no idea how much Dev and Nina had told Vikram.

"Well, Callie, you know what lies ahead for you...for all of us. You have no combat skills and you cannot attempt to face Mahisha, or any of his demons for that matter, without some training."

Okay, so he knew everything. What he said made a lot of sense. I did feel totally unprepared, and if I wanted to have any chance of saving my parents I would have to learn how to fight. There was a lot more I would have to learn, and this was the place for it. Plus it would be kind of a relief not to be so close to Shiv all the time. Or his mother.

I nodded slowly. "So when did you want me to start?"

"Well, you can move in tomorrow. Your combat training will commence immediately. You will also be working with Mr. Perkins, who is our resident expert on demonology. He will bring you up to speed on what you need to know. Given the urgency of our situation, there is no time to waste. Now let me take you to the combat training area."

I followed him down a dimly lit hallway until he stopped in front of a set of double doors. He pushed them open and stood aside to let me enter first. I stepped inside and looked around. It was a lot like the room in Shiv's house, except much bigger. There was one part of the room designated only for weapons storage.

"Some of these weapons are thousands of years old. They have come to us after being passed down to generations of Rakshakari."

"Do the initiates only learn the ancient arts of combat or do you also teach them other forms of martial arts?"

"We certainly try to prepare our guardians in as many different forms as we can, After all, evil comes in all shapes and forms. We wouldn't be so presumptuous as to think that our ancient combat techniques are all that we need to protect the world from evil."

There was a plethora of deadly looking weapons hanging on individual hooks on the wall, but once again my eye went straight to the whip-like sword that I had admired in Shiv's house. Vikram followed my gaze to where the sword was hanging with its companions. He walked over, took it off its hook and turned to me with a knowing smile.

"So it appears that you have a connection. The *urumi* was Kali's weapon of choice as well."

He held out the sword. I hesitated for a split second before grasping the handle. Nothing happened. I don't know what I had expected, but maybe a part of me had hoped that holding a weapon that had been a favorite of Kali's would impart some magical powers to me. But that didn't happen, so I was left standing cluelessly with the *urumi* in my hand and no idea what to do. Vikram looked as though he too had been expecting something along the lines of Xena, Warrior Princess. But he recovered quickly, arranging his features into an encouraging smile.

"Maybe we can start with the training right now," he said, calling over one of the trainers with an imperious wave. A young woman just over five feet tall walked over. She wore a white tunic over a pair of loose-fitting white pants. Her hair was in a long braid that swung down to her hips. As she came over, she bowed slightly to Vikram. He returned the gesture with a quick nod and then turned to me.

"Callie, this is Tara, one of our most talented trainers." Tara's face exhibited the barest hint of pleasure at Vikram's praise, but then she turned to me with a broad smile.

"Callie, it is so great to meet you. We have been waiting."

"It's nice to meet you too," I said, feeling a little awkward at the thought that most people here knew about me, but I knew nothing about them.

"Would you like to try your hand at a little swordplay?" Tara asked, pointing to the training area. I looked over at the students working there. They all seemed very skilled, thrusting and parrying quite effortlessly.

"I don't know if that's such a good idea," I said hesitantly. "I'm not really known for my hand-eye coordination."

"Well, you have to start sometime, so why not now?" Tara said matter-of-factly.

I couldn't think of a good reason, so I just nodded.

"Okay, Tara, I will leave Callie in your capable hands, and when you are done, please bring her to the main house." Vikram turned around and left.

Tara gave me a cursory glance, no doubt regretting her earlier offer. Unfortunately for me, it looked like I was not getting off that easy, because she guided me to the other end of the gym and into the locker room. Except it wasn't your typical high school locker room — far from it. It looked more like a spa than any changing room I'd ever seen. There were large mirrors along the walls. One section of the room had large lockers, beyond which I could see the entrance to the showers.

"I thought you might be more comfortable in something less restricting," she said. I was wearing skinny jeans and a T-shirt, probably not the most suitable for sword fighting.

"Yes, I think you're right," I said, "but don't say I didn't warn you."

Tara just smiled and walked over to a shelf that held stacks of white clothing. She dug around for a bit before pulling out a tunic and pair of pants just like the ones she was wearing.

"These should fit, I think," she said, pointing toward a changing area. I took the clothes, thanked her and went to change. I emerged a few minutes later, suitably attired for battle. The linen tunic was soft against my skin. The pants were of the same material and were probably the most comfortable I had ever worn. We walked back out into gym. Tara brought me a sword, not the *urumi* that I had held earlier, but a regular sword.

"I don't think it's a good idea to start out with the *urumi*. It's a tricky weapon to handle, even for skilled warriors," she said, handing me the sword. I put my fingers around the hilt. It felt odd at first, cold to the touch, but then my fingers warmed the metal. I brought the hilt closer to look at the intricate design. It looked like it was made of bronze, with a leafy motif in silver. All around the top were engravings of Hanuman and Ganesha, as well as peacocks, all intertwined in floral scrollwork.

"This is absolutely beautiful," I told Tara, who was brandishing her own sword.

"Well, are you going to just stand there and admire it all day or are we going to see any action?" she said with an impish grin as she waved her sword around. I decided that I liked her, but not enough to let her cut off any of my body parts. I backed up a little, my competitive nature taking over, and arranged myself in what I hoped was a combative stance. Far from impressing Tara, it seemed that I was amusing her, because I could see a little smile playing at the corners of her mouth. I couldn't believe it, but I actually stomped my foot a little and let the blade of my sword drop to the floor.

"So are you just going to laugh at me or are you

actually going to teach me something? I thought Vikram said that you were one of his best trainers," I said, making no attempt to keep the sarcasm from my voice.

It had the intended effect, because Tara immediately bristled.

"First of all, I am not Vikram's trainer. I am Rakshakari, not his employee. And secondly, yes, of course I will teach you, but I was having too much of a good time watching you pose." The last bit was accompanied by a grin, and in spite of myself I smiled back. It was hard not to like her. I made a mental note to ask Shiv about Vikram and Tara, because I detected a definite note of resentment in her tone.

The rest of the afternoon was spent quite productively. I learned the basics of sword fighting, which, contrary to my understanding, had nothing to do with combat itself but more to do with the different parts of the sword and handling techniques. I got the strong feeling that Tara wanted to make sure I didn't cut of my own or anybody else's parts while flailing around. I didn't blame her but I would have liked to have learned some actual fighting.

Later that day Shiv came to get me and Tara and we met up with his parents at the main house, where dinner was waiting. Vikram asked me if I would like to shower and change before dinner and I gladly accepted. Tara took me upstairs and showed me to a bedroom. It was luxuriously decorated in deep purple and gold, a bit too rich for my taste, but beautiful nonetheless. There was an adjoining bathroom and I marveled at the huge shower as I stood under a jet stream of hot water. A bit later I rejoined the others downstairs, wearing my own clothes and feeling refreshed and ravenous. Dinner was a feast, with spicy, fragrant biryani, fried fish, assorted vegetable and a sumptuous dessert of *rasmalai*. I would have happily skipped the main course for the deliciously soft, sweet balls of milky dough swimming in clotted cream.

During dinner Vikram casually asked me questions about my childhood, the nightmares and everything that had happened afterwards. I couldn't help but feel he was not entirely sure I was the real deal. I didn't blame him. I was still struggling with this new reality. I felt as if my old life had been replaced with this new one where everything was unfamiliar and everyone was a stranger. I missed Ben and all the fun we had together. I missed my parents. But most of all I missed feeling that I had control over my life. I hadn't felt this out of control since I'd first started having the nightmares. But I had built a new life after that, found my tribe and was comfortable again. And then all this happened. And I had no choice but to deal with it. I forced myself to come back to the moment. Vikram was asking me something about my father.

"I'm sorry...I'm exhausted." I really did not want to answer any more questions, but I also didn't want to be rude, especially since Vikram was being such a gracious host. Luckily, Dev saved me from having to answer.

"Vikram, I think Callie has had a very long day. Maybe Shiv should take her home so she can get some rest."

I could tell that Vikram wanted to continue, but he couldn't really say anything without appearing insensitive.

"Of course, you must be well rested for tomorrow, Callie. You have much work ahead of you. Dev and Nina, I will have a car take you home later." I thanked Vikram, said my goodbyes and then waited at the front of the house while Shiv pulled the car around.

SEVEN

THE NEXT AFTERNOON I was looking at the sword in my hand as I stood in the huge training grounds of the Academy. It backed onto a green belt, so there was no chance of anybody seeing us. We'd been training for only a couple of hours and already I was exhausted. Tara watched me expectantly. Did she really think that I would just magically know how to swing the sword around? The thing was heavy.

"Callie, you have to focus. Watch me, remember the stances we went over, and follow my steps." I watched as she jumped around the field, expertly wielding her sword as if it were a feather. I stepped forward, imitating the stance Tara had started with. I held the sword straight in front of me as she had shown me umpteen times then sliced a clockwise arc through the air. That didn't seem too bad. I tried again. This time I stepped into it at the same time. Unfortunately, my hand forgot that it had to hold onto the sword while I was doing the fancy footwork and it slid out and into the air, straight toward Tara, who'd been watching me with a bored look. She jumped out of the way just in time to avoid having her nose cut off.

"Callie, you have to hold on tighter. And you have to concentrate." She was exasperated, as was I. We'd been working on this particular set for hours and I wanted nothing more than to rest my aching feet and eat a cheeseburger.

"Do you think I don't know that? I'm trying, Tara." I took a deep breath and started again. *Step forward, swing clockwise, bring it down, step again, swing counter-clockwise, don't drop the sword.* I repeated this a few times, feeling quite pleased with myself. I deserved credit for not maiming anyone, didn't I? I did a few more turns then came to a stop in front of Tara.

"That's much better, Callie. Now we're going to go over sparring techniques." She spent the next two hours teaching me complicated maneuvers to use while sparring. I tried to focus and absorb as much as I could. I'd always been a quick learner, but this was a little bit different than balancing chemical reactions or solving algebraic equations. As the afternoon turned into evening, I reflected on how unprepared I was to deal with all the challenges coming my way. I was so deep in thought that I didn't realize when the air started shimmering and Tara and the clearing we were standing in disappeared.

One minute I was flailing about with the heavy sword and the next moment everything around me dissolved. I was standing by a lake, the surface rippling softly from a gentle breeze. I was surrounded by trees laden with luscious fruits I didn't recognize. Flowers bloomed in abundance, their unfamiliar but intoxicating fragrance tickling my nose. I knew this was no dream, but it still felt unreal. I spotted two figures under a tree. They were locked in an embrace. I was drawn toward them, so I went, taking care to tread softly, afraid of interrupting a romantic moment. When I got close enough to see them properly, I stopped. The man was facing me and I tried to blend into the foliage as best as I could. His face was hidden in shadows so I couldn't see it clearly, but he seemed young. Curly hair hung down almost to the top of his broad shoulders, and when he leaned back a little from the embrace, I could see the muscles ripple across his shirtless chest. The girl was gazing into his eyes, the fingers of her right hand entangled in his curls while her left hand cupped his cheek. He leaned in and their lips met in a passionate kiss. It felt oddly voyeuristic to watch them, but I couldn't tear my eyes away.

They were lost in each other for some time. It was strange, but even though I was just watching, I could feel the chemistry. A tingle began somewhere deep inside me and worked its way to the rest of my body as

I watched the two of them consumed by their passion. It was a tangible thing, this heat between them. Then they broke their embrace and began to walk toward the water. Just before they turned away, the girl turned and I got a glimpse at her face. I froze. At first my mind was too stunned to register it. I closed my eyes and held them tightly shut for a moment. When I opened them there was no mistaking. I was looking at myself. Not that I would ever wear what she had on. It was too much, like the kind of outfits my parents would make me wear to Indian weddings.

She wore a very elaborately embroidered *lehenga*, the skirt falling around her ankles in swirls. Her bodice was tight, with the décolletage so deep that I blushed when I saw her/my generous bosom peeking out from under it. She was heavily adorned with jewelry; something gold glittered on almost every visible part of her body. She paused to say something to her lover and then she laughed, the delicate tinkle wafting to me as I wondered how this could be happening. I realized I must be looking at Kali, but I was nothing like her. There was nothing delicate about the way I laughed. And I would never wear that much jewelry or show that much skin. I was still trying to figure out the meaning and purpose of this particular vision when the air shimmered again and I was back on the Academy's grounds, holding the sword. Tara was watching me closely as I looked around, slightly disoriented.

"What happened, Callie? Are you okay? You look

a little pale."

"I had a vision...I think," I replied, still trying to sort it all out.

"So what did you see exactly?" Tara asked, carefully taking the sword from my hands and placing it against the metal link fence.

"It was weird...I saw myself with this guy. And we were making out." I could feel the blood rushing to my face as I remembered the tingling.

Tara was watching me with an amused expression. "Do you know who you were making out with?"

I could tell she trying hard to suppress a grin, and I childishly stuck out my tongue. "No, I don't. His face was kind of hidden the whole time."

"But you're sure that the girl was you?"

"I don't know exactly. I'm pretty sure it was Kali I saw, but she did look exactly like me."

"Well," Tara said, "it's not really that strange. If you are the reincarnation of Kali, then it makes sense that you would look like her."

"I guess, but it was weird watching myself with a guy I've never met."

"Then you have something to look forward to, right?" Tara said with a huge grin. She picked up my sword and handed it to me. "Back to work."

"Wow, bossy much?" I grumbled as I lifted the sword.

A little while later we stopped for dinner, and not a minute too soon. For the last hour I had been fantasizing about a nice juicy burger with fries. We joined Vikram in the dining room. After a filling meal, I excused myself and went upstairs to my room. I had moved in early that morning and hadn't had a chance yet to unpack and settle in, courtesy of Tara, who had shown up outside my door minutes after I arrived, insisting that we get started right away. She was very persuasive. So here I was, hours later, feeling gross and utterly exhausted. My muscles were sore and my back hurt. Once I got to my room, I barely made it to the bathroom to undress and shower. I let the water run until it was steaming hot and leaned against the shower wall as the heat dissipated some of the pain. I shampooed my hair and emerged feeling clean and refreshed. I wrapped at towel around myself and another around my hair and then dug around in my bag for sweats and a T-shirt. By the time I was dressed again and had dried my hair, I had just enough strength left to plop myself on the bed before I fell asleep.

I awoke the next morning to the smell of French toast wafting up from the dining hall. I sat up with a groan as my tired muscles reminded me of the torture they had endured the day before. I dragged myself to the bathroom, got ready and went down. Tara and Vikram were already there, as were Dev and Shiv.

"There you are, my dear," said Vikram, smiling benevolently while Tara sat quietly next to him munching on her French toast. She looked up at me and her eyebrows shot up. I knew I looked like a zombie, and it was all her fault. I gave her my best death stare and mumbled a greeting to everyone else. I sat down and poured myself a cup of coffee from the pot in the middle of the table.

"So, Callie, I trust that you are settled in?" said Dev, taking the pot from me and pouring himself a cup.

"Yes, I am, thank you," I replied.

He stirred his coffee as he looked at me thoughtfully. "You look quite exhausted. Did you have a bad night?"

I could hear Shiv choking a little and shot him a withering glance. Tara's face looked as though it was going to explode. Clearly they thought my agony was hilarious. Vikram and Dev were oblivious to what was going on. I just smiled and mumbled something about getting used to everything. They nodded understandingly and went on sipping their coffee. Fortunately, they left soon after and I was free to glare at Tara and Shiv.

"I'm glad that you're enjoying yourself," I said as soon as the two older men were out of earshot. "What's so funny?"

"I'm sorry," Tara said, trying hard not to smile as she spoke. "It's just that you look pretty...well...your hair."

I reached up to pat down my hair, which I knew looked crazy.

"Oh, come on, Tara, she doesn't look that bad," Shiv said, smiling. I just ignored them and sipped my coffee.

"So, what's the plan for today?" I asked after a few moments of silence.

"Well, Dev and Shiv are taking over the combat training today," Tara said.

"Dad is teaching his class today, so you'll just be joining in," Shiv said. "It'll be a great experience," he added. "There are some really good students in his class."

Great, now I would get to make a fool of myself in front of even more people. This day was just getting better and better.

"Okay, lead the way," I said, trying, as usual, to mask my utter terror with nonchalance.

As Shiv and I walked over to the training building, I watched the students as they went to their classes and felt a sense of envy for the natural way in which they fit in. They knew where they belonged and where they were going. From what Vikram had told me, most of them had come from Rakshakari families, or if not, they had spent most of their lives here. Either way, none of them could possibly feel as lost and out of place as I did right now. As we entered the gym, I looked around. There were about ten other students there and three instructors, one of whom was Dev. I counted six girls and four boys, all barely in their teens as far as I could tell. As I watched, one of the girls did a complicated maneuver that included a lot of sword twirling and a few fancy back-kicks. She was a tiny little thing, probably no older than twelve. I shot a quick glance in Shiv's direction, only to find him watching me with a stupid grin.

"I told you they were good," he said with a shrug.

"Yes," I hissed. "But you didn't tell me they were little kids." I was not amused, but I took a deep breath just as Dev noticed me and waved me over. With a parting glare at Shiv, I walked to the center of the training area.

Dev had all the students line up in front of him. "Girls and boys, I would like you to welcome Callie. She is here to train with us."

A murmur passed through the group; they were no doubt wondering why I'd been held back in school. I smiled awkwardly at them and mumbled a greeting of sorts.

"I'm counting on all of you to help Callie as she begins her training," Dev told the group. I could hear tittering and engaged in an immature staredown with a girl in the back. She had two blond braids and looked like a troublemaker. Dev was oblivious to this exchange and continued with his instructions.

For the rest of the morning I learned offensive moves designed to overpower someone much bigger than me. Unfortunately, all my sparring partners were a few inches shorter than me, so I failed to see the benefit of this exercise. On the other hand, I didn't think I was ready to take on anyone my own size, so maybe it wasn't such a bad thing. After lunch, which all students ate in a cafeteria in the school building, I was summoned to the main house by Nina, who had been spending a lot of time communicating with the Elders.

Since Shiv had told me they lived in a cave on Mount Kailash, I wasn't sure how she had accomplished that, but I figured I would find out soon enough. I walked over to the main house by myself after spending the entire lunch hour dodging questions from the students about why I was starting so late. Vikram had made it clear that no one was to know my real story, so it was left up to me to concoct enough details to satisfy the pre-pubescent horde. It wasn't as easy as one might have thought given that these were no ordinary twelve-year-olds. I was glad to escape as soon as I could.

As I walked across the campus, I looked around me. It was so surreal to be here, to realize that this whole other world had always existed right along with the one I knew, and no one had any clue about it. It was well hidden, just another private school on secluded property. I wondered if the students here knew what life was like outside in the world where I had grown up. I reached the entrance to the main house and ran up the steps. Shiv and Tara were waiting in the foyer and took me to a part of the house that I hadn't seen before. I followed them down a hallway, and after a while we turned right into a large conference room. Vikram, Nina and Dev were already there, and we joined them at the large table in the middle of the room. There was a large jug of ice water on a tray with glasses, and I poured myself some. The table was partially covered with printouts and maps. Nina's eyes were glistening as she turned to me.

"Callie, we have great news. Our contacts in India have found the possible location of the sword."

"Kali's sword...that's great," I stuttered, a sudden wave of panic rising.

"Yes, of course," Nina replied impatiently. "We have been trying to pinpoint its location for some time now, but it hasn't been easy. Mahisha's people are also after it, and it has been a challenge to stay one step ahead of them."

"What happens if they do get hold of it?" I needed to know exactly what I was up against.

"Well, then Kali...you...won't be able to destroy Mahisha. It's the only weapon that can destroy him. And you're the only one who can wield it."

I was silent for some time. "But I have no training, no experience. I don't even know if you all are right about this...about me." It was true; they all were convinced that I was Kali, but I didn't feel any different or powerful. I was just confused and overwhelmed.

Dev stood up and came over to my side of the table. He put his hand on my shoulder. "Callie, I know this is hard, but you must trust us. We know who you are, and we have faith in you. It is your divine destiny. Now you must make yourself see how powerful and strong you are." He looked at me beseechingly. "You must do it for your parents."

Even in such a short while, Dev had figured me out. He knew that my parents were my weakness right now. I would do anything to save them, even go to India to get a sword that I had no idea how to use. Then again, I couldn't just stay here, waiting to learn. They may have been too nice to say anything, but I knew Dev and Tara would agree that I seemed a hopeless case when it came to combat training. I could see all of them, Shiv, Tara, Nina, Dev and even Vikram looking at me expectantly. Maybe my imagination was in overdrive, but I felt they were looking to me to save them. To save everybody. And that was a huge burden. I didn't know if I was capable enough. But I did know one thing: I would not let my parents down. I couldn't be sure if my dad had actually come to me in my dream or if I had just been hallucinating, but he had told me to find the sword and that was what I would do. So I squared my shoulders, sat up straight and looked Dev in the eye.

"Okay. I'll go. But before that I need everything you know about what I'm walking into. I won't go unprepared."

They gave a collective sigh of relief. I could feel Shiv's eyes on me, but I couldn't look at him right now. Nothing would distract me. The rest of the day passed quickly as they filled me in on centuries' worth of information. I was glad that I'd always been a bit of a nerd when it came to school, because right now it really helped that I could retain a lot of information in a short time. They told me about the various factions of Mahisha's armies. It seemed that they were spread all around the world. I learned about the tactics they used. Mahisha and his demons fed on humanity's weaknesses. Thus, the most vulnerable members of society were perfect prey for him and his minions. In Kolkata, specifically, that would include the orphans, poverty-stricken widows and pretty much anyone who was cast away. Their lives were so devoid of hope and so full of despair that the promise of a better tomorrow at any cost would be a temptation.

As I listened to the stories of Rakshakaris who had stood guard against Mahisha for centuries, I recoiled with horror at some of the vile acts that humans were capable of committing under the influence of pure evil. Genocide, torture and swindling were child's play to this army of demons. The human recruits gave up their souls in exchange for wealth, security and freedom. A part of me sympathized with the choices these people made, having witnessed first-hand the awful conditions that some people lived in. I could understand how utter despair could turn a mother to the dark side if it meant a better life for her children.

While I had lived in India, some of the harsh realities of a third world country had become part of the daily scenery for me. But after living in Seattle for so many years, I sometimes remembered with horror the things I had seen. Like a mother with little babies who hadn't eaten in days. Their eyes would have a vacant look, the look of someone with no hope. At the time I had been too young to recognize the irony of people living in abhorrent conditions while right next to them others lived in unfathomable wealth. But now that I was older and more informed, it shocked me to the core. As I listened to the others, I realized that thieving politicians and corrupt leaders had one thing in common with Mahisha. They might be human but they were just as evil as the demons we were about to fight. I looked up at the wall clock. We'd been at this for over three hours now. I felt drained from listening to so many depressing accounts and asked to take a break. I got up and went out to get some fresh air. I realized that Shiv had followed me when I heard the door close behind him. He came and sat next to me on the steps.

"That was a lot to take in wasn't it?" he asked, gently taking my hand. His touch was nice, comforting without anything more. It was what I needed right then. For some reason the thought of Ben flashed into my mind. I'd been so preoccupied that I had hardly given him a thought in the last couple of days. But I knew I couldn't just leave without saying goodbye. A part of me recognized the possibility that I might not make it back. I stood up abruptly, my hand slipping out of Shiv's.

"I have to see Ben. I can't just leave without saying anything to him."

Shiv stood up too. He glanced back at the house

and then back at me. "It will take some convincing," he said. "But I think I can figure out a way to take you back. Just go along with me."

We went back into the house. Shiv announced that I needed to go back to my house to grab a few more items since I would be traveling to India, such as my passport and other essentials. His parents didn't suspect anything, so a few minutes later we were on our way back. I had texted Ben, and thankfully he had replied right away. We would meet at our usual spot in the park. Shiv would stand guard. I felt apprehensive about meeting Ben. The last time we had spoken he'd left angry. It was already dark by the time we got there, and Shiv insisted on scoping out the park before I got out of the car. When he signaled that it was safe I joined him and walked over to the swings. Ben was already there on one of the old regular swings that had not been replaced by the weird saucer swings that I detested. I could see from his face that he wasn't too thrilled to see Shiv, but I had been expecting that. I nodded at Shiv to give us some space. He walked over to a copse and then seemed to just blend into the darkness.

I sat down on the swing beside Ben like I'd always done. It was big enough to fit both of us. At first neither of us said anything. Then we both spoke at once.

"Ben. I..."

"Callie, how..."

Ben recovered first. "You go," he said, looking down at his hands. He'd always had big hands, his fingers long and thin, but now I noticed they seemed different. They looked damaged, as if he'd been punching things. There were scars and bruises on them, clearly visible, even in the little light cast by the streetlamp. I reached out to touch his right hand, but he flinched. Something painful flared up for a moment. He was still angry with me. I felt the base of my throat growing warm, but I ignored it.

"Ben, I'm so sorry...I know you have a lot of questions."

He didn't say anything. He just sat there looking down. He wasn't going to make this easy for me. I didn't blame him; he deserved better.

"I'm going away for a while," I began. He looked up then and I gasped. There were shadows under his eyes, but that wasn't what shocked me. He always got those when he spent too many late nights studying for finals. There were bruises on his face, some reddish, some purple, in various stages of healing.

"What happened to you?" I stood up, my pendant growing warmer. Suddenly I felt sick. Out of the corner of my eye I saw Shiv emerging from the shadows by the trees. In the same instant, two men materialized on either side of Ben. I barely had time to register that we were in danger when a dagger flew through the semi-darkness and buried itself right in the chest of one of the men. He disintegrated right before my eyes. At the same time the other one put his arm around Ben's neck, and in the next moment they were gone. Just like that they vanished right before my eyes. Both of them. I stood there, frozen in place, the horror of what had just happened dawning on me. I understood the bruises now and the scars. They must have been waiting for me to make contact with Ben. I had walked right into a trap. And I had just lost my best friend. My legs gave way and I crumpled to the ground. It had all happened so fast, and then Shiv was there cradling my head on his lap as I sobbed into it.

"They took him, Shiv..." I choked on my tears and sat up so I could breathe again. "He had bruises...they must have tortured him to get to me." I couldn't take it. Another person I loved was taken, and it was all because of me. Shiv held me while I cried, stroking my hair until the sobs subsided. It was a while before I could stand, then we walked back to the car and drove to the Academy.

EIGHT

WHEN WE GOT back, Shiv told his parents and Vikram what had happened. He left out the part about the plan to meet Ben, instead making it sound as if we had just run into him. It didn't even matter to me. I was cold inside and felt nothing except icy rage and the burning desire to demolish everything that Mahisha stood for. He would not take one more thing from me.

My fury was boiling over and I could feel the heat in my veins. I had to go somewhere where I could release it before I took it out on someone in the room. I looked at Shiv in a silent appeal. It only took a few seconds. The others were still talking, trying to figure out the next move. Shiv got up, told them we needed to leave and took me to the training hall. Tara was there, already getting things ready for the next day's lessons.

She looked surprised to see the two of us, but Shiv quickly told her what had happened. She nodded, handing me a pair of gloves, and nudged me toward the punching bag that hung from the ceiling in one corner of the gym.

I was hesitant at first, but then the fury took over, guiding every ounce of anger I was feeling into my hands and into every punch that landed on the bag. Each time my fists made contact with the tough material, they exploded with pain, but I couldn't stop...I didn't want to stop. It was as if the hurt kept me from feeling the intense guilt that was threatening to take over. Guilt over Ben becoming a pawn in this cat-and-mouse game. Then there was the paralyzing fear that Ben...*my* Ben was at the mercy of those demons. I couldn't allow my mind to go there. Instead I concentrated on each punch and continued until I felt every bone in my fingers would shatter. I stopped, wiping the sweat from my face and letting my arms fall. Tara and Shiv were watching me with the same strange expression.

"Callie..." Shiv said, clearly not sure what to do next.

"I'm okay." I flopped down on a mat and Shiv and Tara joined me.

"Callie...I'm so sorry about your friend —" Tara began, but I put up a hand.

"I'm sorry, Tara...I can't...I can't deal with this right now." I could feel my eyes welling up and the last thing I needed right now was to have a breakdown.

"What are you going to do?" Shiv asked softly. I looked at him and shrugged, my shoulders rising and falling in defeat.

"I don't know what I can do." I felt utterly hopeless. I had no idea where to even begin. "They used him to get to me. He doesn't even have a clue about what's going on. I lied to him...I never imagined they could get to him." The tears threatened to spill over, and this time I let them as I remembered the bruises I had seen on his face in the light of the streetlamp at the park. He wouldn't have known what was happening and what I was involved in. I couldn't even begin to imagine the betrayal he must have felt when he realized I had kept so many secrets from him. I shook my head, angry for letting myself fall apart like this. I stood up and looked at Tara and Shiv.

"Look...I appreciate that you are trying to help, but I need to focus right now. Ben's my best friend. If anything happens to him...anything else...I will never forgive myself."

Shiv stood up and helped Tara to her feet.

"Callie...whatever it takes," Tara said and Shiv nodded.

"We're here for you. We'll help you train and we won't stop until you're ready to face them," Shiv said. Then he put an arm around my shoulders. "We'll find him, Callie. I promise."

We walked back to the main house in silence. I

knew I had a difficult road ahead of me, but somehow with Shiva and Tara by my side I was less terrified.

When we joined Vikram, Dev and Nina, they didn't ask why Shiv and I had left so abruptly. I had to assume that this was not the first time they had lived through something like this. In their line of work, loss was probably a professional hazard and handling it must be all too familiar to them. I was glad I didn't have to explain myself, and besides, I had other things on my mind.

"I want to know how to channel Kali," I announced. They all looked at me. "You said that her powers will manifest in me. I think that the time has come."

"Callie," Vikram said, shifting in his armchair by the fireplace. "Kali's powers are not something to can turn on with the flip of a switch."

"Well, then tell me what I have to do," I demanded, bristling at his condescending tone. A dark expression crossed his face for a fleeting moment and then it was gone. Nina, who had been sitting quietly in her chair, hastily intervened.

"Callie, I can help you with this. I have spent many years studying the effects that the powers of the Goddess have on her avatars. There are ways to master them, and the sooner you learn them, the stronger you'll be."

There was something about Nina that usually put me on edge, but I had to admit that now she was putting my mind at ease.

"That would be great, Nina, thank you," I said graciously.

"Good, we'll start immediately. Vikram, if we are done here..."

"Yes, of course, Nina, you and Callie go ahead. We can finish up here on our own," Vikram said, waving us off in his usual imperious manner. I decided I most definitely did not like Vikram very much. Maybe I was being childish, but there was something about him I couldn't define that made me uneasy.

Nina and I left the main house, and to my surprise we didn't go to any of the school buildings. Instead she took me to the residence building where I was staying with the other students. We went up to my room. Although it was meant for double occupancy, I did not have a roommate. Nina indicated that I should sit on my bed. I did, not having the faintest idea what to expect.

"Okay, Callie...I want you to relax. Just kick off your shoes and get comfortable. We are going to practice some meditation."

I stared at her in disbelief. *This is how I am going to channel the Goddess. By meditating?*

"Trust me, I know what I'm doing. I have studied the art of Goddess Manifestation for many years. Just close your eyes and take deep breaths."

Was she for real? What the hell was Goddess Manifestation?

I closed my eyes obediently and started breathing

deeply. Soon I was hyperventilating and I was pretty sure that was not what Nina had meant by deep breaths. I'd never been good at yoga or any kind of meditation. When I'd started having the nightmares, my mom had tried to get me to do yoga with her, hoping that would stop them. I would either fall asleep or just worry about all the other things I could be doing instead of just lying there with my eyes closed. This wasn't any better.

"Nina, I don't think this is working," I said, opening my eyes. She didn't reply. She had made herself comfortable on the bed across from mine and was clearly in a deep meditative state. She sat with her legs crossed in a traditional yoga pose, another feat I had never been able to master without toppling over. I toyed with the idea of using my finger to see if she would too, but I restrained myself. Eventually she opened her eyes and looked at me disapprovingly. Her thin lips curved downwards and her even thinner eyebrows arched in a subtle sign of disdain.

"Callie, if you're not going to take this seriously, then no one can help you."

"It's not that...I just can't do this right now. Don't you know some spell or something?" I regretted the words as soon as they came out of my mouth. Nina was not amused.

"Spell?" she said, her voice shrill and loud in the small room. "Do you think I am a witch?" Thankfully, it was a rhetorical question, but I still had to bite my tongue. I didn't want her any more worked up than she already was.

"No, of course not," I managed after gulping down my original response. "I just meant that maybe there was something I could chant or..." I trailed off weakly.

"Look, Callie, this is not going to be easy." She sat down next to me, and when she spoke again her voice was considerably softer. "There is no short cut...you're going to have to do this the hard way. You are a very lucky girl." I smiled at that, shaking my head. "Lucky" was not the word I would use to describe myself these days.

"No, Callie, I'm serious. The Goddess has chosen you, so that must mean that you have the strength. Now you just have to tap into that."

In a way her words made sense. Why, of all the billions of women in the world, would I have been chosen by Kali? There had to be a reason. Even if I didn't know what it was, I did know that it was something. Maybe I would just have to wait to figure out what exactly it was, but for now I had to learn how to channel her powers. Time was running out for my parents and for Ben. I took a deep breath and nodded.

"Okay, I'll try again."

Nina gave me a smile and stood up. "Alright, now this time try to focus your thoughts. Find something you can draw strength from and concentrate on that."

I closed my eyes. It took a few moments, but then I thought about my parents. In my mind I looked at the picture frame that I always kept on my nightstand. It was the three of us at the beach a few summers ago. Ben was with us and had taken the photo, which showed us leaning against a log. It was one of my most favorite family pictures, and it was what I focused on now. I remembered how happy I had been that day with my family, enjoying the togetherness. In my mind I tried to recreate the warmth and love when I was with my parents and how safe I felt. At first, nothing happened. But then I could feel some of the warmth from my thoughts seep into the rest of my consciousness like molasses, slowly coating my insides and leaving me feeling all gooey and soft. Then it changed, becoming something else, something that I could draw strength from. It lit me up from inside, this power, like I'd been connected to a battery and recharged. I opened my eyes, and from the look in Nina's eyes I could tell that she'd noticed a change as well. I wondered if my hair was standing up or something. I reached out and touched it. Nope, my hair was fine.

"How do you feel?" Nina asked, her eyes wide with wonder.

"I'm not sure...I feel strong, I guess...but it's strange...I can't really describe it."

Nina looked a little disappointed. I wondered if she'd thought that I would have some spurt of supernatural power or something.

"Okay, so what's next?" I wasn't going to waste time trying to make Nina feel better; I had plenty problems of my own to deal with.

"Next, you continue preparing yourself. You have little time and much to learn." She put a hand on my shoulder. "I have faith in you, Callie. Perhaps more than you have in yourself right now."

It took a few moments to swallow the lump in my throat. I didn't want to show any weakness.

"I can do it, Nina. I won't let everyone down." I spoke with much more conviction than I felt, but that was all I could do now. I had to believe I had it in me. And I had to train hard.

The next day I decided to get an early start. I ate breakfast and joined Shiv and Tara in the training hall. They introduced me to a different weapon, a set of daggers called *phurba*. They were to be used at the same time. Tara demonstrated, and as I watched her once again, sparring with Shiv, I was in awe of the graceful yet deadly way in which she used them. I could only hope I would be half as good as she was by the time I actually came face to face with Mahisha. When Tara was done and gave the *phurba* to me, I held one in each hand, studying their appearance. They were as heavy as I expected, given that they were made of bronze. They were identical, their hilts bearing images of the goddesses, Durga, Shakti and Kali. Each was inlaid with what I assumed were precious stones.

The blades were serrated and looked terrifying. I didn't know if I could actually use them to hurt someone. But I did know that when the time came and there was a question of saving my parents, I wouldn't hesitate. Tara showed me the correct way to hold them and I gripped one in each hand, my fingers in the grooves of the handles. Shiv picked up another set and we went at it. At first I was hesitant, seeing as I wasn't wearing any protective gear. Apparently at the Academy they did not believe in training with gear that the Rakshakari wouldn't be wearing during a real fight. It kind of made sense to me. I didn't see the point of learning to fight safely, only to end up getting badly hurt when it came to the real action.

I turned my focus back to the action. Shiv was taking it easy on me and Tara was shouting out instruction from the side. It took some time to get into a rhythm, but eventually I did and I could tell from the change in Tara's voice that she noticed it too. I didn't know when it started exactly, but at some point in our sparring something changed. It began deep inside, somewhere in my gut, a small worm of a feeling. It unraveled slowly and spread through the rest of my body until my fingertips tingled with it. The warmth kept building until it spilled over and then it was as if the daggers were just an extension of me. I felt as though I was performing some sort of a dance, the steps of which I had learned in some other existence. It came naturally, and without having to think about it I had

Shiv on the floor with both daggers pointing down at him. It was as if a part of my brain still knew who I was and what I was doing, while another part of me heard echoes from a distant past. It was quite amazing, I had to admit, to feel in control for the first time in weeks. Plus, I loved the way Shiv was grinning up at me, his expression a mixture of smugness at knowing he'd been right and pride because I had finally figured out how to focus.

We took a break and soon it was time for lunch. Thankfully, it consisted of pizza and salad. I was starving and wolfed down four slices. We stayed at the table longer than usual discussing the upcoming trip. After lunch Vikram asked us to join him in the library, where he had laid out several maps. As I sat down, I got a closer look. They looked like older maps, because some of the markings were different. Some were maps of British India from 1860, others were more recent. I noticed that on the older one someone had circled an area about 1,200 miles southeast of Kolkata. It was part of the Andaman Islands, which my parents and I had visited back when we still lived in Kolkata. The Andaman Islands were part of a colony the British government had chosen to use as a prison island of sorts during the centuries of the Raj. Of course, by the time we visited it had long been a resort island for tourists from all over the world. This little island that had been circled in red bore no name.

"What is this place?" I asked, looking at Vikram.

"That is North Sentinel Island," he replied.

"I've never heard of it," I said, pulling the map closer to get a better look. The fact that there was no name on it struck me as odd. Vikram seemed to sense my confusion.

"It's not marked on any maps because it isn't really part of India, or any other country, for that matter. There's a small tribe living there. But they have been untouched by civilization."

"So why are we interested in this tribe?" I asked.

"Well, because they are said to be the first people to come out of Africa around sixty thousand years ago. They have survived and managed to stay completely remote. No outsiders are allowed on the island."

That took a few moments to sink in. My mind was reeling. The fact that there was an area that no government or any other party had been able to take over was quite a feat. I wondered how they had done it. How had they kept everyone out for so many centuries and not fallen prey to the lures of modern life?

"And," Vikram continued, "because we have reason to believe there is an ancient temple hidden deep in the jungles. And that is where we think the Sword of Kali has been hidden."

"I thought outsiders can't go there," I said, confused because none of this was making any sense.

"That's true, but we have accounts that go back thousands of years, and they provide sufficient evidence that what we suspect is true."

"Think about it, Callie," Dev said. "What place is more perfect than one so remote, no one will ever think of looking there?" He looked more animated than I had seen him since we'd met.

It did sound possible. The battle between Mahisha and Kali had taken place about five thousand years ago. Her sword was never found, but according to Nina, even within the anthropological community there were those who believed such a sword existed. So if somehow it had been hidden on this remote island that time had forgotten, it would have been kept safely out of Mahisha's hands. It was the perfect hiding place. A sliver of excitement began to grow deep inside me, as though finally things were beginning to fall into place. I knew there were many other details left to iron out, but at least this was a start. We had a quick dinner of sandwiches in the library as we talked more about the native inhabitants of the island and the very infrequent encounters outsiders had with them. From what I heard it seemed that each time it had been a disaster for those who encroached on their shores.

I listened to them talk for hours, asking questions whenever I felt I was missing a big piece of the puzzle. As the evening wore on I found myself fading. I knew I was done for the day.

"I'm sorry, but is it okay if I go to bed? It's been a long day," I said, standing up and stretching my aching legs. I felt like an old woman, but I knew that tomorrow morning it would be even worse.

"Yes, of course, you need to rest," Vikram said. I wished everyone goodnight and left them to continue. I went upstairs, took a hot shower and got ready for bed. I was asleep as soon as my head touched the pillow. That night I slept without dreams or nightmares. It was the best sleep I'd had in a long time.

NINE

THE NEXT DAY dawned bright and sunny and I woke up feeling refreshed and ready for another day of training. In fact, Seattle was enjoying an unusual string of good weather, and the initiates and I took full advantage and trained outside most days. Tara had me running laps every morning, and I hated her for it. Apparently it was to improve my stamina. I hadn't realized my stamina needed improving, but she was the boss as far as my training was concerned. I was also required to spend time with Mr. Perkins, professor of demonology, in addition to my regular class time. This I did not mind since I had a lot of catching up to do. Plus it was sort of fascinating. Some of the demons we studied were the stuff of horror movies and nightmares. I learned about Makra demons, Kleesha demons, Kaama demons, Agni demons, and Maya demons. Some would burn their victims from the inside out while others would drive them crazy by creating illusions in their minds. Before I knew it, two weeks had passed and it was time for Shiv and I to go on our trip. On some level I think we all knew that this trip could end up being a total disaster, but given the circumstances and the urgency, this was the best option. I felt that Vikram and the others hoped the rest of Kali's powers would manifest somehow in me between now and when I actually came to face Mahisha.

"Callie, are you ready to go?" Tara called from downstairs. Our luggage had been loaded into the cars with all of our equipment while I double-checked the maps and files of research that we were taking with us. Nina had passed on all the information she had been able to find out from the Elders. This included accounts from witnesses dating back hundreds of years. At least I wouldn't be bored on the twenty-seven-hour trip to Kolkata. I nervously touched my skull pendant, looking at my desk, which was strewn with paper and covered in post-its, making sure that I didn't forget anything vital we might need there. Even though a lot of it seemed irrelevant to me, I was not leaving anything to chance. Even though crude hand-drawn maps didn't seem to make any sense to me now, I knew that on the island we would be without phones, GPS, or any of the dozens of other resources we were used to. We would be in unknown, uncharted territory and I wanted to have as much information with me as I could carry in my backpack.

"Tara, I'll be right down," I called out, taking one last look around the room I'd been staying in for the past couple of weeks. Then I closed the door behind me and went down the stairs to the foyer. I picked up the backpack that I'd brought down earlier and went out to meet the others waiting by the cars. Shiv and I were riding to the airport with Vikram so we could go over last-minute instructions. Tara, Dev and Nina were coming in the other car.

When Vikram had first suggested that Shiv and I go on this quest alone, I had been suspicious. After all, he was the head of the Academy and it struck me as strange that he would send someone as inexperienced as me with just one other person. But when I discreetly hinted at it, I found out that the last thing he wanted was to raise suspicion in Mahisha's camp. It was bad enough that they already knew about me and had my parents and Ben. But if they knew what we were planning, we wouldn't stand a chance. So Vikram, Nina and Dev came up with a plan. Shiv and I would pose as newlyweds on our honeymoon in the Andaman Islands. That was so commonplace that no one would notice anything untoward. Of course, the tricky part would be to get from there to the North Sentinel Island. According to articles and reports we had read, there was no way to get onto the island without being attacked. What the Rakshakari were counting on was the fact that

I was an avatar of Kali, and that would protect me from attack. This was all a theory, of course, and we had no way of knowing what would happen.

A few minutes later we were on our way. To the casual observer we would appear calm, but each of us knew that this trip was no game. We had little knowledge of what we might face, and no amount of preparation could disguise the fact that this could be a deadly wild goose chase. Of the five of us I was probably the most apprehensive, but if the others were also aware of that, they were doing a pretty good job of hiding it. By the time we reached the airport we had gone over every detail for the umpteenth time. As Shiv and I said our goodbyes, I couldn't help wondering if I would see them again. I knew I was being maudlin, but in the last couple of weeks they had been my anchor, my link to sanity in a world where everything had suddenly gone insane. I looked at Shiv and wondered what he was feeling. We hadn't had much of a chance to spend time alone, so I didn't have a clue what he thought about this whole plan. We checked in, dealt with immigration then went to find something to eat once we reached our boarding gate. It wasn't too long before we were on the plane, and as I settled into my seat I hoped that on the long, long flight I would delve into the mystery that was Shiv.

"So, Shiv, when was the last time you went to India?" I asked, thinking this a good time to start getting to know more about him. He didn't answer right away and I didn't push him; I knew how it felt. It wasn't easy to leave everything and everyone familiar behind and just start a new life.

"Actually, it's only been three years. But it feels like a lot longer." He turned to me suddenly with a look I couldn't define. "You know who I miss the most?" I shook my head, even though I knew it was a rhetorical question. "My dog, Dobby." He grinned when he saw my expression. "Hey, laugh all you want. I'm a huge Harry Potter fan and I'm not afraid to say it."

Was I surprised at this confession? Sure. Did I think he was absolutely adorable at this moment? Hell yes.

"So what happened to Dobby when you left?"

"We gave him to my uncle. The one we're going to be staying with."

"So you'll get to see him...that's great." Shiv nodded with a smile and leaned back in his seat.

We sat in silence for a while until the attendants started bringing the drinks around. Then we began to go over our plan again.

We pulled down the trays and spread out our stuff as best as we could. We spent the next several hours poring over reports and articles that the Rakshakari had been gathering for years concerning Mahisha's followers and their activities. What I learned did nothing to banish my growing fear. Ever since Kali had all but destroyed Mahisha thousands of years ago, he had been regrouping. It had taken several millennia, but he was finally strong enough to pose a real threat to the Immortals and to humanity. His followers had grown over the last few centuries, and as humans turned against their own kind over land and resources, Mahisha fed off their greed and weakness to lure them into his fold. It didn't take much to convince a desperate person to take the easy way when times were tough.

This wasn't just happening in North America. Reports from Rakshakari members all over the world told the same story. The day was near when Mahisha would arise, having regained his full strength. And from what Vikram, Nina and Dev had told me, once that happened there would be no stopping him.

I had heard the whole story of Mahisha from my dad when I was little. Mahisha had once been loyal to the Immortals. So loyal, in fact, that he felt he deserved immortality. When he brought this request before the Trinity of Vishnu, Brahma and Shiva, the three most powerful gods, they were amused. Their rejection enraged Mahisha, who had spent many years in complete devotion to them. He approached Indra, the King of the Gods, and begged him to reconsider. Although Indra pitied the devoted Mahisha, he could not grant him immortality. He did, however, decide to grant him a boon. This boon would render Mahisha invincible from death by any man or god. Upon receiving this boon, Mahisha rejoiced. He would show the arrogant Immortals what he was capable of. He embarked on a campaign of terror against humans and gods alike. When the Immortals realized they could not stand against Mahisha's powers, they complained to the Trinity, who created Kali. In receiving the boon, Mahisha had neglected to take into account that he could be killed at the hands of a woman. His arrogance would have led to his downfall if not for one thing that went wrong during the final battle. And it was this detail that no one could tell me for sure. No one knew why Kali had failed to destroy Mahisha, and if we didn't figure it out soon, then we were all doomed.

By the time the flight attendants came around with the lunch trolleys, we were both going cross-eyed and were ready for a break. After lunch I tried to close my eyes for a bit but found that I was too restless to sleep. All sorts of thoughts were swirling around in my head, and finally I just gave in and stood up.

"No luck with the rest thing, eh?" Shiv rubbed his eyes and ran his hands through his hair.

"I can never sleep on airplanes," I said. "I think I'll just walk around for a bit."

I almost ended up on his lap trying to squeeze out into the aisle. Muttering about how airplanes should really have more legroom, I walked to the lavatory and freshened up. By the time I returned to my seat the tea and coffee carts were being wheeled around, so I asked for a cup of tea. Fortunately, by this time Shiv had moved over to my seat, so I didn't have to climb all over him with a hot beverage. I could see the dark circles under his eyes. I glanced at my watch and did a quick calculation. We'd been in the air for almost eight hours, so I knew we'd be landing in London soon. I was looking forward to the opportunity to get out and stretch my legs before getting on another plane for the nine-hour flight that would take us to Kolkata.

I finished my tea and placed it on the cart as it passed by again. I leaned back in the seat and closed my eyes. I was about to doze off when a sudden wave of nausea washed over me. I tried to open my eyes, but it was really difficult and I just gave up and waited for the nausea to fade. It started to abate but then something strange happened. I could hear Shiv saying my name, but it sounded like it was coming from far away. I could feel his warm cinnamon breath on me as he spoke and I felt a tingling that started deep in my belly and worked its way up to my chest then into my head, and then I was floating away. I wondered if I was having another vision, but this was different. I was weightless, as if floating on clouds.

I looked around, but there were no bodies, no screams, only serenity. I felt a touch on my shoulder and turned around. Shiv was standing there. But he wasn't really the Shiv I knew. He looked different, celestial somehow, his dark hair long and falling in curls around his shoulders. His chest was bare, muscular and over his right shoulder he wore a strap from which hung a sword. He wore some sort of loose trousers, the kind Indian men often wore for formal occasions. He was smiling down at me, and when I looked into his eyes I could see my reflection. Only it wasn't really me. I looked exotic, with long, dark tresses cascading down past my shoulders. I was wearing a lot of jewelry and a gold sari. Then the reflection disappeared and I was drowning in his eyes again. I opened my mouth to ask what was going on, but no sound came out. Instead, he started moving away, as if pulled by some invisible force. He seemed to be calling out to me, but I could hear nothing. I reached out to touch him, to hold him to him, but he kept moving away until he was a speck in the distance. I felt myself floating again, getting heavier. My eyelids fluttered until I could not keep them open any longer, and then blackness took over.

TEN

WHEN I CAME to, the first thing I felt was a cool hand on my forehead. I opened my eyes and found myself looking into Shiv's eyes. Once again I felt the tingling, but this time there was, thankfully, no floating away. I was still in the airplane seat with Shiv leaning deliciously close to me. I decided that I wanted to relish the moment a little longer, so I closed my eyes again.

"Callie," Shiv was saying softly. "How are you feeling?" He sounded really worried, and against my better judgment I decided to let him out of his misery. I opened my eyes as slowly as I could.

"I'm okay, Shiv," I said, straightening and sitting up.

"Did you have another vision? What did you see?"

"Nothing different from what I've seen before," I

lied. I was not ready to tell him what I'd really seen until I had a chance to figure out what it meant.

"Can I get you anything? A sandwich? You should have some ice water."

He reached up to press the call button, and when the flight attendant came Shiv asked him for a glass of water for each of us. By the time the water came I was feeling a little better already, but my throat was parched so I gratefully took big gulps and emptied the glass in no time. Something had been nagging at the back of my mind for some time, and I decided this was as good a time as any to discuss it, seeing as I wasn't about to get any more rest on the plane.

"Shiv, something's been bothering me for the longest time...how exactly did Mahisha escape?"

"Well," Shiv, taking a sip of his water, "from what I've read, Mahisha was able to evade Kali by changing forms. The myths say that during the battle he took on the form of a buffalo, a lion and a warrior. It was when he was in buffalo form that Kali last fought him."

"Exactly, and Kali was able to sever his head while he was a buffalo." I distinctly remembered reading that as a child, which was why I was so confused.

"Yes, that's what popular legend tells us about the Great Battle between Kali and Mahisha," said Shiv.

"But that's not what really happened, is it?" I knew the answer to that question even before I asked, but I couldn't help it. I needed to hear it again, just in case this whole thing was a crazy mistake.

"No, but no one knew right away. It wasn't until after Mahisha started recruiting that anyone figured out what was going on."

"But does anyone know exactly how he survived?"

"Well, one theory is that he knew Kali's weakness and was able to stop her from killing him."

"What was her weakness?"

"That's where the problem lies. Only Shiva, Vishnu and Brahma knew her weakness. When the gods created her, they each gave her some of their powers so that she would be all-powerful."

"Okay, so whose bright idea was it to leave her with a weakness? I mean, wasn't that the whole point of creating her — to make sure she would be able to destroy Mahisha?"

"Yes, but you are overlooking an important fact. The gods aren't all that different from us humans. They're just as insecure when it comes to their power. The Gods of the Trinity, Shiva, Vishnu and Brahma, have always been considered the most powerful. They weren't about to risk losing control of an all-powerful goddess they had created."

I was beginning to think that maybe the gods weren't as all-knowing as we made them out to be.

"So they left one thing about her vulnerable to attack, and somehow Mahisha knew about it and used it to his advantage?"

"That's right," said Shiv. "And no one really knows what can hurt her."

At that moment the flight attendants started coming around with the in-flight meals, and the next few hours went by with little conversation. I even managed to take a short nap before the pilot finally announced our arrival in London. We had about three hours here before getting on another plane that would take us to India. We used our time at the airport to stretch our legs and just look around. Before long we were on our final leg of the journey and eventually the pilot announced our descent into Kolkata's international airport. I couldn't wait to be out there, breathing in the humid air, pushing my way through the sea of people.

After an excruciatingly slow exit through immigration and customs, we finally made our way toward the exit. As soon we walked through the massive sliding doors that led to the outside, the air engulfed me. It was thick with humidity and carried with it familiar smells. Some of them made me gag momentarily. Others evoked memories I had not visited in a while. The smell of deep-fried *pakora*s like my grandmother used to make. The fragrance of jasmine flowers permeating everything. For a brief moment I felt as if time stood still while I inhaled Kolkata. Then it was over. The shrill sound of a whistle broke the spell, and I was jolted back into reality. Reality was swarms of sweaty bodies jostling for space, trying to make their way to the pre-paid taxi stands. Young men and boys vied to carry our bags.

Shiv looked at me and grinned. "It's great to be

back, isn't it? I never realize how much I miss all this until I'm here."

I just nodded, too overcome by emotion to actually speak. Shiv was scanning the crowd, looking for his uncle.

"There he is. He's seen us." Shiv started making his way toward the moving mass of people. Contrary to my instinct, which was telling me to turn around and run back into the cool refuge of the terminal, I followed him into the crowd. A minute or so later we came to a stop in front of a middle-aged, slightly balding man.

"Ah, so you are the young Callie I've been hearing so much about. I'm Suresh, Shiv's uncle. I hope the flight wasn't too bad?" As he spoke, he took the carry-on bag I was holding and handed it to a young man standing behind him.

"It's so nice to meet you, Uncle Suresh," I said, folding my hands in the traditional *namaste*. "Thank you for all the trouble you've gone to. Shiv's told us that you've been a great help getting everything arranged for us."

It was funny how I was still able to switch into that super-polite version of myself when faced with an adult in India. When I was in Seattle I was always amazed at the dichotomy of being an Indian teenager. There was one way you were with your friends and another when you were around the more traditional Indian adults. It sounded duplicitous but it really wasn't. It was more like self-preservation, as well as a way of being respectful. My friends would tease me about it all the time. I even had a different accent when I spoke to my relatives; I tended to revert to my Indian accent when I was around them, a remnant of my years living in India. It hadn't always been easy. Sometimes I wished I could just be the same around everyone, but that was just the reality of my life. And it wasn't that I didn't love my Indian heritage; I loved all the richness and warmth and color it brought to my life. But I had to admit I did not like some of the complications that came along. Luckily, I had found a pretty good balance.

Before we landed Shiv had filled me in on all the details of his family. Uncle Suresh was Nina's brother. We would be staying with him while we were in Kolkata before beginning our journey to North Sentinel Island.

Our drive into the city was a trip down memory lane. We drove across the Howrah Bridge. It was still as huge as I remembered from our family trips years ago. It was strange to be there again, as if nothing had changed, but everything was somehow different. From the bridge I could see the rows of slums that lined the banks of the Hooghly River, but as we approached the city center tall buildings reached up into the sky as if they were trying to grab bits of cloud to shelter them from the sun. Giant billboards advertised all the latest brands and fashions while voluptuous Bollywood heroines pouted down as we drove beneath them. Traffic in India had never been light, but clearly things had changed in the ten years I'd been gone. We didn't move for what seemed like hours. It was nearly dark by the time we reached Uncle Suresh's house, and I was exhausted. Shiv had somehow managed to take a nap during the long drive, but I felt a headache coming on and needed to rest.

Uncle Suresh's home was in an upscale neighborhood judging by the luxurious homes with sprawling gardens we passed on the way. Tall wrought iron gates separated his estate from the outside world. I realized this had to be a requirement of any Rakshakari home, given the kind of lifestyle they led. We went down a long, winding driveway and finally stopped in front of a massive entrance flanked by actual armed guards in uniform. I saw Shiv raise an eyebrow as we pulled up.

"Uncle Suresh, what's with all the security?" he asked.

His uncle turned to him with a wry smile. "Things have changed since you were living here, Shiv. We cannot take any chances."

Shiv didn't respond as we got out of the car and went up the marble steps to the main door. All of a sudden a flash of black and brown shot out the front door and jumped on Shiv. The next moment he was on the floor of the entrance rolling around with his beloved Dobby. I just stood and watched. The expression on his face was one of sheer joy.

After they both calmed down, Dobby came to me

and put his cold nose on my hand. As I ruffled the fur on his head, he wagged his tail and gave me kisses. I was in heaven. After a while I looked up and saw a young woman trying to greet us. She wore a white sari with a thin yellow border running along the bottom. Because she seemed so young, I was surprised to see her in white, the color of widows. She folded her hands in a *namaste*, as did we, and after giving her some instructions, Uncle Suresh ushered us into the lavish interior of his home. The living room, or drawing room as it was called in India, was tastefully furnished with antiques. By the time we were seated, the young woman had brought in a tray of tea and assorted cakes, cookies and other goodies. I was starving and wasn't shy about helping myself, while Uncle Suresh and Shiv made small talk about relatives and acquaintances. I was curious about the young woman, so with the excuse of having to use the washroom, I went to find the kitchen. She was there, chopping vegetables, and was a bit startled when I walked in.

I asked in Bengali for her name, but she replied in English. This didn't really surprise me; given that there were around twenty-six different languages spoken in India, English was often the only common language, a remnant of two centuries of British rule. Her name was Aruna.

"Aruna...I'm Callie. Thank you for the tea and cakes. They were delicious." She didn't respond, but her shy smile told me that she was pleased. I waited for her to say something and was rewarded for my patience.

"I have heard about you from Mr. Suresh and the others." She glanced up from her vegetables and looked directly at me for the first time. "I didn't think that you would be so young," she said softly.

I smiled. She was really pretty, with delicate features. She wore no makeup yet her skin was flawless, her doe-shaped eyes dark and fringed in long black lashes. Once again I wondered about her white sari, but I couldn't very well ask her something so personal. Even though I'd just met her, I felt profound sadness when I looked at her.

"Can I help you with anything?" I asked, feeling bad that she was stuck in the hot kitchen, no doubt preparing our evening meal. As soon as the words came out of my mouth I regretted them. She looked up at me pleadingly.

"Please...no, thank you...I can manage on my own." She nodded toward the living room. "Why don't you go and relax with the others, it's so hot in here."

I got the distinct feeling that I had been dismissed, so I turned around to go back. She was probably worried that she'd get in trouble if Uncle Suresh found me helping her. As I walked back I could hear Shiv and his uncle. It sounded like they were arguing. All I caught was a snippet of what they were saying.

"...talk about this later," Shiv was saying as I walked in.

"Callie, there you are. You must be exhausted from your long trip."

Uncle Suresh looked over at Shiv. "Why don't you show Callie to her room and let her freshen up. Dinner should be ready soon."

"Uncle Suresh, I don't think I can eat anything tonight. Would you mind if I just went to bed?" I asked.

"Of course, I understand. I hope you will be comfortable. If you need anything at all, please just ask Aruna. She sleeps downstairs and can bring you anything you need."

I thanked him and followed Shiv out of the living room into the foyer. A spiral marble staircase led up to the second floor. As we walked up I ran my hand over the smooth mother-of-pearl inlaid banister. And I couldn't take my eyes off the richly colored tapestries that hung on the walls. These Rakshakari sure knew how to live. Shiv led me up the stairs, down a hallway and came to a stop in front of a heavy wooden door.

"You should get some rest, Callie. We still have a lot of preparation to do before we head off for North Sentinel Islands." I nodded and he turned away to leave, but I grabbed his sleeve.

"Shiv...wait. What were you guys talking about when I walked in? Is everything alright?"

"Yes, of course. We were just talking about some family stuff...don't worry." And with that he turned around and walked away. Something didn't feel right, but I figured I was just really tired and needed to rest.

With the twelve-hour time difference I knew I was going to feel awful in the morning. I went in and realized that someone, probably Aruna, had already brought up my luggage, and I gratefully took my PJs out and changed. I barely managed to brush my teeth before passing out. The last thing I remembered was the heavenly softness of the pillow as my head sank into it.

ELEVEN

THE NEXT MORNING I rose bright and early, feeling well rested and eager. I showered, changed into jeans and a light cotton tunic and made my way downstairs. Shiv wasn't anywhere in sight, but breakfast was served. It looked delicious and I was ravenous. Uncle Suresh was up too, and we made small talk over light, fluffy *poori*s and curried chickpeas. Dobby came around and vacuumed any crumbs that fell from the table. Every now and then he would come and stand conveniently close enough for me to scratch his ears. Shiv joined us after a while and announced that since Uncle Suresh was still waiting for some permits to come through, we would be taking a trip to the Kali temple. I perked up, thinking that maybe we would get some leads or at least some information. I doubted the same *sadhu* who had given me the pendant was still there. So many years had gone by, and he had already seemed so old back then. Either way, it couldn't hurt. Plus I really wanted to get out and see the city...my city, which still held so many memories.

I was sad that I couldn't go visit my aunts and cousins, but I'd decided already that it would be too difficult to tell them about my parents, and I knew I wouldn't be able to lie to them about why I was really there. My grandmother had passed away a few years ago. She would have been able to help me. I knew this deep inside because I had always felt a deep connection to her.

After breakfast we were on our way. Uncle Suresh insisted we take his car and driver. I was grateful for the air conditioning as we cut across the insanity that was Kolkata traffic. I knew the heat would be unbearable once we got out of the car, so I sat back and enjoyed the ride. I was struck by the fact that it didn't feel as though any time had passed since I was last here. What should have taken a mere ten minutes ended up being an almost hour-long drive that involved many twists and turns along Kolkata's winding alleys. Finally we were there, and as I stepped out of the car, the humidity slapped me in the face. There was no other way to describe it. It was a physical thing that made your clothes stick to you in a highly unflattering manner and turned your hair into a ball of frizz. Luckily, I was not concerned with my appearance right now.

I was desperate for anything that would lead me closer to finding my parents. It was no coincidence that the *sadhu* had insisted on giving me that skull pendant here all those years ago. As we walked up the concrete steps to the inner temple, I filled Shiv in on the events of that day ten years ago. He didn't seem too surprised, which made sense given the fact that his whole life had been about all this. We went inside to find the priest, and it turned out it was Mr. Bhandal, the same man whom my parents had come to see ten years ago. I didn't want to get my hopes too high, but I felt I finally might get some information about what had happened to my parents. I knew it was a long shot, but there was a voice inside me, probably born of desperation, that was telling me I would find answers here. I took a deep breath and began to tell Mr. Bhandal about our visit years ago. It took him a while, but eventually he did remember.

"Yes...I do recall a couple from America. The wife was Indian but the husband was white, I remember," he said, tugging at a little tuft of hair at the back of his head. He wore a saffron-colored *dhoti* and had white sandalwood paste on his forehead. Even though it had been a long time, being here brought a rush of memories. Or maybe it was just that I wished I could travel back in time to when my parents were safe.

"Do you remember what kind of information they were looking for?" I asked, realizing with a sinking feeling that I was about to be disappointed.

"Actually, your parents came back again once more after that day. I could never forget that visit," he said, his eyes narrowing, as if just realizing who I was.

"I don't understand...when did they come back?"

"You were very young. They said they needed help. They said they had to find a *sadhu*, someone they had met outside the temple."

My mind was reeling. If my parents had come back here, it must have been after the nightmares started. Why would they have been looking for the *sadhu* unless...unless they knew it had something to do with the pendant? Which brought me back to my original dilemma. Had they known about all this the whole time? So many questions were swirling around in my head, I felt as if it was going to explode. But I had to focus and I couldn't afford to lose it right now.

"Mr. Bhandal," I said as calmly as I could, "would you be able to tell me why my parents came to you the first time? It had to do with some research they were doing."

"As a matter of fact, I may have copies of some of the papers they brought with them. But you have to understand...it has been a long time, it may have been thrown away," he said apologetically. He started walking further into the temple and Shiv and I followed. The inside was darker and therefore much cooler, a relief from the heat. He took us to a room at the back, off the main hallway. It was small and cramped, with a desk overflowing with papers in one corner. Against the wall were a couple of tall bookshelves, also filled with cardboard boxes. There was a tiny fridge in the corner and he reached into it to pull out two cans of soda, which he offered to us. I took mine gratefully since my throat was parched.

"Please have a seat while I try to find the papers. It may take some time," he said, squatting on the floor in front of the bookshelves and pulling down a couple of boxes. As he rummaged around in them I had to resist the urge to sneeze as dust flew around the room and settled on every surface.

"Mr. Bhandal," I said after what seemed an interminable time, "maybe if we all look together, we could find it faster."

He stood up, surprisingly limber for someone with such a large frame, and swatted the dust off his *dhoti*. Then he looked at me with his bushy white eyebrows meeting in the middle.

"You are not a patient one, are you?" he said, waving a sheaf of papers. "I think I have found what you are looking for."

I had to stop myself from jumping up and grabbing them from his hand. Shiv must have noticed because I could feel him glaring at me. I think I was actually embarrassing him. I chuckled inwardly at the thought and then turned my attention back to Mr. Bhandal, who was spreading the papers on top of the desk. I stood up and walked to the other side to look over his shoulder.

"It looks like your parents were very interested in

Kali's weapons. Most of what is in here is about the six weapons she carried." He picked up the top few sheets and handed them to me. I walked back over to where Shiv was sitting and sat back down next to him. I skimmed the first couple of pages quickly and then handed them to Shiv. Mr. Bhandal was right. All the information on these pages was about the stuff I'd been learning about at the Academy. It talked about the sword, the mace, the bow and arrows, the thunderbolt, the chakra and the trident. I put the papers down and looked at Shiv.

"They knew...and they never said anything..." I felt so betrayed and angry, I could hear my voice rising. Shiv shot me a warning glance and moved his gaze over to where Mr. Bhandal was still poring over the rest of the papers. I got it. Trust no one. Vikram could not have been more paranoid about the fact that Mahisha's people were everywhere. I tried to keep calm, but it was difficult. Mr. Bhandal seemed completely oblivious. I could see his lips moving as he read what looked like handwritten parts on the paper. It was probably my mom's writing, in which the letters always looked like they were falling off the page. All of a sudden he looked up.

"I remember now," he said, looking quite excited at this sudden revival of his memory. "They were particularly interested in any information about Kali's sword."

"Kali's sword?" I repeated, not wanting to face the

163

reality that I was the last to know what was going on with me. Everyone had known about this...Shiv, the other Rakshakaris and now my parents.

"Yes, Kali's sword," he repeated slowly as if talking to a particularly young child. "Are you alright, my dear? You look a little pale." I nodded slowly, thinking of all the years I had spent agonizing over losing my mind. All the friends I had lost because I was the weird girl who screamed from her nightmares during sleepovers.

"Yes, thank you, Mr. Bhandal, I'm fine. Thanks for all your help." I gathered the bunch of papers that were scattered on the desk. "Do you mind if I take these?"

He shook his head, handing me the rest. I looked at Shiv and he stood up. I had to leave. I felt as if I couldn't breathe in here, and I needed to get some fresh air.

We both thanked him profusely and left. The driver came running back to the car from the tea stall across the street when he saw us coming down the stairs, and we rode back to the house in silence. My head was spinning, the questions and anger creating a maelstrom of emotions that threatened to boil over at any moment. Shiv must have understood what was going on inside because he did not press me to talk, and for that I was grateful. By the time we got back it was past lunchtime, not that I could have eaten anyway. But Aruna made me a cooling mango smoothie and I felt it would be rude to refuse. I took it up to my room and sat down on the bed. I had to sort out all this new information and what it meant. According to the priest and his papers, my parents had gone to him looking for answers about Kali's weapons. One thing was certain: they had known what was going on all along. What I did not understand was why they wouldn't have told me. But even through all the anger and resentment I was feeling toward them at the moment, I was certain about another thing — they loved me unconditionally and they must have had a good reason for not telling me.

Thinking about that calmed me. I would find out their reasons soon enough...I hoped. Now I had to figure out if their research could help me in some way. In my dream my dad had told me not to worry about them and to focus on finding the sword. That was what had kept me going until now. Even when Ben was taken and I felt as if I should have done something to stop it, I had kept reminding myself that my parents were still alive, and somehow they would guide me through this. And I would get Ben back. I had to, because if I didn't I could never make it up to him for being such a rotten friend. It occurred to me that although I was supposedly a reincarnation of Kali, it wasn't as if I suddenly had superpowers. I would have to rely on my own strength and ability. Strangely enough, this thought did not fill me with trepidation; rather, it fuelled my determination. I was not going to wait around for some goddess manifestation as Nina had suggested. When I'd trained with Tara back in

Seattle, I had actually surprised myself sometimes. Even though at the time it felt like Kali's powers seeping through, making me so strong and focused, I realized now that my own anger and passion had given me the ability to fight. And I could do better, much better. I went downstairs after a while, and soon it was time for dinner.

"Uncle Suresh, when do you think we will be traveling to the island?" I asked between forkfuls of *biryani*. The spicy rice and vegetable casserole made me reach for my third glass of water.

"It may take longer than we had expected, Callie," Uncle Suresh said, helping himself to some more cucumber and yogurt salad. "We have run into some problems with the transport and the permits."

"Permits?" I was confused.

"North Sentinel Island doesn't fall officially under India's jurisdiction. It has to do with the indigenous inhabitants of the island who've never had any contact with the outside world," Uncle Suresh explained.

"So it's been difficult to get people who are willing to take us there. The island is not exactly known for being welcoming," Shiv added.

I realized this could actually work for me. "Uncle Suresh, I would like to spend more time training. As you know, I haven't really had much time, and I have a lot to learn."

Uncle Suresh looked pleased. He picked up his glass, drinking almost half of the water before he answered. "Aruna might be able to help you with that," he said to my surprise. "She's an expert in *kalaripayattu*. And we have plenty of space here for you to train."

"I've heard of this before...kalari...?" I said, intrigued since he had mentioned Aruna.

"It's an ancient form of Indian martial arts. It is practiced with a regular sword as well as the *urumi*. You are familiar with the *urumi*, yes?"

I nodded, totally sold on the idea.

"I would love a chance to learn from Aruna," I said, full of anticipation.

"I must warn you, Callie, it is very difficult." Uncle Suresh sat back in his chair, considering me thoughtfully. "Do you think you are up for the challenge?"

I sat up straight, looking him in the eyes, just so there was no doubt left.

"I'm ready Uncle Suresh. Bring it on."

He stood up, nodding slowly. "Good, then we shall begin tomorrow. I will inform Aruna that she is relieved from her normal duties."

We said goodnight and went to our respective bedrooms. After a quick shower, I changed into shorts and a T-shirt. I sat down on the edge of the bed, picking up my cell phone out of habit. I looked at the last text Ben had sent on that fateful night. I wondered where he was. I couldn't even think of how he was, because horrible images of the two demons flashed through my mind. At least I knew my parents wouldn't be harmed for the time being, but I could only hope that Ben was still alive. I shook the thought from my mind. I couldn't dwell on that or I would not be able to focus on the task ahead. I lay down, hoping to get some sleep, but it eluded me for quite a while.

TWELVE

THE NEXT MORNING found me full of resolve. It felt good to be proactive and I was looking forward to spending more time with Aruna. After a hurried breakfast, I went to find her in the back of the house. As I walked out the French doors of Uncle Suresh's bungalow, I was greeted by a fragrance that took me back to my grandmother's blooming garden. There were *madhumanjari* creepers, their tiny trumpet-shaped flowers in varying shades of pink and red. Then there was my favourite, the *champa*, its cream-colored flowers spreading their sweet scent. I took a deep breath and walked over to where Aruna was practicing in solitude. She had hitched the lower part of her sari up and tucked it into her waistband, a common practice for Indian women when they needed to allow their legs free movement. Practicing martial arts while maintaining the elegant drape of a sari could be hazardous.

Unaware that I was watching, Aruna moved with the grace of a classically trained dancer, her sword cutting the air effortlessly in a smooth motion. Her intricate steps belied the danger that I knew her opponent would face. Her arms swung the sword overhead like a feather while her legs moved to the rhythm of an unheard melody. Wanting to get a closer look, I stepped forward. The crunch of a twig underneath my feet alerted her to my presence and her head shot up. She looked startled, almost as if she'd been lost in a world of her own. Then her face lit up with a smile of recognition as she realized it was me, and her demeanor underwent a subtle shift, from fearless warrior to submissive girl. It bothered me, although I wasn't sure why. I had spent the first few years of my life surrounded by domestic help; it was the norm here. So was the blatant division of social classes. I decided that because I'd been away for so long, the reality of it jarred my senses.

I walked quickly to where she was waiting in the center of the garden. On my way I passed a koi pond filled with large lotus flowers with fish darting about underneath them. Tall betel nut trees stood like sentries all around while palm trees competed for airspace. In a far corner mango and tamarind trees formed a cluster, creating some nice shade from the powerful sun that was already evident even this early in the day.

Aruna held out a long stick, gesturing for me to take it. It looked like a baton, and any delusions I had of doing the graceful warrior dance today were shattered in minutes. I spent the next couple of hours learning how to twirl the baton over my head, under my legs and around my body. Even that was a challenge since I dropped the stick every few minutes. By the end of the two hours I had managed to master it to some small degree, but I needed a break. My arms ached from the unfamiliar strain, my muscles protesting the rigor. For someone so petite, Aruna really resembled a drill sergeant when it came to training. Luckily, just then Shiv came out with some fresh lemonade, which I gulped down in an instant. After that small break we went at it again and I realized that Shiv had used the lemonade as an excuse to watch me. When I heard him chuckle for the fourth or fifth time, I shot daggers at him with my eyes. Of course, he just deflected them with a lazy smile as he leaned nonchalantly against a coconut palm tree. I tried to ignore him, which was an exercise in futility. Shiv was not somebody to be ignored. I looked at him out of the corners of my eyes while trying not to lose my grip on the stick. He was tall, dark and handsome, which I realized was a terrible cliché, but there no denying it was true. Under different circumstances I might have been more inclined to dwell on the fact that there was obviously some chemistry between us, but there was no time for distractions. I just forced my mind back to the stick I was twirling.

Finally, after what seemed like forever, Aruna said we were done for the day. But she wanted to teach me some of the history and theory behind *kalaripayattu*. I was fine with that as long as it didn't involve anything more physical than listening. I could barely feel my fingers at this point and I didn't think I could even lift one to turn a page. We went in and washed up before lunch, which consisted of a simple pasta salad. Or it was simple by Kolkata standards. It actually contained several kinds of delicious fresh vegetables and a spicy sauce. Food always put me in a good mood, so I had regained the bounce in my step as I made my way to Aruna's room in the servants' quarters, which were in the back of the house. As I entered, my eyes had to adjust to the dark interior. Even though it was late afternoon, it was still bright and sunny outside. Aruna was sitting on one of the traditional woven cane and bamboo stools that could be found in every household. There were three more arranged in a circle. She looked up when she heard me come in.

"Are you ready to learn some more?" she said with a smile.

"Sure. As long as there's no stick involved," I replied, grinning.

For the next hour she taught me about the various moves and stances that were used most frequently in *kalaripayattu*. Even though I knew this was important, I found my mind wandering as she spoke. I waited for her to pause before I jumped in.

"Aruna, can we take a little break?"

"Of course. Would you like some fresh coconut water?" she asked, standing up and moving toward the kitchen area, where a small refrigerator hummed in the corner. I got up, following her in case she needed help. As I watched, she took two fresh green coconuts off a shelf and put them on the little table in the middle of the kitchen. Then she picked up a curved knife and proceeded to cut the tops off the coconuts. She put a straw in each one and handed one to me. Next she took two plates off a shelf and went to the fridge. From it she removed a box of Indian sweets. She placed an assortment on the plates and gestured for me to walk back over to the stools. As we sat and sipped our coconut water, she began to open up about herself.

"Callie, have you heard about the Priestesses of Kali?" she asked as she picked up one of the little sweets and popped it in her mouth.

"I heard Shiv's parents mention them back in Seattle," I replied. "They said many people believe they didn't really exist."

"Actually, they did," Aruna said. "They were chosen by Kali herself to bring her sword to a safe place and guard it. My grandmother and her mother before her...they were all descended from one of the Priestesses. The knowledge is supposed to be passed down from generation to generation."

I took a moment to lift my jaw from the floor.

"So you're telling me that you are actually a

Priestess of Kali yourself?" My voice had risen considerably from disbelief, and there were not enough emojis in the world to adequately describe my level of excitement at this little tidbit. Aruna seemed alarmed at my reaction, because she jumped up and went to the door to check if it was closed all the way. She came back and sat down once more.

"Callie, no one here can know," she said in a low voice.

"Why not? They are Rakshakari, wouldn't they be thrilled?" I couldn't imagine why she would want to keep it a secret, but whatever it was, I wanted to know.

"It's not that simple...if they knew..." She didn't finish her sentence; she seemed to get lost in her thoughts.

I couldn't stop myself from probing further. This was too important. If she knew something that could help me find my parents and the sword, I had to know.

"What do you think would happen if they found out?" I asked gently, not wanting to pressure her too much.

"There are a lot of things you don't understand yet, Callie. It's hard to know who to trust."

"Well, you can trust me." Even as I said it, I had to wonder why she put her faith in someone she'd just met. I knew I wouldn't. The fact that I was even here went against every instinct, but the catalyst had been my parents' disappearance. But for Aruna my presence didn't really change anything, so I understood her reluctance to confide in me. I decided to try another angle.

"Aruna, you must know about my parents...that they've been taken. I will do anything to find them." I took both her hands. "If there is anything...anything at all you can tell me, I will be in your debt for the rest of my life."

Aruna raised her head to look into my eyes. I hoped she would see my desperation and take pity on me.

"Callie...the priestesses...they've been ostracized for centuries. It's not the way it used to be." She was silent for a while, and again, not wanting to push her, I waited patiently. Finally she went on.

"There was a time when they were revered...but things changed. They became powerful and had many devoted followers."

"So what happened?"

"I'm not sure exactly, but I think that society changed and a group of women having so much influence wasn't a good thing for the rulers at the time."

"You think the rulers felt threatened?" I could see that happening, especially hundreds of years ago.

"My grandmother and mother told me some stories about it. The priestesses would step in whenever women were being abused or treated unjustly. Because they had so much influence, they were able to bring many of the perpetrators to justice. Sometimes that included the sons and brothers of prominent people."

It made sense. Not much had changed from the time Aruna was talking about. I still heard on the news that women and young girls were being raped and assaulted while their attackers got away scot-free because of their connection with influential politicians. It must have been even worse long ago.

"So what happened to the Priestesses?" I asked.

"It started slowly at first...a few were assaulted as they walked home alone from the river, then someone's hut would catch fire and they would be burned alive."

"But if they had supporters...?"

"They did, but then the village elders would start with allegations of theft, or children would mysteriously disappear. They would accuse them of practicing dark magic. Slowly, their supporters dwindled and so did the number of Priestesses." Aruna looked down at her hands. Once again she seemed lost in thought. When she looked up, there was something in her eyes that spoke of a deep hurt.

"You know, Callie, I've never told anyone this, but my mother...she was raped when she was sixteen. She worked for a wealthy family and their son was about her age. They knew she came from a line of priestesses and the son would mock her for it, saying she was cursed and that no one would ever want her. He would come into her room at night, knowing she would never tell anyone. She didn't because she knew they would never believe her, but when she got pregnant with me she tried to tell the boy's mother. She laughed, saying that my mother was nothing but a lying whore who wanted to get her hands on their rich son. They threw her out in the middle of the night with nothing but the clothes on her back." The tears that had pooled in Aruna's eyes now rolled down her cheeks, and my heart broke for her. I put my arms around her, pulling her head onto my shoulders. I couldn't even begin to imagine the horror of knowing that your existence was based on such an act of violence.

"She went back to my grandmother. For a few years it seemed that my mother was fine, but then one day she was taking me to the market and saw my father driving by."

Aruna's mouth turned down in disgust at the corners as she spoke. "Later that night my grandmother found her hanging from the ceiling fan in her room. We never spoke about her after that."

Now it was my turn to cry. It all just seemed so unfair and cruel. We held each other for a little bit and then Aruna pulled away and wiped her eyes with a tissue. I grabbed the one she offered me and dried my own tears.

"What a fine pair of warriors we make, no?" She smiled wanly, shaking her head.

I didn't know what to say. I was still in shock after hearing the horror that Aruna's mother had gone through and what she herself must have had to endure. No wonder she didn't want anyone knowing about her lineage. To her it was a reminder of everything she had lost.

Taking a deep breath, I stood up and held out my hand to help her up as well.

"I think we've had enough training for one day," she said, her voice still slightly tremulous.

"I couldn't agree more. Is there any chance that we could go and watch a movie?" I hadn't watched a Bollywood movie in ages, and it was just the thing to get our minds off all the heavy stuff for a little while.

Aruna's face lit up and she nodded enthusiastically. "There's a new one out that I've been wanting to watch. We can get *panipoori*s too."

Paanipoori. Another one of my favorite street foods. I could just taste the sweet and tangy water as the thin, crunchy balls of fried dough exploded in my mouth. There was nothing that compared.

THIRTEEN

THE NEXT MORNING I woke up to agony. As expected, my muscles were sore and my hands had several blisters. I felt good, though, because of last night. It had been a good idea to go out and do something fun. There had been a pang of guilt, though, when I thought that I should be using the time on more productive pursuits, but in the end I realized I desperately needed some down time. I also felt genuinely bad for Aruna and blamed myself for forcing her to dredge up bad memories. On the other hand, I was convinced she possessed some vital information. I didn't know why I was so sure of that, but I was.

I got dressed and ready for another day of training. After a light breakfast of toast and tea I met up with Aruna in the vast garden. The fragrant jasmine and tuberoses filled me with calm and positivity. Aruna was waiting for me as I passed the koi pond on my way to the open space where we had practiced the previous day. She looked a lot better than she had when I'd left her after we got back from the movies. There were some dark shadows under her eyes, but she smiled when she saw me coming and it lit up her face. We spent the next few hours practicing with the *urumi* and I had to admit I began to feel more and more confident and less like a klutz. We broke for lunch and a little rest but got right back to it until late afternoon. My muscles protested as I sat down on the edge of the koi pond and Aruna joined me. It was cooler now that the sun was setting, and the koi swam lazily around between the lotus pads.

"I have something to give you, Callie," Aruna said shyly, reaching into her jute bag to pull out something wrapped in cloth. She handed it to me and I removed the soft cover. It was a dagger, the blade of bronze as far as I could tell from its color. The handle was beautifully adorned with a pattern of red, blue and green gems. I didn't know if they were precious stones, but it didn't matter. It felt heavy and ancient, but I didn't know why Aruna was giving it to me.

"My grandmother gave this to me before she died," she said, getting that faraway look in her eyes again.

"Did it belong to your family?" I asked.

She nodded. "It's been handed down to the women in my family for generations. Along with this." She handed me a piece of paper, folded carefully in four. I took it from her. It was old brown parchment and the creases where it had been folded were so deep I was afraid it would tear if I wasn't extremely careful. I unfolded it as delicately as I could. It was a map. A really old map, judging by the fact that the Indian subcontinent was divided into a multitude of kingdoms. The names were in Sanskrit, so I turned to Aruna.

"What does it say? Is that Kishkinda?" I asked, referring to the kingdoms that were part of the *Ramayana* and the *Mahabharata*, India's ancient texts.

Aruna nodded. "My grandmother told me this map is of the utmost importance to the Priestesses of Kali, that I must guard it with my life." A cynical smile played across her lips. "Everything I've experienced in my life had made me doubt the truth about the Priestesses. But now, seeing you here, I believe that I must give this to you."

I didn't know what to say. My heart raced and my hands trembled, whether from excitement or because I was touched by her actions, I did not know.

"Aruna...you have no idea what this means to me. Does this really show the location of the sword?" I couldn't really make sense of the map, but I did look to see whether North Sentinel Island was visible. There it was, not a tiny speck in the Indian Ocean like on the other maps, but much larger and clearly visible. But if I'd expected some quick fix, an X that marked the spot, I was disappointed. A part of me had hoped it would be that easy, but of course it wasn't. I was grateful that I at least had a map, and that Aruna had seen fit to pass it on to me, even though she knew that it was of precious value to her ancestors.

"I'm not sure whether the sword is actually there, Callie," she said with an apologetic shrug. "My grandmother never talked about it with me. She just told me it was very important and that I would know what to do when the time came."

"The time for what?" I was confused. Her grandmother couldn't possibly have known about me.

"I don't know that either. I'm sorry I can't be of more help. But I know that you should have it, that's all."

I turned the dagger over in my hands and decided I needed to go and find Shiv, but there was something I had to do before that.

"Aruna, I want to ask you something. I know you don't want anyone to know about your secret. But in order to use this map and dagger, I need help from Shiv. He'll want to know where I got it." I felt like a really bad person asking this of her, but she was already nodding her approval. I enveloped her in a big hug. She was smiling when I let go.

"I trust Shiv," she said. "I've known him for many years and he will keep my secret."

I was relieved.

I headed back to my room with the dagger and map tucked safely away in the waistband of my yoga pants, covered by the loose cotton tunic I had worn for today's practice. Once there I put both on a desk by the window and went to shower and change before dinner. I got dressed and went to the dresser to pick up my skull pendant, which I had taken off that morning. Then I plucked the map off the table and was about to go back down, hoping to catch Shiv before his uncle joined us. Just as I opened the door to the bedroom, I felt a cool tingling in my throat. I put my fingers on the spot, looking down, only to realize that my pendant was glowing with a blue light.

That's weird.

I undid the clasp and pulled off the pendant. It was still glowing. I put it down on the table next to the map. It began to glow even brighter, the blue light so blinding that I had to avert my eyes. I picked it up gingerly. My fingers tingled where the pendant touched them, but it wasn't painful, just cold. The light seemed to dim. I put it back down and immediately the light brightened again. I did this a few times, feeling a little foolish. Each time I put the pendant down the light grew stronger, but it faded when I picked it up.

I put it back down again for the fourth time. It began to emit a buzzing kind of noise and I realized that I had put it directly on top of the map. An excited thought occurred to me. What if the pendant was reacting to the map? It wasn't that inconceivable. After all, Aruna had said that the map was handed down in her mother's family for generations. What if there was some ancient connection between it and the pendant? I picked it up off the map then put it back on top. There was definitely something going on here. I left it there this time as the buzzing grew louder and the blue light seemed to get stronger. As I stared at it sitting on the map, I suddenly noticed that some lines on the map were brighter than others. I peered closer at it and gasped. The lines that were highlighted formed a route, and it was directly on the island. I shot up, adrenaline pumping as realization dawned. The pendant was marking a route on the map to what I could only assume was the location of Kali's sword.

I put the pendant away carefully in my overnight bag, picked up the map and went off to find Shiv. He was in the garden by the koi pond with Dobby. Clearly this was a popular spot. Dobby got up and came running over. Shiv turned his gaze to follow and smiled when he saw me. I realized I had barely seen him in the last few days, what with my training and then my Bollywood escapade with Aruna. I was brimming with impatience and the words stumbled over each other as I recounted what I had learned about Aruna, the map and the pendant. If he was as excited as I was, he did a much better job at containing his enthusiasm.

"So...Aruna is a priestess," he said after I stopped for a much-needed breath. A pang of annoyance briefly stabbed through my happy glow, but then it disappeared. Nothing could bring me down right now. This was the first time I felt that I was doing the right thing, that I wasn't crazy for putting my trust in these people or this whole notion, for that matter. It had given me hope that I could find the sword.

"Yes, Shiv, she is. But she made me swear that I wouldn't tell anyone but you." I glared at him. "You better not tell anyone...not even your uncle."

He smiled at my failed attempt to be stern. "I won't. I would never betray Aruna's trust."

"She told me you've known each other for years." I hoped I sounded casual because the last thing I needed was for him to think that I was jealous.

Shiv nodded. "She's been coming here since she was a little kid. Her grandmother worked for my uncle before she died, and she would bring Aruna with her."

I wondered if he felt bad that she'd never told him about being a priestess or about her mother.

"We would play together whenever I visited my uncle. I had no idea that she was hiding such an awful secret." His voice trailed off and he was lost in his thoughts. I knew I would be pretty shocked too if I found out that Ben had been hiding something like this from me. *Ben.* The thought of him made my heart ache. I could physically feel the pain as I allowed his face to swim into my mind. I had purposely shut out any memories of him, because to indulge in the guilt I felt over what had happened because of me would serve no purpose other than to make me weak. And that was one thing I could not permit. Shiv stood up, thankfully preventing any further melancholy from taking over.

"So let's go and take a look at the map," he said. "Maybe I can figure out something about the route."

We decided it would be best to wait until after lunch, when Uncle Suresh was gone. For some reason I was reluctant to share this with him. I expected Shiv to argue, but to my surprise he agreed and we went in to eat.

"Callie, Shiv...there you are." Uncle Suresh was already seated and seemed very pleased to see us. "I have good news." He paused for dramatic effect. The look on my face must have given me away as usual because he smiled affectionately before continuing.

"We have all the tickets and necessary permits ready for both of you to go to North Sentinel Island." He turned to me, put an arm on my shoulder and looked me straight in the eye.

"I hope you're ready, Callie. You have a great challenge ahead of you."

Great. No pressure at all.

FOURTEEN

THE NEXT MORNING I woke with a sense of anticipation I hadn't felt for quite some time. We were all packed and ready to go to the airport after lunch. We would fly to the Andaman Islands, only two hours away. We would spend the night there before traveling by boat to the shores of North Sentinel Island. My excitement grew as the morning wore on. Finally, I was doing something that would bring me closer to my goal. A month ago I would never have believed this about myself, but I was ready for battle. It was strange, but all the training, practicing and everything I'd seen in the last few weeks had changed me in a way I had not imagined possible. Shiv looked the way I felt. His eyes were bright, his movements precise and I remembered the day he had saved me from the demon in my parents' bedroom. I was so relieved that he was coming with me because even though I felt ready to go on this quest, I did not want to face any demons by myself. The last two times had not gone well for me, and this time I didn't want any surprises.

When we arrived at the airport Aruna enveloped me in a tight hug. "Take care," she whispered. "Don't be afraid. The Goddess is with you."

If she was, I wasn't aware of it. I still thought of myself as just me. Regular old Callie, nothing more. But I was different. I had been chosen, for some reason that was beyond my understanding. I still didn't feel any special powers, nothing that made me goddess-like. But I knew that I believed in it more now than I did before. I felt stronger and surer of myself than I ever had before in my life. The memories of the nightmares I'd had for so long were undeniable proof that I was meant for something bigger than the life I'd been leading up to now. And I was fine with that. I would do what I had to.

After Shiv and I said our goodbyes, we went to get something to eat while we waited to board. We were sipping our coffee when I noticed Shiv watching me closely.

"Is something wrong?" I asked, my hand flying to my hair, wondering if I'd forgotten to brush it this morning in my rush to get going. It would be just like him to neglect telling me that it was sticking out in all directions.

He smiled disarmingly. "No, don't worry, your hair is fine."

"Then why are you staring at me?"

"I was just remembering...when we first met..."

"You mean like a month ago?" I said sarcastically.

"I know...it's only been a month. But I'm just saying...look at you now, all ready for war."

He was making fun of me. Of course.

"Well...I know I'm ready to hurt you if you don't shut up," I said, only half joking.

He put up his hands in mock defense. "Seriously though, Callie...look, I know I'm not good at talking about stuff like this..."

"Stuff like what?" I asked impatiently.

"Just that...I'm really impressed. I mean, not many people could handle something like this. And you're doing a pretty awesome job of it." He played with the wrapper from his breakfast sandwich, not really looking at me. I was glad for that, because I could feel a blush slowly creeping into my cheeks, and the last thing I wanted was for him to know how much his praise affected me.

"Hey...I know I'm awesome. I'm just glad you figured it out too," I said flippantly. One of the skills I'd always been proud of was the ability to hide behind humor and sarcasm whenever I was nervous or shy. It had always worked before and I knew it did this time too, because Shiv grinned. He was saved from having to say more on the subject because boarding was announced.

The next couple of hours passed uneventfully as our little plane made its way to the Andaman Islands airport. The islands had once been used by the government of nineteenth-century British India as a prison for political dissidents. Now it was a must-see tourist destination for honeymooners and just about anyone who wanted a few days in paradise. I gazed out the window as we descended and couldn't believe that such a place existed. A lot of it was covered by dense forest surrounded by blue water. As we landed I got a view of the airport. We had landed in Port Blair, which had only one runway, a little tidbit the pilot shared as he informed us that there would be a wait until we could disembark.

When it was finally time to get off, I could smell the ocean, even as the humidity in the air transformed me into a troll doll. I could feel my hair getting frizzy as we walked to the terminal, and Shiv's look of amusement did nothing to improve my mood. I decided that after all this was over I would shave my head and start a new trend. I would be a bald goddess. It would save a lot of time in my daily grooming ritual.

We went through customs, where, thanks to special permits obtained by Shiv's uncle, I was not arrested for carrying a dagger. I had carefully wrapped it in a sheet of cotton and tucked it into my backpack. We didn't have any suitcases with us, for obvious reasons, so everything we might need was stuffed into our backpacks. Apparently the permit had mentioned something about research being conducted by two university students from the U.S., and Uncle Suresh knew an important government official who had facilitated all this. I was sure that by "facilitated," he had really meant bribed. It was a fact of life in this part of the world.

Once out of the airport we were met by a driver who took us to the hotel where we would be spending the night before embarking on the rest of our journey. I was glad because I needed time to strengthen my resolve and also because Shiv and I had to pore over Aruna's map to make sure we hadn't missed anything vital. Once we reached the island we would hit the ground running, since everything we had learned indicated the islanders would not be thrilled to see us. We were going to be sitting ducks, but there was no other choice. At least we wanted to be prepared. My bravado from earlier that day had abated, leaving me with a sense of impending doom. I couldn't shake the feeling, even after Shiv ordered us some dinner. No amount of seafood was going to make me feel more prepared for what was to come. However, the plate of spicy crab legs that showed up deserved to be appreciated, so I decided to drown my sorrows in it.

After dinner, Shiv and I decided to take a walk. It was as if we both knew this might be the last time we could do something as normal as taking a stroll by the water. We walked along Marine Drive, the spectacular scenery doing away with the need for conversation. A thought struck me as we stopped for a moment to admire the twinkling lights of the city from our vantage point. The only other person I felt this comfortable with was Ben. With Shiv, I was content just being there without having to say anything.

We stood in silence for a while before Shiv turned to me. In the lamplight, his eyes shone with something I couldn't define, and despite myself a delicious shiver ran up my arms. My mouth felt dry and my palms were getting clammy. I looked up at him and opened my mouth to speak just as he lowered his to mine. As our lips met in a warm, gentle kiss, I could feel my racing heart beat even faster. Of their own volition, my hands traveled up his arms and my fingers locked behind his neck as I stood up on my toes to get even closer to him. His hand pressed against the small of my back as our kiss deepened, sending little shock waves of pleasure all through my body. I quieted the small voice in my head that tried to remind me of where I was and what I should be doing. This felt right...Shiv and I...together like this. I knew I might regret this moment as soon as it was over, but I was powerless against the emotions that coursed through me. I had assumed from the very beginning that the attraction I felt toward Shiv was mostly physical. After all, I didn't know him well enough to feel the kind of inexplicable, everlasting love that I read about in books. Also, to my mother's great disappointment I'd never really bought into that whole love-at-first-sight romantic nonsense. So logically, it made no sense that I should feel anything deeper for Shiv than just physical attraction born from the fact that we were venturing into the great unknown tomorrow.

But my mind was feeling anything but logical at the moment as Shiv broke off the kiss and brushed hair away from my face. Then he just looked into my eyes and I felt myself melting, for lack of a less nauseating word. Warmth flowed through me, making my fingertips tingle. I had to do something.

"Shiv..." I began, with no clue what I was going to say. But luckily he beat me to it.

"Callie, I'm sorry...I don't know what came over me. I didn't mean to make you uncomfortable."

Clearly he had no clue what I was feeling. "Uncomfortable" was not the word I would choose.

"I...you don't have to be sorry..." I really didn't know how to finish that sentence.

"I don't mean I'm sorry that I kissed you," he said hurriedly.

I swallowed the big lump that was suddenly in my throat.

"Me neither," I said softly. He reached down for my hand and pulled me closer. Then he turned me so we were both facing the water and said nothing more. We just stood there, our bodies close, watching the boats go by. It felt right. After some time, we pulled away in a mutual unspoken agreement and headed back toward the hotel. The entire time Shiv never let go of my hand.

FIFTEEN

THAT NIGHT MY father came to me in my dream once again. What I saw shook me to my very core. His face was gaunt with scars in different stages of healing.

"Callie..." he whispered hoarsely. "You must hurry...he's getting impatient."

"Daddy," I cried in my sleep. "Where are you? Where is he keeping you?"

"I don't know...Callie...Mom is..." And with that he was gone, leaving me gasping for breath as I broke out of my dream and sat up in a panic. Something had happened to my mom...something bad. I was sure of that. I looked at the clock on the nightstand. It was 4:45, almost morning. There was no way I could go back to sleep. I fought the urge to go to Shiv's room and wake him up, busying myself instead with repacking my backpack.

I went out to the adjoining balcony to get some fresh air. The sun was just rising, casting an orange glow over everything. From here I could see the ocean and it brought back vivid memories of another time...a happier one when my parents and I had come to the Andaman Islands for a vacation. I must have been five or six, but I still remembered the thrill of standing under an icy waterfall as the water hit me and the drops fractured into a thousand little beams of light in the bright sun. Now I looked at the ocean and all I felt was dread. It filled the pit of my stomach, leaving a bitter taste in my mouth.

I went downstairs in search of some food. The lobby was already abuzz with employees and tourists as I walked toward the restaurant. I sat down, ordering some coffee and toast with jam. I had no appetite, but I also didn't want to feel sick all day, especially since we were going to be on a boat for a few hours. My breakfast came fairly quickly, by which time it was getting brighter outside and the restaurant was beginning to fill up. I was sipping my coffee while debating whether I should check on Shiv. I got up, grabbing the cloth napkin that lay folded like a pretty fan beside my plate. As I brought it to my mouth, something white fluttered to the ground. I bent down to pick it up. It was a note. On it in small neat, handwriting were the words: *Do not trust them. They are not who they seem.*

I stared at the note for a second then quickly looked up and around to see if anyone was watching me. There were people just walking in and others in the middle of their breakfast. No one had come near my table except the waitress who had brought my food. I scanned the room trying to locate her, but she wasn't there. I sat back down, thinking that she would probably reappear in a moment with somebody's order. For a second I thought that this could be Shiv's idea of a joke. I contemplated that possibility for a bit longer as I waited for the waitress to show up again. I decided to go find the restaurant manager. I asked a passing staff member and was told that he would be there shortly. A few minutes later he approached my table.

"How can I help you, madam?" he said.

"I'm looking for the waitress who served me about an hour ago," I said.

"Is everything alright, madam? I hope the breakfast was to your satisfaction?" His brow was furrowed and I feared I might be getting the girl in trouble.

"Yes...everything was great," I said quickly. "I just wanted to ask her something."

"Let me go check. I'll be right back."

I thanked him and waited. True to his word he was back in a few minutes.

"I'm sorry, madam, but I was just told that she left due to an emergency. Is there something I can help you with?"

"No...thank you," I said, an uneasy feeling

blossoming. The manager left and I sat there trying to process what the note might mean. Who were *they*?

I decided it was time to go and find Shiv. I knocked on his door and when he opened it, it was clear that he had been fast asleep. His hair was disheveled and his eyes bleary as he stood lazily looking at me.

"What time is it? I thought we didn't have to leave until after lunch," he said.

"It's just after six, don't worry," I assured him, wondering if I should mention the note to him. He peeled himself off the doorframe and waved me in. I followed, deciding that for now I was going to keep the note to myself until I'd had time to figure out what it meant. My thoughts threatened to go to a place of doubt and fear where I would begin to question the wisdom of embarking on a quest with someone who might pose a danger to me. But the side of me that did not want to deal with this right now won. I pushed aside any potential worries and focused on the present. He walked into the bathroom as I looked around his room, taking in the half-packed backpack and last night's clothes strewn carelessly about.

"I saw my dad again," I blurted out. He stopped midway through brushing his teeth, holding up his toothbrush and foaming at the mouth. I could see him from where I stood and had to suppress a laugh. Then I realized he was trying to ask me something.

"What did he say?" he was asking after he rinsed his mouth.

"I think they're in danger," I replied. "He also started to say something about my mom, but he couldn't finish. It sounded bad, though."

Shiv came out of the bathroom, still in his pyjamas and T-shirt. He walked up to me and took my hand. "Callie, we will find them and they will be fine."

"What if we're too late?" I asked. "I tried to ask my dad where they were but he couldn't say anything. He looked so bad...he had scars on his face...I..." My voice trailed off as I pictured my father again as he had looked in my dream.

"Callie, we're so close. You can't give up now." Shiv squeezed my hand gently and I drew comfort from him. He was right. This was not the time to lose hope.

I took in a deep breath and let it out with a sigh. "You're right...thanks, Shiv. It's just...seeing my dad like that...I couldn't think straight." He pulled me in for a quick hug.

"I'm going to shower and get ready. Do you want breakfast?" he asked, releasing me and stepping back.

"I had some already. But you go ahead and I'll get ready too." I left him and went back to my room. I took a quick shower, changed, put my toiletries in my backpack and then I was ready to go. I didn't really want to wait until after lunch to leave. I went back to Shiv's room. He had ordered room service and was ready as well. We went down to the front desk, paid our bill and got a taxi to the pier, where we would have to locate our designated boat person and see if we could leave earlier. That turned out to be easier than I had anticipated. A couple of hundred rupees and we were on our way.

It was going to take over four hours to make our way to North Sentinel. Since it was illegal to travel to the island, there were no official modes of transportation that we could have taken. Uncle Suresh had used his Rakshakari contacts for special arrangements to get us there. The special arrangement turned out to be a medium-sized motorboat and a boatman who was happy to make some extra money as long as he didn't have to go too close to the shore.

We had been warned before leaving Kolkata that there was a bit of swimming involved. I was glad my years of swimming lessons were going to pay off. When all this was over, I would be thanking my parents for the many things they had pushed me to do, including all those summers of swim camp. The water was not too choppy as we slowly moved away from the shores of Port Blair out into open sea. We had packed sandwiches from the hotel restaurant before leaving and shared these with the boatman a couple of hours into our trip. By now the sun was beating down mercilessly and I was glad for my floppy hat that protected my face from the blaze.

The boat ride was pretty uneventful, and a few hours later we were as close as the boatman was willing to take us. I could see the shore from our position and didn't think that we would have to swim for too long.

Our backpacks were going to be covered in a tarp-like material to keep the contents dry and we would just drag them along with us. It didn't seem to be the best way, but I couldn't think of anything better. At least we would have our supply of dried fruit and nuts, as well as water-purifying tablets.

When the boat came to a stop, I hesitated before jumping in. Shiv thanked the boatman and took the leap into the ocean. I swallowed the lump in my throat and followed. As I hit the cold water I gasped at the initial shock but quickly realized it wasn't as bad as I had anticipated. I began to follow Shiv with fluid strokes, the backpack slowing me down a little. I tried my best not to think of sharks or anything else that might be lurking in the water. The boatman had assured us that nothing dangerous came this close to the shore. The worst thing, he said, would be some curious fish nibbling at our toes.

I'd been swimming for a while and was beginning to tire, so I decided to tread water for a bit to get my bearings. The backpack certainly wasn't making things any easier. I squinted against the glare of the sun on the water and saw that Shiv had almost reached the shore. As I watched he stood up, waist-deep, and began to walk onto the beach, his backpack dripping as he dragged it behind him. He flopped onto the sand, clearly winded. I took a deep breath and began to swim again. I was pretty close to the shore when I felt my backpack pulling away from me. Assuming it was just the current, I turned back to pull it closer when I noticed my pendant was floating in the water on the black string around my neck. It was glowing red. I was immediately overcome by a feeling of dread. Something was very wrong.

I looked around as I treaded water, but there was nothing that I could see. I began to swim again, this time faster, kicking harder. I was so close I could see Shiv rooting around in his backpack for something. I knew I could make it. Just then I felt something pull at my right leg and I was pulled under. I barely had time to suck in a huge breath before my head was under water and I was frantically kicking at whatever had grabbed my leg. I forced my eyelids open against the water. At first I couldn't see much but then my vision cleared and a scream lodged in my throat. It was a crocodile, large and scaly, its jagged teeth glinting in the refracted rays from the sun. It had let go of my leg and was probably waiting to pounce once again.

I was frozen in sheer terror. I knew that I should try to kick my way up to the surface, but I could not move. Above me I could see movement. Shiv was swimming to me. I knew no more than a few seconds could have passed but it felt like a long time. And that's when it happened. At first I thought it was just the water and the lack of oxygen that was playing tricks with my mind, but then it dawned on me that my worst fears were coming true. The crocodile was changing, right in front of my eyes. It appeared to grow but then its features changed as I looked on in horror, fear immobilizing me. It transformed into a creature that stood on two legs, its torso covered in scales. At first it just watched me with an ominous glint in its eyes. I could see Shiv getting closer. I turned toward him and my eyes widened in horror. There was another one. I could see that it was going to intercept Shiv. I was on my own.

I turned back to the one in front of me just as it lunged. I burst into action. Survival instinct kicked in and as I swung my left arm around to hit it with the backpack, I aimed my right hand at its eyes. I dug my fingers as deep as I could into them, touching something slimy that I did not want to identify. That bought a momentary reprieve as the creature backed off. It must have howled in pain because I saw bubbles erupting from its mouth. I remembered I had Aruna's dagger and reached around to grab the backpack and as quickly as I could, removing the waterproof covering until the front pocket was exposed. I unzipped it and reached in for the dagger. My fingers had just closed around the hilt when I felt my head being yanked back painfully. Not letting go of the dagger, I kicked and flailed my legs as hard as I could until I was facing the creature. It held my hair firmly in its grip and my scalp began to lose sensation.

Somewhere in the periphery of my vision I thought I saw Shiv, his body strangely distorted by the water, as I tried to focus all my strength on maneuvering the dagger closer to the creature. At some point during our struggle we must have broken the surface, because I was able to suck in another long breath. As I was dragged down a second time, I felt renewed energy and swung my right arm as hard as I could, plunging the blade deep into the creature's body with all the strength I could muster. Its eyes widened in surprise even as it loosened its grip on my hair, and then I was free. I frantically kicked my way up to the surface and gulped in lungsful of air as soon as I broke the surface. Then Shiv was there and he dragged me the rest of the way to the sand. I coughed and sputtered as he checked me over for injuries. But other than a massive headache from my hair being pulled, I felt fine. Shaken to the core, but fine nonetheless.

"Callie, are you alright?" Shiv fell back onto the sand once he was satisfied I was no longer in mortal danger.

I was still breathing heavily and my throat burned from swallowing the salty water. "I think so. What about you?" I hadn't been able to see how he had killed his crocodile demon or if he was hurt in the process.

"I'm fine, but..." he said, looking down at the sand.

"But what...?"

A look of guilt settled on Shiv's face. "I should never have gone ahead...I thought you were right behind me."

"I was, but there were two of them. Were you planning to fight them both off?"

"I'm so sorry, Callie. I should have..." His voice

trailed off.

"Shiv, look, you can't be there every second to protect me. I have to defend myself too." He was killing my buzz. "This was just the beginning. And I survived. So let them bring it on...I'm ready."

He smiled, finally. It made me feel better. But mostly I felt great that I had kicked ass. Demon ass.

SIXTEEN

WE SALVAGED WHAT we could from my now completely soaked backpack. I ended up with a few bottles of water, a change of clothes and my dagger. Luckily, the map and most of the food supply had been in Shiv's backpack. After drying off, we entered the cover of the jungle. Aware that we were walking into territory restricted to outsiders, we both kept a vigilant eye out for any angry inhabitants. Secretly I hoped that if I could convey to them that I was an envoy of Kali, so to speak, they would welcome me. Of course, I had no idea what awaited us. My incident with the crocodile demon had not attracted any unwanted attention, but I knew that could change at any moment. The map gave us some sense of which direction we were headed in. Since high-tech gadgets were completely useless here,

Uncle Suresh had the foresight to include an old-fashioned compass in our supplies. It came in handy now. According to the map, the temple was located somewhere on the northern tip of the island. The dense forest provided a welcome reprieve from the sun's intensity, and it was alive with birds and all kinds of tropical flowers. I could not identify a single one, but that did not stop me from being awed by the sounds and scents that filled the air. I had lived in cities all my life and the air here was so fresh, it was unlike anything I had inhaled before.

We walked along for a while before stopping for a rest. We had packed fruit and other dry foods, which we now rationed to last us as long as possible. After a little while we continued on our way.

"Should we stop here for the night, Callie?" Shiv asked as it began to get dark. "This seems like a good place."

I looked around. We had arrived at a small clearing where a few fallen trees formed a sort of cover. Luckily for us, in this part of the world the temperature rarely went below eighty degrees Fahrenheit, so sleeping out in the open was not going to be dangerous as far as the weather was concerned. The chances of us avoiding being killed by wild animals were not so optimistic.

"That actually sounds good," I said. "We should try to find some food. I think there were banana trees back there. I'll go see if I can get us a few." I turned and walked back the way we had come. Soon I reached a cluster of banana trees heavy with fruit. I poked around a bit, looking for a ripe bunch. It took a bit of muscle and the Swiss Army knife I had salvaged from my backpack to break off the right bunch but eventually I was holding six bright yellow bananas for our dinner. I walked back to the clearing and saw that Shiv had been busy too.

"How on earth did you get those?" I asked, looking at the pile of green coconuts on the ground beside him.

"It wasn't easy, but I still remember how to climb up and get these," Shiv replied, looking quite proud of himself. "When I was little, my dad would bring me to Kolkata to visit my grandmother. I'd watch the gardener climb up the trees and get the coconuts. I begged him to let me try it too, so whenever we visited I was allowed to get some. I haven't done it for a few years, but I guess there are some things you don't forget."

"I guess not," I replied, sitting down beside him on the log and handing him a couple of bananas. We ate them in silence, and then I helped Shiv cut the tops off the coconuts with his knife. The water was refreshingly cool and sweet.

The sun had set by then, so we had no choice but to settle in for the night. I decided to keep first watch, since I knew I wouldn't be able to sleep anyway. I had too much on my mind and there was a lot to process. The night brought with it a whole new arsenal of sounds. Some were soothing while others made the hairs on the back of my neck stand up. I started thinking about all the dangers lurking in the night but stopped before I gave in to hysteria. All the stories of man-eating tigers I'd heard as a child did nothing to ease the worry, but I didn't have the luxury of worrying about that now. I watched Shiv sleep, his right arm stretched out over his head. He slept peacefully, his thick, dark lashes fanning out over his cheeks. I was glad he was able to get some rest. At least one of us would be well rested to take on whatever tomorrow would bring. Suddenly I felt a burning on the back of my neck. My fingers flew to where it was stinging the most. The skin there felt raw, and when I looked at my fingers they were smudged with blood. In a panic I shook Shiv awake. He sat up immediately, alert, ready to defend.

"Shiv, there's something on my neck," I said, picking up the flashlight.

He took a look and gasped.

"What is it?" I asked impatiently. I was sure it was some nasty tropical bug that had laid eggs under my skin and now they would hatch inside me...I could feel myself becoming hysterical.

"It's a skull tattoo," Shiv said calmly. I whirled around to glare at him.

"Really? You think that's funny? Whatever it is...get it off me."

"I'm serious...it's a small skull tattoo."

"How is that even possible?" I was convinced he was teasing me.

"I don't know Callie, but I'm telling you what I see. It's a tiny little skull."

I was officially freaked out. This was way too weird. Even with all the strange things that had happened to me in the last few weeks, this still qualified as bizarre.

"Maybe it's something to do with that demon you killed."

"What do you mean?"

Shiv shrugged and put up his hands in mock defense. "Hey, I'm just as in the dark as you are. I'm just throwing out ideas here."

I shook my head. The stinging had stopped, and only a slight throbbing remained. I decided there was nothing I could do about it now, here in the middle of the jungle.

"Why don't you get some sleep? I'll keep watch until morning," Shiv said.

Surprisingly, I fell asleep immediately. I didn't know how long I slept but I was rudely awakened by a loud chattering. I sat up, disoriented, and determined that the sound was coming from directly above me. I looked around for Shiv. He was gone. In a panic I stood up, scanning my surroundings. Then I heard him. Or rather, I heard him swear loudly. Then he appeared from under some low-hanging branches.

"What's going on?" I demanded.

"The monkeys...they took our stuff." He picked up an empty coconut husk and threw it up against the nearest tree. In response, the forest echoed with the amused chattering of the little thieves. This was not good. All our supplies were in that backpack. Without it we could be going around in circles for days. Food-snatching monkeys were not an oddity in Kolkata, so I was not terrified of them. I was more annoyed than anything else because we really didn't have time for this kind of game. We had to get our stuff back and it had to be now. Only I had no clue how to do that. I started waving my arms about and yelling at them. Nothing. A couple of them swung down on lower branches and just stared at me mockingly. Shiv picked up some more coconut husks and threw them into the trees. Of course the monkeys dodged them easily. Just then something fell from the sky. It hit my head on the way down, which prompted me to say something very unladylike. Shiv bent down to pick it up, but not before I saw his grin.

"What is it?" I gingerly touched my head. There was going to be an ugly bump soon.

Shiv looked up at me, still with the goofy grin. "You're not going to believe this."

"What is it, Shiv?" I snatched it from his hand and gasped. "No way. That's not possible." It was the compass. "Where did it fall from?" I looked up, which was a big mistake, because just then something soft and slimy hit me. "What the hell was that?" I spluttered, furiously wiping at my face.

By now Shiv had lost it and was bent over with

laughter, which was ironic, because the next instant I looked up again just in time to see a monkey throwing a half-eaten banana and hitting Shiv square in the face. *Hah,* I thought, *revenge is sweet.* I was laughing so hard that I didn't see the next missile coming at me, this time a granola bar. It bounced off my face, landing on the ground. I ducked just in time to avoid the next item, a water bottle. That would have taken me out.

"Shiv, I think they're trying to return our stuff," I yelled over the cacophony up in the trees. There were at least a dozen monkeys and they were chattering very loudly.

"You think?" he yelled back, barely dodging something wrapped in cellophane.

We were running around in circles picking stuff up while the monkeys followed us overhead. After some time things stopped falling out of the trees. Shiv and I surveyed the lot. It seemed that we had most things back. At least everything we needed right now. The monkeys had disappeared too.

"Okay, that was weird," said Shiv, fiddling with the compass. "But at least we have our stuff back."

Suddenly there was a crashing sound that reverberated through the trees. It was followed by another one, this time a thunderous boom, and then the ground shook. Suddenly I felt a strong breeze out of nowhere and then to my utter disbelief a small funnel cloud descended upon the little clearing, blowing dust and leaves all around us. We were momentarily blinded, and when everything settled, I rubbed the dirt out of my eyes. When I opened them, I froze. Before me stood Hanuman. The King of Monkeys. Not Tarzan, but the beloved god from Hindu mythology. Son of the wind god. Savior of Sita. The stories about him were endless. As a child I would beg my grandmother to tell them to me over and over again. I loved his heroism when he saved Lord Rama's beloved Sita from the demon Ravana. He was the son of a celestial nymph and the wind god, Vayu. Stories of his childhood antics filled my memories, as did those about his powers of shape-shifting. Now he stood before me in all his simian glory. His body was covered in hair but his face was more human than ape. His long tail swished as he stood before us. He was smaller than I would have imagined, but I suspected that had something to do with the fact that he could change his size at will. All these thoughts swirled in my head as I stood in front of him, at a complete loss for words. I stole a glance at Shiv beside me. He was apparently suffering from the same affliction.

Hanuman smiled at us.

"I apologize for my naughty children," he said in a deep, booming voice that echoed around us.

"Lord Hanuman...I can't believe it..." I had finally found my voice, but I still couldn't trust what I was seeing.

"Yes, my dear. It is I, Hanuman. I have been waiting for you."

"I don't understand..."

"I have something to give you, my child." An object appeared in his hand from thin air, as far as I could tell. I had seen one like it before, in a temple in Kolkata. It was a *gada*, a mace, the favored weapon of Hanuman. He handed it to me. I reached out to grab it by the handle, which was thin on the bottom but increased in girth until it ended in a bulbous top. In the stories my grandmother would tell me, the *gada* was used in the epic battles of the *Ramayana* to destroy the armies of Rakshasas. Now I held one in my hand. It was not as heavy as I had expected. My fingers fit comfortably around the bottom and I swung it, hesitantly at first, then with more confidence. I looked up at Lord Hanuman. He was smiling at me.

"It seems that it is made just for you, isn't it?" he said with a wink.

Then his expression became grave once more.

"You have a difficult journey ahead of you, my child. This *gada* will help to protect you against the many dangers you will face. It is more powerful than it appears. Use it well."

And with that he whipped around so fast that all we could see was a cloud of dust and leaves and then he was gone, as quickly as he had appeared. When the dust settled I looked at Shiv. He looked stunned, which was exactly how I felt. In all my life I had never anticipated that one day I would be standing in the middle of the forest having a conversation with Hanuman. He was one of my favorites of all the Hindu deities. His ability to leap over mountains in a single bound, to change his size at will and to heal were all part of my fascination with him. But most of all I loved his loyalty and his willingness to fight for the weak. And now he had given me a *guda*. I held it close, admiring the intricate patterns etched into the wood. I looked up to see Shiv looking at it longingly.

"Here," I said, handing it to him. "You can hold it for a while."

It was like giving candy to a kid. His face lit up and he took it almost reverently. It seemed I wasn't the only one who was a fan of Lord Hanuman.

Now that we had our stuff back, we sat and ate the rest of our bananas from last night, along with some of the crackers the monkeys had so generously dropped on our heads. There was more coconut water too, so I was quite content when we started back on our trip. A quick consultation of the map and confirmation with the compass indicated that we were still on the right track. Back in Kolkata I had read that a big tsunami a few years ago had altered the geography of the island quite a bit, but it seemed that the interior of the forest had remained unchanged. I wondered when and if we would come into contact with any of the few hundred inhabitants. I'd been fascinated to read in several articles that this particular tribe and its descendants had lived on the island completely untouched by civilization for thousands of years. They kept to themselves and attacked any outsiders with spears and arrows before they got too close. Based on that, I thought we'd been pretty lucky so far. We hadn't seen anybody at all.

We walked in silence for some time, stopping only to rest briefly so we could make the most of daylight. At one point we were caught up in a monsoon shower that stopped as abruptly as it started, leaving us drenched. However, once the sun came out it took very little time to dry off. We seemed to be making good progress so we decided to stop and eat after a few hours of trekking through the jungle. According to Shiv's calculations, we would be there by nightfall.

We were just finishing up and getting ready to leave again when I noticed a movement out of the corner of my eye. I immediately reached for the *gada*, which I'd tucked into the waistband of my jeans. I looked toward the trees, where I thought I'd seen something move. But now there was nothing. Shiv noticed me standing very still and stopped as well. He dropped his backpack, reaching for his own dagger. For some reason my eyes were drawn to a particular tree. There was something about it that didn't seem right.

I walked a little closer and stared at the trunk. The markings seemed uneven. Not that I knew that much about trees, but this one looked like it had...eyes. I jumped back just in time as a part of the trunk seemed to come to life. A figure seemed to peel itself right from the tree. It did not seem friendly. In fact, it came straight at me with arm-like limbs that ended in sharp claws. Shiv jumped in front of me and plunged his dagger into the creature. It staggered back, slowing down for a brief moment before straightening up and coming at us again. This time I put myself between the creature and Shiv, swung the *gada* and brought it down on the demon's head. A piercing sound erupted from it as it fell to the ground. But just as swiftly it regained its balance and lunged for me again. I swung again, this time aiming for the torso. It fell again and this time it stayed down. Shiv had come up behind it and stabbed it again with his dagger. It screamed in agony and in that scream I was sure I could make out words. I could have sworn it said "Mahisha is coming for you." Then it slumped down and its body turned to ash, leaving nothing other than a few tendrils of smoke that floated up into the air. Shiv and I watched, stunned.

"Did you hear what it said?" I whispered, terrified that he hadn't.

"Mahisha is coming? Yes I heard that," Shiv said grimly.

It was strange, the way hearing the words from the demon made this whole situation seem more real than all the conversations I'd had with the Rakshakari. I felt the dread growing stronger. At the same time it also had to mean that we were getting close. That gave me hope, and hope was something I needed badly right now. I could see by the determined set of Shiv's jaw that he shared my sentiments. Our eyes locked for a moment and then in unspoken agreement we moved on.

"So...this *gada*," I said, swinging it around as we began walking again. "It's pretty cool, isn't it?"

"Yeah, somebody sure enjoyed using it," Shiv said, grinning.

"Hey, a girl's gotta take care of herself, you know," I said, playfully punching him on the shoulder.

I didn't know how long we'd been going when it happened. One moment we were walking along and the next Shiv disappeared. It was as if he had been lifted right off the ground. It was a good thing I looked up, because there he was, hanging in a net from a tree branch, looking as stunned as I felt. But only for a moment. Then I took a few steps forward, too late to hear him shout out a warning. I felt my feet slide out from under me as I was hoisted high up into the trees. Once I'd caught my breath, I tried to find Shiv. Thankfully, I could still see him. He looked shocked, probably due to the profanities coming out of my mouth, or maybe it was the situation in general. Either way, we were stuck there, defenceless and at the mercy of whoever had set the traps.

"Are you hurt, Callie?" Shiv's voice sounded shaky, which was exactly how I felt. I checked myself as well as I could, given the awkward position I was in. It didn't feel as if anything was broken.

"No, I think I'm okay. What about you?" I craned my neck to get a better look at him, but the more I moved the more twisted the net got. It was hard to face in one direction.

"Yeah, I'm okay too, I think. Can you see anything from there? I don't see anyone and I have quite the vantage point here."

I looked around, turning my head as far as I could without dislocating my neck, but there was nothing. "No, Shiv, I don't see anything either. Do you think it's the locals trying to keep us away?"

"I think that's about right. Remember how my uncle said they're not very friendly? This is probably how they keep outsiders away."

"Well, we need to figure out how to get down. Any ideas?" I was getting a cramp in my legs and it was starting to get dark. I did not want to be hanging all scrunched up in a net when night fell in the jungle. Suddenly I heard a loud thud and then a grunt. "Shiv?"

There was no reply. I tried to swing my body to face in his direction. There was nothing to push against, so the best I could do was a rocking motion to get myself moving and hope that I ended up facing the right way. After several attempts, I ended up facing where I thought Shiv had been hanging. He wasn't there. I swung around again, changing directions, but I couldn't see him anywhere.

"Shiv, where are you? Shiv, say something if you can." Panic began to set in and I fought the urge to scream. The next thing I knew there was a tug from above me, and I was falling. As the ground raced up to meet me, I screamed in terror and then mercifully everything went black.

SEVENTEEN

WHEN I CAME to, I couldn't move. I opened my eyes and immediately shut them again as the bright light assaulted them. I tried again, just opening them the slightest bit. I didn't know how I was being restrained because I couldn't even move my head to get a look. The only thing I had to rely on was my vision. At least there was light.

I squinted against the brightness and slowly my eyes got used to the glare. I looked around and gasped. I was in a very small cage. It was barely large enough to fit me, which explained why I was stuffed in there like poultry. I strained my eyes as far as I could to get a better look. I was about to scream for help when my cage was rattled loudly. I heard the door being opened and then I was pulled out unceremoniously. My entire body hurt from being all twisted up for who knew how long. I looked at my captor. He was about my height, all of five feet tall, but stocky with curly salt-and-pepper hair. He wore only a loincloth and a held a staff in one hand. His eyes bristled with anger. Clearly I had pissed him off. Then he spoke to me. I didn't understand the words, but the way he was jabbing at me with his fingers made it abundantly clear I was not welcome. Something twisted in my stomach. I didn't see Shiv anywhere. I tried to open my mouth and speak, but my throat was dry and scratchy. All that came out was a croak, which made my captor look at me in confusion. I tried again.

"Shiv?" I called out. Nothing. *Where is he?*

The man yanked me roughly forward. I tried to get a better look around. There was a circular arrangement of shelters made from what looked like bamboo and dried grass. The structures had no walls and only provided cover on top. A few women and children were outside. The children chased each other while the women called out to them every now and then. But I still couldn't see Shiv.

"Shiv," I called out again. This time some of the children stopped to stare at me, and the women turned around to look too.

My captor regarded me disdainfully before turning to his right and shouting something. A few seconds later Shiv appeared, hands behind his back. He was dragged over to where I stood by another man with a similar build as my captor. Shiv looked disheveled, his T-shirt torn in a couple of places, but other than that there didn't seem to be any visible damage. As soon as he saw me his eyes mirrored my relief. Now we just had to figure a way out of this pickle.

When he came closer, I pulled away from my captor's grasp to reach out to him. That earned me a hard knock on the head.

"Callie..." Shiv shouted, pushing toward me. His captor hauled him back roughly. Then we were both thrown to the ground and pulled back up so that we were kneeling in the dirt. Shiv's captor produced a knife and held it to Shiv's neck. I screamed and tried to pull away. I must have dislodged my skull pendant during the kerfuffle because it began to glow and I felt a familiar warmth at my neck. Our captors staggered back, dropping their knives. They exchanged words then turned around to gesture wildly at the women and children. I stood up, watching them, not moving a muscle as the women herded their children into the shelters. The captors looked at us, but their eyes held a very different look now. I recognized it as fear and confusion. My pendant was still glowing, and the way that the two men were eyeing it told me that they knew something we didn't. Shiv got up to stand beside me, rubbing his wrists.

"They're afraid of the pendant," I whispered.

"Do you think they know something about it?"

"That...or they're just freaked out by the light." I

touched the pendant and moved toward them. They backed away. It wasn't warm anymore and when I looked down I saw that it had stopped glowing too.

"It's okay," I said coaxingly as I inched slowly forward. I had a feeling in my gut that these people knew something. If they had really never been in touch with the outside world for so many centuries then the stories might even be true. Maybe they knew where the temple was and what was hidden inside.

The men had stopped moving backward, which I took as an encouraging sign. When I finally came close enough, one of them picked up a small stick and began to draw in the sand. Shiv came over too and we watched as the man worked fast and furiously. As we watched, it became clear what he was trying to depict. He had drawn a structure that resembled a temple. He had also drawn the figure of a woman. I bent down to get a closer look. It was unmistakeable. He had drawn Kali. She held a sword and a *gada*, along with an assortment of other weapons. It was a crude drawing but clear enough to erase all doubt in my mind that the inhabitants of this island knew about Kali.

He must have sensed my excitement because when I pointed to the sword and mimed a question, he nodded vigorously. I hoped that meant he would help us. But it appeared I would have to wait to find out. He turned to the women, who were peeking out from the shelter, and waved for them to come out. At first they hesitated, but then slowly a few of them ventured out with their children in tow. Soon they were standing behind the two men with shy smiles. Other men had also joined them.

A little girl with curly black hair came closer than any of the others. She hid her face bashfully but then reached out to touch the hem of my shirt. A collective gasp rose from the little congregation. I kneeled down so that I was at her eye level and gently touched her hair. It was dry and springy, no doubt from the salt water and sun. I smiled at her and she returned a shy smile of her own. Then she ran back to her mother to hide her face in her lap.

I stood up. There was a strange feeling in the pit of my stomach, but this one wasn't bad. It was the first time I had a sense of being part of something much bigger than myself. Something that had been in play for millennia. After all, these people had inhabited the island for over sixty thousand years and had never relinquished their independence and original culture. They were untarnished by the trappings of the modern world. It was no wonder that Kali's priestesses had chosen this piece of paradise to keep the sword safe for all this time.

I bent down once again and pointed to the sword in the sand drawing. The men both nodded. I spoke to them in Bengali, even though I knew they spoke a different language. But I felt weird miming and speaking in English didn't make much sense either. After a lot of gesturing I was able to deduce that they would show us the way to the temple. At least I hoped I was right. It was already dark by now, so when they urged us to sit and brought crude bamboo mats for us to sleep on, we didn't argue. There were several fires going by now, and the women prepared a meal of fish and some kind of vegetable I couldn't identify. It was simple and delicious. After we ate, we went to sleep. It was strange that neither of us felt the need to keep watch after the way they had initially treated us. We agreed that they were just defending themselves against outsiders and that they must have been very suspicious of two strangers who had dropped in uninvited. After the almost reverent manner in which they had been treating us the whole evening, I could not bring myself to mistrust them.

We slept soundly through the night and awoke to the happy squeals of children running around. After a breakfast of bananas, our former captors waved us over to where they sat on their haunches looking at another drawing they had made in the sand. As Shiv and I joined them, we realized they were showing us the way to get to the temple. Apparently it was accessible only through a series of caves and tunnels. Then the drawings became quite graphic. We saw bodies that had been torn apart by enormous wild-looking creatures. At first I was confused but soon I realized what I was seeing. The passage to the temple was guarded and the bodies were those of others who had attempted to get there. Over the centuries numerous people must have tried to get to the temple and the sword. Even without tangible proof, there were always those who believed. The Sword of Knowledge, as Kali's weapon was referred to in the many accounts I had read, was known to have many powers. One of those was the power to do away with evil and ignorance. This must have made it attractive to both good and bad people. After all, who wouldn't want to have such glory?

If the two men had intended to alarm us with their drawings, they had succeeded. But one look at Shiv and I knew that like me, nothing was going to deter him from trying. On the other hand, it was good that we knew what to expect. The last thing we needed was a surprise attack while we were in the caves.

We gathered our meager belongings and followed the men back into the forest. We had no way of knowing just how far we were going, but we were grateful nonetheless for having personal guides. We ended up walking for about three hours with a break for some coconut water and mangoes. It was a nice change from the bananas we'd been eating since we got there. I had a feeling that I wouldn't be eating that particular fruit for a long time after we got back home.

After that it wasn't long before we came to a clearing. There, a few feet from the center, was a large rock covered in shrubs growing right out of it. The sides were also covered by greenery, and as far as I could see there was no entrance of any kind. Puzzled, I turned to the two men. They pointed to the rock and said something. I didn't understand most of it, but one word was perfectly clear. Kali.

Shiv and I went closer to the rock, looking for a way in. The vines of whatever plants were growing on top stretched all the way across the top and down the sides. I tugged at one of them but it was thick, with a diameter of about an inch. Unfortunately, upon touching it I realized it also had tiny, sharp thorns. I quickly let go of the vine and looked at my fingers. There were tiny puncture marks with blood dotting the tips. Other than a little stinging, I was fine.

"You okay there, Callie?" Shiv asked. "Looks like the entrance is pretty well concealed. We'll have to cut through."

I nodded, turning around to look at the two men. They hadn't moved from where they'd been standing a few moments ago. When I gestured to them to come and help us, they shrank back. Clearly they had come as far as they were willing to go. I walked back over to them and Shiv followed. Since words were not an option for me, I communicated my deep gratitude by putting my arms around first one and then the other man. When I pulled away, the looks on their faces were priceless. They smiled, their embarrassment evident in their downcast eyes. I hoped they knew just how much they had helped. After a moment they began to retreat into the forest. I waved and then they were gone, swallowed up by the dense vegetation. We were on our own.

"Okay, so I'm going to cut the vines. Hopefully there's an opening in there somewhere." Shiv pulled his dagger from the waistband of his jeans and walked purposefully toward the rock. I rummaged in the backpack for my Swiss Army knife. I watched as Shiv slashed a couple of the vines closest to him and then made his way down toward the ground. I started hacking away with my little blade in another spot. After a few minutes I turned to look at where Shiv was working. He had made a lot more headway than me, but there was still no trace of any sort of entrance. It was getting dark and I was worried that we would end up spending the night out here. It was frustrating because we were so close. We worked as fast as we could and then suddenly Shiv called out.

"I found something."

I scampered over. Sure enough, there was an opening, still partially covered by thorny vines, but large for a person to squeeze through. I let out a sigh of relief. Finally, a break.

"I'll go first," Shiv said, grabbing the backpack and pushing his way through the entrance. I followed as soon as he was fully inside. It was pitch black, and I was glad that Shiv still had a working flashlight. An added bonus was that my pendant began to glow as soon as I entered the cave. A pattern was clear. The skull pendant would glow and emit heat whenever I was in danger. Now it didn't get warm, and the light was blue rather than red. Based on prior incidents, red was for those times when I was in mortal danger and blue for when I just needed some help. I counted my blessings for the handy little skull pendant. The light cast an eerie glow on the walls of the cave, bathing everything in a bluish hue. It also bounced around as I walked, making me feel slightly nauseated. I took it off, thinking it might be better to hold it by the string like a little lantern. But as soon as I dropped it from my fingers to let it dangle, the light went out. That was weird. I picked it back up. The light came back on. Shiv turned to me in confusion.

"What are you doing?" he whispered, his voice echoing off the cave walls.

"The pendant...watch this." I demonstrated.

"Huh...I guess it has to touch your skin to work."

We walked along the narrow passage, the walls cold and hard whenever we brushed up against them. The light from the pendant and the flashlight was enough to prevent us from slamming into the rock or each other as we carefully navigated the unexpected twists and turns. Eventually the passage widened, opening up into a fairly large chamber. I almost tripped over something as soon as we came out of the narrow part and shone my light on it. A scream escaped me as I looked in horror at a skull on the floor. Shiv shone his flashlight all around and we both gasped. There were more skulls and other assorted bones strewn all over the ground. I looked at the pendant. The light was still blue, not red. Hopefully this meant that no wild creatures were lying in wait to kill us and rip our limbs off. But something had killed all these people. I counted at least twelve skulls and didn't bother with the other bones. I wondered who they'd been...these people who had dared to come in here, risking their lives. I couldn't help thinking that this might very well be a trap, one set by Mahisha or his minions. They could have led us to believe that the locals were being helpful, when in fact they were leading us straight to our deaths. I could feel the paranoid thoughts threatening to take over, and right now, here in this dark cave, so close to my goal, I was not about to allow that to happen. So I took a deep breath and stood up straight.

"Callie...come here and take a look at this," Shiv called out. He was pointing his flashlight at something on the wall. I went over and pointed my pendant to the same spot. What I saw rendered me speechless. The entire wall was covered in drawings, scenes of battle alive with vibrant colors. They depicted the gods and goddesses of ancient lore in battle with the demons.

"Who do you think did these, Shiv?" I asked breathlessly, stunned by the vivid details.

"I don't know. I've never heard of anything like this. It couldn't be the locals...they were too afraid to come near."

"Well," I said, running my fingers along the wall, "it must be really old, so maybe things were different back then."

"When we get back we're going to have to ask the

Elders about this," Shiv said, walking alongside the wall until it ended and a new one began. I followed closely, shining my light just above his head.

I realized that the drawings were divided into panels, each depicting a particular scene. Most of the stories they told were old, familiar ones from my childhood. Here was Brahma creating the world, populating it with plants, animals and insects. In a next panel he was giving them seven gifts: the sense of touch, taste, smell, sight, hearing, the power to move and the power to reproduce. In another he was riding a lotus boat, enjoying the wonders of his own creation.

I moved on, and now I was looking at a drawing of Brahma dividing himself and creating Saraswati, the Goddess of Knowledge. Together they created humans and endowed them with the seven gifts, plus an additional one, the power of reason.

"This is so amazing," I said, still unable to process what I was seeing. "I can't believe this has been here for centuries and no one has discovered this place."

I walked ahead, stepping carefully over a skull. As I shone my light on the next panel I saw the Immortals granting boons to humans. The humans in turn worshipped them, made sacrifices to them, sometimes animals, sometimes young girls. I shuddered to think that there was a time when killing an innocent child was considered an act of worship.

I moved on, and there was Mahisha begging to be made Immortal. Then he was depicted in all his wrath after his request was denied. He hadn't always been the bad guy. He had spent years in prayer and meditation, all so that he could be granted a boon. In his eyes it must have been the Immortals' arrogance that prevented them from giving him what he felt he deserved. The ultimate betrayal. I looked at the next few panels in horror as they told the story of Mahisha after he had turned into a demon. He had unleashed his massive army upon unsuspecting mortals, men, women and children alike. As his terrible deeds grew, so did his might.

I turned a corner with Shiv close behind me now. Neither of us spoke. The panels on this wall told the story of the trinity, Brahma, Vishnu and Shiva, as they met to discuss the problem of Mahisha's growing power. It told of the creation of Kali as she sprang forth from the fire poured from the mouths of the gods in anger. She was born with multiple arms, in each of which the gods put the weapons with which she would destroy Mahisha.

I looked long and hard at the drawing. The goddess was glorious in her power and beauty. Her eyes blazed with purpose. She sat tall and erect on her lion as she rode into battle, ready to destroy evil, prepared to defend humanity. I continued down along the wall, watching as Kali fought valiantly against Mahisha and he escaped each of her attempts to destroy him, first by changing into a lion, then a man, then a buffalo. We had come to the last panel and stopped in front of it. As I studied it, I realized that this must be the only account of what had really happened in that battle. For centuries it had been believed that Kali had cut off the head of the buffalo-demon, as Mahisha was usually referred to. All the ancient religious texts and the stories that I'd heard as a child told the tale of Mahisha's destruction at the hands of a most powerful goddess. This definitely shed a different light on things. It was all becoming clearer.

"Callie, I think we should keep moving. Judging by the skulls, I think we're lucky we're still alive." I couldn't agree more.

We kept moving. The chamber narrowed into another seemingly endless stretch of tunnel. When we finally reached the exit, it was dark. Thankfully, because the trees were not quite as dense as in other parts of the forest, the moonlight and the stars provided some light. It was enough to see the hill in the distance and the temple perched on top of it. A sudden burst of energy made us both run up to where steps had been carved into the hillside.

"I can't believe it's held up so well," Shiv said when we reached the top.

I could only stare up at the spires rising majestically into the starlit sky.

"I can't believe they had the tools to do such intricate carvings such a long time ago," I said, completely awestruck.

As we walked up to the main entrance I saw the traditional mandala design on the floor, a square intersecting a circle. I knew that each point of intersection had a special significance. I vaguely remembered a story my dad had told me of how the mandala became so crucial to the design of the temple.

I tried to remember the details. It was something to do with Shiva sweating in the midst of a fierce battle. A drop of his sweat fell on the ground and from it sprang a tremendous demon that proceeded to destroy everything in its path. To stop him, several gods had to join forces. In fact, once they had overcome him, they had to sit on different parts of his body so that he could not rise again. This became the basis of the belief that a temple had to be constructed in a particular way so as not to allow any evil to enter.

Nice theory, I thought. Clearly it didn't work so well or there wouldn't be demons running amok right now.

We looked up at the ornate arched double doors. We tried to open them but they wouldn't budge. There was no lock or anything, so I wasn't sure what was keeping them closed. I looked around for any hidden latches but found nothing. I tried to channel the Relic Hunter, one of my mom's guilty pleasures. She would have found a way to get in by now.

"Shiv," I called out over my shoulder, "I'm going to look at the carvings again and see if there's some sort of a clue there."

"Okay, Callie," Shiv replied, walking away. "I'm going to check for another way in. The front can't be the only entrance." I barely caught the last of his words as disappeared around the back.

I turned my attention to the carvings. They seemed ordinary, typical of any Kali temple around the world. They depicted Kali on her lion, with a snake wrapped around one of her six arms. Further down the wall she was surrounded by the Immortals who had created her. Then a series of depictions as each of the gods gave her a gift: the lotus, the bow and arrows, the trident, the thunderbolt, the discus and finally...the sword. I looked at the sword with a longing that started deep in my gut and blossomed. If only I could get my hands on that sword, all my problems would be solved. I had to get in somehow. Not knowing what else to do, I kept staring intently at the carvings, hoping to glean some information by osmosis. I must have stared at them too long, because suddenly I thought I saw something move. I blinked and shook my head, trying to clear my vision. I looked at the carving again. Nothing had changed. I was looking at Kali with the snake around her arm when it happened again. This time I was sure of it. The snake had blinked. That was what had caught my attention earlier. I stood frozen in front of the carving. Was I finally losing my mind? Not that a snake with blinking eyes was the strangest thing I'd encountered recently.

"Shiv," I called out, sounding only slightly panicked. "I think you should come here...now."

He must have heard the panic in my voice

threatening to take over, because he was at my side in a flash.

"What happened, Callie?" he asked breathlessly.

"Look at the carving...right there." I had to know if I'd really seen the snake blink at me or if I was stark, raving mad.

"What am I looking at, Callie?" He looked at me, then back at the carving. "It's Kali and her weapons and...oh my god...did that snake just blink at me?"

I smiled. I was still sane. "Phew, I was worried there for a moment...thought I was losing it. So you saw it too?"

"Umm, yes, Callie, it's kind of hard to miss that. What do you think it is?"

"I don't know...maybe it's watching us...Wait, Shiv, I don't remember much about snakes from my parents. The only thing I do remember is that Manasa, the snake goddess, was supposed to be the daughter of Lord Shiva. Is that true? Hmm...but what did she have to do with Kali?" I mused, absentmindedly stroking the carving.

Suddenly we heard a rumble, quiet at first, then becoming louder. I couldn't quite tell where it was coming from, but then I realized it was coming from inside the temple.

"What was that, Shiv?"

"I don't know, but there's definitely something inside."

The rumbling stopped. We still had no way of

getting in. I turned my attention back to Kali and the snake on her arm. I laid my hand on the cool stone surface and waited. Nothing. I wasn't really sure what I expected to happen. Maybe a way in would have been nice. I figured if the snake was guarding the temple, then maybe it would let me in. I was an avatar of Kali, after all. Still nothing. A thought occurred to me. I looked closer at the etching of Kali to confirm. Yes, she was wearing the skull pendant around her neck. I put my hand on it. Again nothing. I was about to remove my hand when I felt a strange sensation. A slight tingling, almost imperceptible, but definitely there. I felt my own pendant getting warm.

"Callie, your pendant...it's glowing," Shiv said softly. I looked down at it and saw the soft amber light emanating from it.

"I feel something, Shiv. I think..." Before I could finish speaking, there was another loud rumble. This time it sounded like thunder, but really close to us. I kept my hand on Kali's pendant and when I looked at the snake on her arm it was glowing too.

I turned to look at Shiv, but he had walked up to the double doors at the entrance and was staring at them.

"Callie..." he called out. "The doors are open. Hurry up, I don't know how long they'll stay that way."

I was afraid to take off my hand, but I had to take the chance. I ran over to the doors and we both entered at the same time. As soon as we crossed the threshold into the cool darkness, the doors closed with a loud bang that echoed throughout the interior of the cavernous temple. It seemed to be a great deal bigger than it looked from outside. I had a brief moment of panic when I realized we might not have a way of getting out, but that soon passed when my eyes adjusted to the darkness.

EIGHTEEN

As I ENTERED the temple, the cool darkness enveloped me, offering a welcome relief from the hot, humid air outside. Beautifully carved relief panels adorned the walls. I walked toward the inner sanctum that housed the statue of Kali. No matter how many times I had been to these temples, it never got old. The sense of awe was always there, humility that people thousands of years ago created such beauty by hand without the help of any modern technology.

Shiv and I silently took in the wonder of what stood before us. In the center of the enormous hall stood a statue of Kali. It was big, a little taller than me, but shorter than Shiv, who stood at almost six feet. It was adorned with the traditional jewels and garments that could be found on any statue in temples throughout

India. Then, just as Shiv and I began to walk toward it, we heard a growl. I looked around and to my surprise I saw that standing all along the wall in a wide circle were statues of monkeys. Not small, cute ones like back in the jungle. These ones looked ferocious, like they could rip your throat out. Or bash your skull in. I couldn't help thinking of the skulls we had seen in the cave. But they were statues, not live monkeys.

I looked at Shiv in surprise. "Were those there when we came in?"

He shook his head. "I don't know, I didn't notice them until now. Do you think that's where the growl came from?"

"I don't think so." A second later I wanted to take back my words. Out of the corner of my eye I saw movement but before I could check to see what it was, the statues came alive around us. My blood ran cold as I watched, my mind working almost in slow motion as it registered what was happening. Shiv looked at me, and my terror was reflected in his eyes as we realized that we were surrounded by monkeys that didn't look particularly pleased with our presence. Also, we were trapped inside the temple with no way out.

I could feel my pendant beginning to get warm. A tingling started to travel from my gut, up my body and down my right arm. I raised my arm and brought my hand closer to my face to see what was happening. The monkey to my immediate right must have noticed the movement, because it growled, low and menacingly.

Then it charged. My response was automatic. I didn't hesitate or think about my action. I just let the energy shoot out of my arm with a blast of light and the monkey was down. I had just enough time to see the entire herd closing in on us and I knew this was the end. But then the earth shook and we all froze. Me, Shiv and the monkeys. A loud roar thundered through the temple. It felt as if the very walls trembled from the sound. I closed my eyes in terror and when I opened them I saw Hanuman standing before us. He stood over seven feet tall this time. His tail was draped around his right arm. His large black eyes seemed to see deep into the soul of me.

"We meet again," he said, in a deep rumble that echoed through the temple. "And you have just killed one of my own." I looked around at the monkeys, who were now prostrate on the ground before their master. I was in shock. I had no idea where that blast came from and I certainly had no idea that I could kill with it.

"Forgive me, Lord Hanuman. I...I don't know what happened...my hand..." My words trailed off as I surveyed the damage I had caused. I could not look at the monkey that lay lifeless on the ground. The walls behind where it had been standing had scorch marks on them. This was insane. The pedant had gone from just giving me a warning glow to turning me into a killing machine. I turned to Lord Hanuman, desperate for his forgiveness.

"I had no choice. I thought they were going to kill

us. Please...can't you do something?" I rushed over to where the monkey lay and gently put my hand on its face.

Hanuman walked over to us. He placed his right hand on the monkey's forehead. A soft light emanated from his hand into the monkey's body and in just a moment the its eyes fluttered open. As it saw the face of its lord and master, it rose to its haunches and then touched Hanuman's feet in an age-old gesture of respect and gratitude. Tears of remorse sprang to my eyes as I realized what I had done.

"It seems that you are not yet in control of your powers," Hanuman said, rising and standing before me. "It will bring you much pain and regret if you do not master them soon."

And with that he disappeared in a cloud of dust and wind as quickly as he had come. The monkeys reverted back to their statue forms.

I looked at Shiv, who still seemed to be in shock. "So...you have a pretty deadly power there," he said, nodding toward my hand.

"I honestly don't know where that came from," I said, looking at my palm to see if there were any burn marks. Nothing. It was as if fire had not just come shooting out of it.

"I think my connection with the pendant is getting stronger somehow." I couldn't think of any other plausible explanation. The one good thing about this debacle was that finally I felt like I had an actual power.

I'd thought that I was going to have to develop some serious ninja skills to pull this off. I looked at the monkeys and felt a lump in my throat. It was hard to believe that they could have been here for thousands of years.

"It looks like they were just protecting the temple for Kali...or you," Shiv said, pulling me toward him. He put his arms around me and held me as I sobbed softly into his shirt. I wasn't really sure why I was crying except that I was so relieved we had made it here alive. After the sobbing had subsided, I wiped the tears on my sleeve and took a deep, shaky breath. Shiv stepped back and studied my face.

"That was something else, wasn't it?" he said.

"I can't believe we finally made it...in one piece," I said with a watery smile.

"Well, I guess now we start looking for the sword," he replied.

We walked over to the statue of Kali. She was all arms. She was magnificent, proud and powerful, black hair flowing down her back in long tresses. Eyes blazing with anger, dark as the night. This was no demure goddess; her beauty was not traditional. She represented other strengths, fierce protectiveness, fearlessness and above all a desire to fight against evil. Her beauty was the fire in her eyes, the anger in her grimace. She inspired fear in her enemies and loyalty in her devotees. She held all the weapons that had been given to her by the gods. One of them was a sword. Of course, the weapons were usually not real, but rather replicas. However, since we were in this particular temple, I wanted to think that this sword was the one. I touched it and pried it out of her statue hands. Despite my wishful thinking, this one was made of wood, too light to do any damage at all, other than a few splinters maybe.

"Any luck there?" Shiv asked wryly from the other side of the statue.

"A girl can hope, can't she?" I quipped. I walked around the statue toward another exit. I peered around the doorframe. A short hallway connected this larger room to another.

"Shiv, I'm going to check out that other room, okay?" I called over my shoulder.

"I think I'll keep looking around in here," he replied.

I went quickly down the hallway and entered the room on the right. It was much smaller than the main hall I had just left. There were no statues here. Instead I saw a few brass pots covered in cobwebs sitting on the floor by the wall. On one wall there were little indentations. Curious, I went closer to take a better look. There was a tiny object in one of them. At first I couldn't tell what it was because it was shrouded in cobwebs. Suppressing my disgust, I brushed away as much as I could and peered at it.

It was a ring. A beautiful silver ring in the shape of an eternal knot. As I held it and tried to figure out what it was doing here, I felt my surroundings fade away. I blinked in confusion, and when I opened my eyes, I was still in the room. Except it was bright and clean with sunlight streaming in from tiny little windows set high close to the ceiling. There were four young women in the room, but none of them seemed aware of my presence. They wore pretty yellow saris with red borders running along the bottom. Each had a garland of jasmine flowers twisted in her braid. One of the girls stood by a small fire, where she was pouring heated milk into small vessels. Each of the other girls then took one, picked up a small platter of sweets, fruits and nuts and walked out of the room. The one who remained sat by the fire for some time. Then she looked around furtively before reaching into the folds of her sari and producing a ring. She put it on her middle finger, admired it, then changed her mind and put it on her ring finger. Suddenly she looked up and I froze, afraid that she would see me. But although her gaze was pointed in my direction, she saw right through me.

Then a couple of the other girls came back. I decided to return to the larger room. I went down the same hallway, but this time it was clean and well lit by sconces that lined the walls. I looked down at my hand as I walked into the large hall. I was still holding the ring. Somehow I knew that I was having this vision because of it. I wanted to know what was going on and felt that I was witnessing this because something important was going to happen. I stood by the entrance.

The girl stood in front of Kali, pouring water over the statue and washing it with slow, careful strokes. Then she dried it with a cloth and put garlands of marigolds around Kali's neck. She carefully placed the tumblers of milk and the platter of sweets on the ground in front of her. Then she sat on her haunches and proceeded to create a *rangoli* pattern on the floor. I watched as she made intricate designs with different colored powders, all the while humming a pretty tune. I put the ring in my pocket and instantly everything around me transformed. I still stood in the same temple, but now it was dark and musty. Shiv was still looking around in every nook and cranny.

"Shiv, you'll never guess what happened," I called out.

He came bounding back from the other side of the room. I held out the ring. I sort of expected that I would have another vision, but I didn't. Shiv looked at me in confusion.

"A ring? Where'd you find it?"

"In the other room. But it was so weird...as soon as I picked it up, I had a kind of vision."

I told him what I'd seen.

"So you think they were the priestesses of Kali?"

"Yes...think about it. Who else could they be?" I wish I could know what time I had been transported to. From their attire, I wasn't able to hazard a guess. Women still wore saris like that.

"The vision stopped when I put the ring in my

pocket. I thought I would see it again when I touched it." I was a little worried that I might never be able to get it back. I didn't know why, but it seemed important.

"So maybe it only shows you what it wants you to see and when it wants," Shiv tried to reason.

I nodded. That made sense for now. "Have you had any luck here?" I asked. Even though I wanted to find out more about the priestesses, I knew we had to find the sword quickly and get back.

"Not really. I was thinking maybe there was some hidden panel or compartment or something, but if there is I haven't found it." He shrugged. "I'm just going to keep looking."

I decided to return to the room. Maybe I would find some clue there. I walked back down the hallway and entered the room again. I took out the ring and stroked it absentmindedly as I walked around. Suddenly everything shifted and I was in another time once again. This must have been a different day, though, because the girls were not wearing the same saris. They were preparing for some ritual; I could smell incense and there were trays with garlands of marigold and other ones with sweets. Once again, all the girls left except for the same one as last time. But this time she put the ring on her finger and went to the wall farthest away from where I was standing. There was cloth hanging over a part of it like a curtain. To my surprise, she pushed it aside to reveal a small opening, just large enough for her to slip through. I ran to the spot where she had disappeared and followed her out.

After I squeezed through the opening, I found myself outside. I stood in a beautiful garden, surrounded by blooming marigolds and jasmine. To my left was a shaded corner where the trees made a little canopy, providing shelter from the sun. That's where I found the girl. But she wasn't alone. A man sat on the grass with her and held her hands in his. I was pretty sure I was witnessing a secret rendezvous, because according to what I had read about the priestesses, they were celibate. They devoted their entire lives to the worship of Kali, protecting her sword and guarding the temple. But of course that didn't mean that they weren't subject to the same desires as the rest of us. This priestess had obviously fallen in love.

The man began to caress her, running his hands up and down her arms. Then he brought his face close to hers and kissed her. She responded timidly, but then as his hands became bolder she pushed away and said something to him. He smiled and then continued the same way. This time she pushed him away a little harder and his face darkened with anger. He grabbed her by the arms and shook her. I could hear her protests getting louder and looked around, hoping that the others would hear her. But we were at the at the back of the temple in the far end of the garden, and I didn't think they would hear her. I had to do something.

I shouted, knowing it was futile. I ran to them and tried to pry him off her, but my hands just touched air.

She was crying by now, desperately begging him to let her go. I didn't understand the words, but I didn't have to. It was clear she was afraid of what he was going to do to her. She fought him, at one point managing to scratch his face with her fingernails. As they raked across his cheek, leaving a bloody trail, he began to transform. Right in front of me his face changed into something grotesque, his thin lips bared, exposing sharp teeth. He grabbed her and threw her on the ground as if she was nothing more than a doll. He ripped off her sari and then began to shred her blouse until she was exposed. Suddenly everything disappeared and I stood in the middle of a patch of jungle that was overgrown with vines and grass. Where the trees had made a canopy, now there were thorny branches growing into each other. The ring was on the ground by my feet. I must have dropped it and somehow been expelled from the vision. I had to go back. I had to help her.

I picked up the ring and went back instantly. But I was too late. She lay on the ground, naked and bleeding, her clothes in shreds around her. She wasn't crying, she was probably beyond tears, but mine ran down my cheeks. I went to her and tried to touch her, to comfort her, but she could neither hear me nor feel my presence. Then as I stood helplessly, she got up, gathered the torn sari and blouse and dragged herself back through the opening in the wall. I followed her inside and watched as she covered it up carefully with the cloth and went into a small area in the room that I hadn't seen before. It was a washroom, with a pitcher of water and a bowl. She cleaned herself up as well as she could and put on a fresh sari and blouse. Then she walked out to the main hall and joined the others.

I walked right behind her, wondering if she would tell them. She must have, because a few moments later they all huddled around her in tears. They embraced her and checked her over. When they saw the bruises and scratches they cried some more, but I could also see anger rising in them. They must have realized that her lover was just another demon, using her to get to the sword. But this time one of their own, their sister, had been hurt. I wondered what they were going to do next. I didn't have to wait long.

They had talked for some time and then one of the others left the hall. She returned after a while with an assortment of bowls and incense sticks. It looked like they were going to perform a ritual. I thought that they were doing some sort of healing thing, but then to my surprise, one of the other girls went to the statue of Kali and removed the sword. My eyes widened as I saw the girl's arms bend under the weight of it and I realized that this was not the wooden sword that the Kali statue held now. This one was the real one. I watched as they chanted an incantation and in front of my eyes the sword disappeared. Then they gathered their things and left. At the same time my surroundings changed yet again and I was back in the main hall with Shiv staring at me in concern.

"Callie...what happened? I heard you cry out, but you couldn't hear me. Are you hurt?"

I shook my head. I was still in shock at what I'd seen. But it all made sense now. After Kali had given the priestesses the task of keeping the sword safe from Mahisha and his demons, they had devoted themselves to this duty for generation after generation. Even though they did not marry, there were always plenty of young women ready to take their place when they died. They must have fended off many ploys and had kept the sword safe for centuries. But this attack must have hit too close to home. So they decided to put it somewhere where no one could find it. Unfortunately for me, knowing the story behind it still didn't tell me where it was hidden. But deep down inside I knew that it was somewhere here in the temple.

"I'm going back to the room," I said. I had a strong feeling that I would find something there.

"I'll come with you," he said. "I don't think there's anything here."

Shiv looked around the parts I'd already covered. I went to the corner where she had cleaned herself up. There was a tiny hallway that led out of this chamber, which I hadn't noticed at the time. I went through and ended up in a small alcove. It was empty. I looked around just to make sure I hadn't missed anything. I was about to turn around and leave when I noticed that my skull pendant was getting warm. It was glowing, but the light was blue, so no danger. It could only mean one thing. The sword was hidden somewhere in here. But where? There was no place to put a sword. Still, I walked around once more, not know what I was looking for. I was about to give up yet again when I noticed that the pendant's light was getting brighter, casting a bluish glow throughout the room. I stopped and looked at the wall. Could it be hidden inside? It made sense. The priestesses wouldn't have wanted to take a chance after what had happened with the demon. What better place to hide it than buried deep inside the structure of the temple itself?

"Shiv," I called, hoping he could hear me. He was there in a flash.

"Did you find something?" he said.

"I think it's in here," I said, pointing to the wall. I looked at my pendant, which was now straining away from me. It was getting warmer, uncomfortably so, and the string was beginning to cut into my skin. I thought I felt a vibration and looked at Shiv in a panic.

"Did you feel that too?" I asked.

He nodded. "I think we should get out of here. I have a bad feeling about this."

I did too, but I wasn't about to leave without the sword. The vibrations were getting stronger and the pendant burned my fingers when I tried to pull it back. It wouldn't budge. I had to get the sword out. This was my only chance. Unfortunately, the ground began to shake and I knew we were running out of time.

"Callie," Shiv said in a warning tone. "We have to

go now. I think this place is going to blow."

"What do you want me to do?" I yelled over the loud rumbling that accompanied the vibrations. "I'm not leaving without the sword."

Shiv looked at me for a moment then wordlessly pulled out his dagger and began to hack at the spot on the wall that my pendant was pointing to. I picked up the *gada* and joined in, hoping the blows would loosen the spot enough to expose the sword. But then a loud crash told us that we had just run out of time. We ran for cover and didn't even have enough time to make it out of the hallway. Shiv threw himself on me and all I heard was an explosion, followed by a huge cloud of dust and debris that filled the hallway, almost choking us. When the vibrations subsided and the dust settled, Shiv picked himself off me and helped me up. We still couldn't breathe without coughing, but it appeared that the hallway had protected us, since it was still intact. The same couldn't be said for the alcove. The ceiling had caved in, as had one of the walls. But the one that held the sword still stood erect. Once we could see again, we looked up and gasped. There, wedged into the rock where the priestesses must have hidden it thousands of years ago, was the sword. Kali's sword, the Sword of Knowledge. *Finally.*

I stood frozen, my mind unable to register what was right in front of me. Then Shiv cleared his throat rather loudly and shook me out of my moment. I reached over to pry the sword out of the wall. But as soon as my fingers closed around the hilt, everything went crazy. A million images flashed in front of my eyes. I closed them as intense pain seared my brain, but the images kept coming. It was an assault on all my senses as I saw what I realized must be Kali's memories. I tried to remove my hand from the sword, but my fingers were welded to it. I saw Kali on the battlefield, riding on her lion, wielding her sword as she destroyed an army of demons. I saw her with Lord Shiva in an intimate embrace and then both of them fighting more demons. From a distance I heard someone calling my name. I tried to focus on that sound and gradually the images slowed down, until my vision cleared and everything was back to normal again. When I opened my eyes Shiv was standing right in front of me.

"What happened?"

I shook my head. My hand wasn't touching the sword anymore, and it still sat in its spot in the wall.

"I don't know...as soon as I touched it...it must be connected to Kali's memories somehow."

"So...what did you see?" Shiv asked.

"It was too much, so many things all at once. I've seen some of it before in my nightmares..."

I stopped as I felt a slight tremor, followed by a louder rumbling.

"Callie, grab the sword," Shiv shouted. "We won't make it out of here if the whole place comes down."

I nodded and ran toward the wall. This time, as I

closed my fingers around the hilt, I felt a current of electricity. It zapped me, leaving a strange tingling in its wake. At first I couldn't get it to budge, but then as I pulled more firmly it came loose and I lifted it out. I only had a second to relish the feel of it in my hand because Shiv was yelling at me to get out. I ran behind him, through the hallway into the small room, then back out into the main hall. We had just made it to the enormous doors when we were forced to come to a stop. The entrance was closed. I'd forgotten about it, but now I looked at Shiv in panic. We were trapped.

Shiv grabbed the large metal handles and tried to pull the doors open. They didn't budge. The rumbling was deafening now and the ground shook with strong vibrations. As a last desperate resort, I lifted the sword and touched its blade to the line where the two doors met. A blue light sparked briefly. I was too afraid to check if it worked, but Shiv was not. He grabbed the handles again, and this time when he pulled they opened. We ran out, getting as far away as we could from the structure. Once we were under cover of the trees, we stopped and turned back just in time to see the temple crumble until there was nothing left but clouds of dust and a mountain of rubble.

We collapsed onto the jungle floor, exhausted and relieved at the same time. I couldn't believe that this temple had withstood the effects of time for thousands of years and now it was nothing but a heap of debris. No one would ever know the sacrifices of the priestesses and the pain they had endured. Although it had been horrible to watch, I was glad I had witnessed some of it. I still felt awful that I had not been able to save the young priestess, but at least I would never forget what she had gone through to protect the sword.

Kali's sword.

My sword.

There was no denying it anymore. I felt it in my bones now, the connection with the sword when I touched it, the firepower when we fought against the monkeys. It was undeniable proof, although by this point I no longer felt I needed proof. Something had changed deep inside of me. Now that I had the sword, I was ready to take charge. I would rescue my parents and destroy Mahisha once and for all.

NINETEEN

IT WAS WITH this new resolve that I set off with Shiv on our trek back through the jungle. We had to make it back from North Sentinel Island to the Andamans and then back to Kolkata. We had no time to lose. I hoped that the Rakshakari had made some headway in locating my parents while we were gone. I was impatient to get back. We walked for hours before stopping for a break, with only our compass to guide us. We had run out of food and relied on bananas, mangoes and coconuts to sustain us. I had to admit that I would have killed for a pizza right now, but I tried not to think about it. Although we both felt much more hopeful now than we had on our way to the temple, we were still wary. After all, now that we had the sword, Mahisha and his minions would try to take it from us. But my newfound firepower and the sword gave me new confidence. We had been walking for most of the day and I was getting cranky. I was hungry and the mosquitoes were particularly vicious. After I had slapped myself for what seemed like the twentieth time trying to kill the little winged devils, I gave up. Suddenly Shiv stopped mid-stride.

"Callie do you hear that?" he asked, looking around.

"Hear what?" I strained but I couldn't hear anything over the infernal buzzing of the mosquitoes.

Shiv took a few long steps ahead and I hopped after him while trying to squash a mini army of the bugs that was trying to set up base on my left calf. I still couldn't hear anything.

"It sounds like crying." He looked in the same direction as I did. "We should check it out."

"What if it's a trap?" I wasn't too sure I wanted to deal with any more demons. And I still couldn't hear anything.

"We'll be careful. And you have your sword now."

I had a bad feeling about this, but I decided to follow him against my better judgement. The sword was securely strapped to my back in a handy little sheath that Shiv had brought with him from Kolkata. The *gada* was tucked into the waistband of my jeans. My pendant hung from its black string around my neck, comforting me with its presence. We walked in the opposite direction of where we were supposed to go.

Shiv stopped abruptly, making me walk right into him.

"What is it, Shiv? What do you see?" He didn't reply but just stood looking at something.

That's when I heard it. At first I wasn't sure what the sound was, but then I realized it was sobbing. Who could be out here in the middle of the jungle? Could it be one of the local kids?

I caught a glimpse of something moving, just a flash of white between the trees. That was what Shiv was staring at.

"Who do you think it is?" I asked. He didn't answer, just walked ahead. I followed him and a little farther up ahead was a small clearing. There, sitting under a tree, was a young girl. The twigs under our feet crunched as we walked, and she looked up when we came close. Her eyes were red from crying and she wiped at them with the hem of her white sari. I signaled to Shiv to stay while I went up to her.

"Are you lost?" I asked her softly in Bengali, not really expecting her to understand. I didn't want to scare her, but I was really concerned that she was here all alone. She looked young, probably our age, but she was really thin, her watery eyes huge in her gaunt face. She looked up at Shiv, who had walked up behind me, and answered in Bengali.

Several thoughts occurred to me simultaneously. How did she understand Bengali? The native inhabitants didn't speak it. And how had she managed to make it onto the island without being attacked or captured, as we were?

"I've been here for days," she was saying, looking only at Shiv. "I ran away from my village, but now I'm all alone here and I'm so scared they'll find me." She started sobbing again. I tried to comfort her but she shrank away from me.

Shiv walked around me and came to stand by her side. "I think we should give her something to eat and then we can figure out what to do," he said to me. To her he spoke in Bengali. "You must be hungry. Sit here for a bit and eat something. We have food and water for you." He took her gently by the arm and sat down on the ground with her.

"Callie, get out all the food and water," he said impatiently. As I opened the bag and took out the fruit and our last bottle of water, I wondered again who she was and what we were going to do to help her.

"What's your name?" I asked her, offering her a banana. She shook her head and looked at Shiv.

"My name is Rohini. My parents arranged my marriage to a man I don't love. So I ran away."

Shiv picked up one of the mangoes from the bag and started peeling it with his utility knife. He cut off small pieces and handed them to her. She ate them eagerly and watched hungrily as Shiv cut off more pieces.

"Where are you going to go?" Shiv asked.

"I will just stay here. No one will follow me and I can start a new life.

"So how were you able to hide from the locals?" I asked. It all seemed a little strange to me.

"Callie, maybe you should stop interrogating her and let her rest," Shiv said, handing her a bottle of water.

"Shiv, I'm not interrogating her. I'm just trying to figure out what's going on here. And so should you," I said pointedly.

"Yes, Callie, we're all trying to figure out what's going on. But right now this isn't about you. It's about helping Rohini get to a place where she can be safe."

With that he took her by the arm, helped her up and started walking away. I stood there for a moment, dumbfounded, looking at our bags and all the stuff in them just spilled on the ground. What had just happened? What was wrong with Shiv? He was acting very strange and I had no idea why. I did know, however, that it had something to do with this girl.

Angrily, I shoved all the remaining food into the bags and tried to catch up to them. I found them after a while, huddled by a tree. Shiv was holding Rohini, who looked as though she was going to collapse.

"What took you so long, Callie? Rohini needs water. Give me the bottle," he ordered.

And that was it. That was just about as much as he was going to get away with.

"Shiv, come here," I said, stepping just out of earshot from Rohini. "What the hell is wrong with you?"

"What do you mean?" he said. "I'm just trying to help her."

"Don't you think it's just a little bit suspicious? She shows up here all by herself...how did she even get here?" I glanced back at her.

She was looking in our direction, intently watching my face. I knew she couldn't understand what we were saying, but I was sure our tone spoke volumes.

"Look, I know it's weird. But she needs our help. And I'm going to help her. If you don't want to come with us, then that's your choice." And with that he turned around and walked away from me.

I stood there, completely stunned. What had just happened? He walked back to Rohini, helped her up and they both walked away. Then Rohini threw a brief glance my way before turning back around. It was enough for me to confirm what I suspected. There was no mistaking the glint in her eyes. It was one of triumph. I knew that Shiv was in danger.

I waited until they were just out of sight. Then I followed them as closely as I could without being seen. I didn't know where they were headed, but from what I could see, it looked like Rohini was leading the way. I now knew with absolute certainty that she was a demon and had somehow brainwashed Shiv into believing he had to help her. If this was about the sword, which I was sure it was, then it made sense to separate us and leave us more vulnerable. I didn't know what her game plan was, but I did know that Shiv was not going to be hurt under my watch. Suddenly, I was racked with guilt. If anything happened to Shiv, I would never forgive myself. How many more people were going to suffer because of me? Then I shook those thoughts off. They were not helping right now. I realized that I had come upon a clearing and Shiv and Rohini had disappeared. I looked around, trying to figure out in which direction they might have gone. I had almost given up hope when I saw something that looked out of place here in the jungle. There was something caught on one of the branches. I picked it up and looked at it carefully. It was a piece of cloth from the shirt Shiv was wearing.

I felt a trickle of hope. There was still a chance I could find them. Darkness was fast approaching, and I knew before long it would be impossible to see anything. I walked as fast as I could, but I still hadn't found them by the time the sun had set and the jungle was blanketed in darkness. Soon only a few trickles of moonlight were all I had to guide me. I stumbled along, tripping several times and cursing when a sharp root scraped some skin off my right ankle. My pendant began to get warm, and a red light began to emanate from it. That meant they were close. It also meant I was in danger, and so was Shiv. I was able to move faster now that I could see where I was going, thanks to the pendant. I noticed that the ground was getting softer. There hadn't been any rain, so I figured that I must be getting close to some other source of water. I was right. Soon the trees became less dense and I was out of the jungle. I could see much better now because the moonlight bathed everything in a soft glow. I was at the edge of the ocean. I could see footprints in the mud, and there were two sets of them.

I followed them for a bit until I could see two figures farther up ahead. I slowed down to assess the situation. They didn't appear to be moving. I could see the girl gesturing with her hands. It looked like she was pointing at the water. Shiv was standing still. Then he started moving toward the water. I looked at the waves softly crashing against the shore. A little farther out was a group of jagged rocks. The water hitting them sent up a fine mist and in the moonlight I could clearly see that if Shiv went in there, he wouldn't stand a chance. Even if he was a strong enough swimmer to hold his own against the current, the rocks would kill him. I had to stop him. I started sprinting toward them. They couldn't hear me coming over the sound of the water crashing against the rocks, so I had the advantage of surprise.

I called out when I was close enough. They had their backs to me, and I saw her face first when she turned toward me. In the moonlight I could see her as she really was. She barely resembled the young girl I had seen in the jungle. Her skin was leathery and sallow and her eyes drooped on either side of her face. When she saw me her eyes gleamed and she turned around. But just before that I saw the air shimmer and her face transformed once more into the young girl's. Shiv was facing me now and I saw the look in his eyes. They were mesmerized. And now he was walking away from her again, into the water.

"Shiv, stop!" I screamed, running toward him. He turned to look at me but just continued walking. I don't think he even recognized me. I had almost reached him when something slammed into me from the front and knocked the air out of me. I fell back onto the muddy ground. I got up and started running again, desperate to get to Shiv. I could see her out of the corner of my eye. She was pointing toward me and muttering something. Well, two could play at this game. I didn't know what powers I had, but I wasn't going down without a fight. I pointed my hand at her and channelled all the rage and frustration I felt. I didn't know how I knew to do that, but I just did.

Nothing happened at first. Then I glanced at Shiv again. He was almost in the water. No time to think. I just wanted to destroy her. That's all I could think. And feel. She would not take one more person from me. My hand was getting warm. Really fast. I concentrated all my anger into my hand. Suddenly, a blast of heat came out of my palm. It knocked me back, and when I regained my balance, she was gone. A small plume of smoke billowed where she'd been standing. I ran over, but there was nothing left but a small pile of ashes. My brain couldn't really process what had just happened, which was good, because I was out of time. Shiv had disappeared.

I ran to where he'd been standing just a few

seconds ago and into the cold water. In an instant it was up to my waist. I sucked in a deep breath and dove in. I opened my eyes, but at first I saw nothing. Then I detected movement a little to the right. It was Shiv. But he wasn't alone. Something else was there with him, dragging him farther away from me. It was a strange diaphanous shape, vaguely resembling a human. It looked at me as I swam closer, and I froze. It had a face, but the mouth and nose were barely there. The eyes stared at me for a moment, bright and blazing red. Then it looked around and suddenly I was surrounded. There were dozens of them, the floating shapes. I could feel them as they tugged on my clothes, pulling me deeper. I knew I wouldn't last long; I was running out of breath.

I kicked and struggled and managed to shake them off. I kicked harder and tried to swim back up. I was able to break the surface and get just one gulp of air before they pulled me under again. Then I saw Shiv. He was swimming toward me, kicking at the shapes pursuing him. The sight of him gave me energy and I too kicked as hard as I could. I could see him reach out to me and I stretched as hard as I could until I felt his fingers close over mine. Together we kicked our way up to the surface, fighting then as they repeatedly got a hold of us and tried to drag us back down. Finally we made it up the surface. Shiv was on his feet first and pulled me up. We staggered to the edge, desperate to get out of the water and onto dry land.

We fell on the ground but crawled as far as we could away from the water's edge before collapsing in a heap. My lungs were on fire and after our coughing subsided we got up wordlessly and went back into the cover of the trees.

Neither of us spoke for a few minutes. I had so many questions but I didn't know where to begin.

"What happened back there?" He didn't say anything for such a long time that I didn't think he was going to answer. But then he spoke.

"I don't know what happened. The last thing I remember is finding that girl in the jungle. Then I was drowning and those things kept trying to drag me under."

"You mean you don't remember anything that happened in between?" Well, that was convenient.

"No, I don't, Callie." He looked pretty miserable, so I guessed I'd have to believe he was being truthful.

"Okay, fine. I don't know what happened to you, but I can tell you what you did. Once we ran into the girl, you turned into a real jerk."

"What do you mean, a jerk? What did I do?" Shiv looked really uncomfortable, so I decided to tell him what I'd seen.

"Well, I'm pretty sure Rohini was a Maya demon. She brainwashed you somehow, so you did whatever she said. And you were a real jerk to me." I don't know what I expected him to do about it. It wasn't as if he had known what was happening. But I was still really angry with him.

"I'm sorry, Callie, I really am. But I don't remember any of it." I believed him. Maybe it was because the alternative was unbearable. I didn't want to believe that he could ever be that mean to me intentionally.

"This is seriously messed up," I sighed. "How are we supposed to know what to trust? Or whom to trust?"

"Well, I think we have to trust our own instincts. I mean, that's what you did this time, didn't you?"

He was right. I had listened to my gut, and thankfully it had been the right decision.

"Let's just get going," I said, shivering slightly and remembering that my clothes were soaking. We walked back into the cover of the jungle. We had nothing to make a fire with so we slept very close to keep as warm as we could. When I woke the next morning I was stiff from the uncomfortable night. We ate a little and got started on yet another long walk. Once again we walked most of the day, only stopping to eat and rest briefly. The thought of rescuing my parents and Ben was what kept me going, even when every single bone in my body ached.

We kept a lookout for anything out of the ordinary, but we had no idea what form our next attacker would take. We had been going for a while after our last stop when I thought I saw a flash of something bright in the trees ahead of us. Immediately I reached for my sword. I was not taking any chances. Shiv pulled out his dagger. We walked cautiously forward, taking care not to step on any twigs or dry leaves. When we reached the spot where I'd seen the flash we stopped. There was nothing there. I let the sword fall to my side. Maybe I had imagined it.

"What did you see?" Shiv put away his dagger after taking a good look around.

"I'm not sure. I thought I saw a flash of color...but I guess it was nothing."

Shiv checked the compass to make sure that we were still headed in the right direction and we had just turned left around yet another small cluster of banana trees when I nearly tripped over someone. I was about to pull out my sword when I realized that it was a meditating yogi. He wore a white loincloth and nothing else. Although that wasn't technically true. His entire body was covered in tattoos of snakes of different shapes and sizes. My pendant started to get warm and I felt a wave of panic sweep through me. I kept my hand on the hilt of the sword and began to step away from the yogi.

Shiv followed my lead, keeping a hand on his dagger the whole time. We still kept an eye on the yogi as we retreated. Then, unexpectedly, an eye appeared on the middle of his forehead and opened. Talk about cliché. But then something happened that I did not see coming. His tattoos came alive. Suddenly he was covered with hundreds of writhing snakes while he chanted something incomprehensible. At least to us.

Not to the snakes. They slithered off his body and came toward us. That was all the incentive I needed to run faster than I ever had in my life. I looked back and saw Shiv right on my heels.

We ran as far as we could but when we turned around, the snakes were still right behind us. Time for Plan B. I stopped and pulled out my sword. Shiv must have had the same idea, because he stopped at almost the exact same time and turned toward them. As the first wave of snakes came within range, I swung my sword. I didn't feel guilty about cutting down the snakes. Clearly they were up to no good. But just as we thought we were getting the upper hand, a fresh wave rushed at us. To my horror they appeared to converge and join into one large serpentine creature. I had never been so terrified. I called out a warning to Shiv just as the creature fell upon me. I held on tightly to my sword, but it was impossible to gain much wiggle room with the tight grip that the serpent had on me. It was wrapping itself around my upper body so that my arms were just hanging loosely at my sides and it was getting very hard to breathe. As I tried not to pass out from a lack of oxygen, I could see Shiv attacking the creature from the back. He must have irritated it just enough to let go of me, because it unwound and turned on him. I gulped in air as soon as I could, my ribs hurting fiercely with each breath. Then I picked up my sword and smoothly cut the serpent's head off just as it was about to squeeze Shiv to death. As its lifeless body fell to the ground, Shiv fell to his knees, noisily sucking in air. His ribs must have been worse than mine. I sat down next to him and waited until his breathing calmed again.

"You know what, Shiv? I think we've been attacked by just about as many demons as I can handle. I think it's time for Mahisha to make an appearance, don't you?"

I didn't wait for his answer. Instead, I stood up and yelled into the forest.

"Stop hiding behind your goons. Come out and show yourself."

My voice echoed angrily throughout the forest, but besides scaring some innocent birds off their perches, there was no response.

I was reminded of the Mahisha myth, in which he was said to have known fear for the first time in his existence when he heard Kali roar. I think the only person who felt fear from my yelling was Shiv. He looked quite terrified, most likely because he thought now he was stuck with a crazy person in the middle of the jungle island. I dropped myself down. Shiv hadn't said a word yet. The poor guy was probably having trouble breathing, let alone talking.

"Shiv," I said after a while. "Can I tell you something?"

"Sure."

"I'm really glad that you're here. I mean I'm not glad that we're here, obviously...this is horrible."

I felt a blush creeping into my cheeks and hoped he

wouldn't notice how nervous I suddenly was.

"What I'm trying to say is...well...if I have to be here with someone, I'm just glad it's you."

There. I'd said it. And now he was probably really uncomfortable. I knew this wasn't the appropriate time or place but what we'd gone through in the past couple of days made me realize there was a good possibility I might never get to say how I really felt. The demons, the temple exploding, it was all so insane. I didn't want to regret keeping my feelings to myself. I'd never been the kind of girl who gushed and fell in love with every second guy she met. I was very practical when it came to matters of the heart, especially mine. I had learned early on that even your best friends could turn on you if you were different, and I was pretty guarded when it came to emotional stuff. But these last months, meeting Shiv, getting to know him and spending all this time together in the worst possible circumstances, did something to me. He was kind, loyal and fiercely protective. I knew a lot of it was part of his job description as a Rakshakari, so I was aware that my feelings might not be reciprocated. But after this last demon attack I decided to throw caution to the wind. At least I was being honest with myself and with him. Of course, there was a good chance he had no clue I was talking about romantic feelings. It might have sounded like I just thought he was the perfect guy to bring along on a suicide mission where one might run into a multitude of demons. I decided to give it another try.

"Shiv..." I began but didn't get any further because he brought his lips to mine and then we were kissing, just like on that evening in the Andamans. Except this time there was something deeper, more passionate. I felt that several near-death experiences might do that to people. A chuckle escaped me and he broke the kiss to look at me quizzically.

"I'm glad you find my kisses amusing," he said, looking at me tenderly.

I laughed, partly from relief that he felt the same way and partly because it was all so crazy.

"I'm laughing because I was thinking that dating anyone else after this will seem so boring."

"What makes you think I'll let you date anyone else?" he growled softly into my ear, making shivers go up and down my arms. Then he brought his lips to mine again. This kiss was meant to show me that I belonged to him. After a while I had to come up for air. My legs felt like jelly, and it was a good thing I was already sitting down.

"Well," he said, sounding very satisfied with himself, "now that we've settled that, what's the plan, my Goddess?"

"Shut up...don't call me that," I said, playfully punching him in the shoulder. Unfortunately, he winced in real pain and I immediately felt awful. I had momentarily forgotten he was recently crushed by a serpent.

"I'm so sorry," I said, covering his shoulder with

little kisses.

"You'd better stop doing that," he warned. "I know you think I'm capable of superhuman restraint, but there are limits to my powers of self-control."

For a moment I toyed with the idea of testing those powers, but then I came to my senses. This brief escape didn't change the reality that we were still in danger and so were my parents. That thought sobered me instantly and brought with it a wave of guilt and shame. What kind of a daughter was I, flirting and laughing while my parents were missing? Shiv noticed the change in my demeanor and put his arm around my shoulders.

"We are going to find them, Callie. And do you really think that they would want you to be alone? Don't you think they would rather know that you were safe and loved?"

He had a point. That was why he was so great — he got me. No explanations necessary. It was only later that night as I was drifting off to sleep that I remembered what he had said.

He said he loved me.

TWENTY

THE NEXT MORNING I woke achy all over from fighting the serpent demon. But inside I felt warm and fuzzy, especially when I realized I had been lying in the crook of Shiv's arms all night. I sat up, careful not to wake him, but he stirred anyway. When he opened his eyes and smiled lazily at me, I melted. All my teenage years I had scoffed when I read about gooey-eyed girls so madly in love with a guy that they couldn't think straight. It had all seemed so over-the-top that a person could lose the ability to reason all because of a guy. And although what I felt wasn't nearly as silly, I was beginning to understand some of those emotions. For example, when we reached the edge of the forest and Shiv pulled off his shirt to jump into the water, I found myself longing to run my fingers along his tattoos. This was not normal for me. And when he came back to me, water dripping from his black curls, I felt the urge to run my fingers through his wet hair. Also, not normal. But since I had decided not to do just normal anymore, I wasn't going to worry about it.

Since we had reached the edge of the forest, we were hoping the Sentinelese would help us get back to the Andamans. We had no way of contacting anybody so we had to figure out a way to get back on our own. At first there was no one in sight, but then our former captors emerged cautiously from their shelters. Behind them, a couple of children tagged along. One of them was the cute little girl who had come close to me before. This time she ran over as soon as she saw me. She stopped right in front of me and smiled. I drew her in for a hug. Her little hands held on to me tightly, and it was the sweetest thing. Then she let go, ran back into her shelter and returned a few seconds later carrying something. When she handed it to me, I smiled. It was a bracelet made with the most beautiful shells, all in different shades of white, gray and black. I put it on immediately and I could tell that she was pleased.

"Thank you," I said as I gave her another hug. "I love it."

I didn't even care that she didn't speak English. I was convinced she knew what I meant.

The two men approached us, this time with smiles. They were saying something and I wanted to think they couldn't believe that we had returned alive with Kali's sword. I was pretty sure they were saying that we were amazing and all sorts of other great things. Unfortunately, I would never know. Shiv was smiling and nodding and I was sure that he was thinking the same thing. It was quite comical really.

"I'm going to draw a boat and see if we can get them to help," Shiv said as he started drawing lines in the sand. Soon the men were nodding vigorously, which I took as an indication that we were going home.

They took us to the water's edge and helped us get into a dugout canoe. Then one of them, the one with the graying hair, got in as well. Strangely, I felt a little sad at the thought that I would probably never see them again. The little girl stood next to her mom. I couldn't help myself, so I jumped out at the last minute and ran over to give her another hug. Then I got back into the canoe, nearly capsizing it, and waved to them. They waved back as we pushed away. The man took us to a remote part of the shores of the Andamans. Luckily, we didn't have to swim this time, because he was able to bring us right to the edge. As we disembarked, I smiled at him in gratitude. We would have been lost without them. I squeezed his shoulder and he nodded. Shiv did the same and then we waved goodbye. We stood and watched for a while as he rowed away, then turned to make our way back to town. We had to find a phone. We couldn't exactly go traipsing about with a big old sword, looking as bedraggled as I was sure we did. So I waited behind some trees while Shiv went off to find a place to call. Luckily he came back soon, because I was beginning to attract some attention.

"My uncle's sending someone to pick us up and take us straight to the airport," Shiv said. "He'll make emergency travel arrangements and they even have some special permit for us to carry the sword on board."

I raised my eyebrows. These people must have some serious contacts. Shiv read my mind.

"Something about valuable and ancient artifacts..." he said.

"Well, as long as it isn't out of my sight, I'm good." I just wanted to get home.

Before long, a sedan with tinted windows pulled up and the driver got out to help us with our things. Luckily, it was the same man who had picked us up at the airport earlier, otherwise I would have hesitated to get into the car. We made a pit stop at the hotel we had stayed in. He said that we had time to clean up before our flight, which I gladly did. I was surprised to find that a loose cotton tunic and *churidaar*s had been laid out on the bed. I took a hot steaming shower and came out feeling human again. I put on the clothes, enjoying the feel of the soft linen pants that tapered and bunched around the ankle. The tunic was light and comfortable, perfect for travel, especially after the jeans and T-shirt I'd been running around in for days. I threw them in the trash. They could not be salvaged. I noticed a beautifully embroidered cloth on the table with a note and picked it up. *For your belongings*, it said. I looked at my backpack. Everything was already in it. Then I looked at the sword. Of course. I couldn't just walk around with the sword sticking out. I wrapped it carefully in the cloth and tucked it into the backpack. Then I changed my mind. It would be easier just to carry it. Now I would just look like hundreds of other tourists who bought traditional items to take back with them. I met up with Shiv in the lobby, where he was waiting for me by the indoor fountain. He too was wearing clean clothes. He looked very Indian in a traditional tunic and loose-fitting cotton pants. As I walked up to him, it occurred to me that we would have to be careful with the touchy feely stuff while we were here and in Kolkata. Public displays of affection were generally frowned upon and I certainly did not want to draw any attention.

"So, tell me this," I said when I was standing beside him. "Who are these people that anticipate all our needs? Should we be worried?"

"No, it's perfectly safe," he said with a laugh. "There are staunch supporters of the Rakshakari everywhere. They work for government and private organizations. Many of them are wealthy and have great influence."

"So they help however they can." I could understand that. In exchange for knowing that the Rakshakari were keeping the world safe, people were willing to do their part when it came to certain formalities and expenses. Back in Seattle Nina and Dev had explained to me that the Rakshakari had to operate in secret because otherwise it would be impossible to track Mahisha's progress. After the encounters we had on North Sentinel, as well as the visions I had in the temple, it was clear to me that Mahisha's reach had always been far and wide. I had come to the conclusion, though, that for whatever reason, Mahisha was not ready to face me himself, instead sending demon after demon to do his dirty work. That had to mean that he was still weak and I was determined to use this to my advantage.

I felt Shiv's intent gaze on me and looked up at him.

"Why are you staring?"

"I'm just thinking of everything that happened. I mean, I've fought demons for most of my life. Mostly, they were fairly easy to detect. Now, with you in the picture, everything is more intense."

"Yes, but you said it yourself, there hasn't been an avatar for some time, right?"

He nodded. "That's true. It's just...I feel I can't trust my judgement any longer."

I knew that he meant the encounter with Rohini.

"I should have seen it coming. I've known about Maya demons and how they operate all my life. But I still fell for it. And I didn't protect you."

I should have known he still felt guilty about that. His very existence was tied to my protection. I would have to do something about that. I did not like the idea that everybody thought I was some helpless little goddess that needed protection. Plus, as far as the Rakshakari were concerned, their purpose was to protect all of humanity from evil. I knew that they'd been waiting for Kali for a long time and that it was their sacred duty to initiate me and teach me the ways of the goddess, but I felt that now we were past all that. After all, Shiv and I had found the sword and had survived some badass demons. I also thought I had held my own pretty well. I no longer felt that it was appropriate for Shiv to see me as someone who needed protecting all the time.

I needed Shiv to know that too, so as we left the hotel and were driving to the airport, I told him so. After I was finished, he didn't say anything for some time.

"Rakshakari are wired to think of themselves as protectors. So it's difficult for me to change that." He hesitated.

"But not impossible?" I asked.

"No...not impossible," he said. "It might take some time, though."

"I have time. Look, I'm not saying I know everything now and I can do it all on my own. I know I still have a lot to learn. I have several thousand years to catch up on. But I want to be one of you, saving everyone along with you. I don't want you to see me as a helpless newbie anymore. I think I've earned that, don't you?"

I looked down at my hands on my lap. They used to be smooth and soft. Now they were calloused and rough. And I realized I liked it, the thought that I was physically capable to defend myself and others. With time I would get even better and stronger. Shiv reached over and put my hand in his. We sat like that for some time. If the driver was watching us in his mirror, he showed no indication that there was anything untoward going on. I almost laughed out loud at the thought that hand-holding was still scandalous in this part of the world. Not that it didn't happen all the time, but everyone was just really good at hiding it. We got to the airport fairly quickly and were hustled through customs in no time. Soon we were on the plane bound for Kolkata. We arrived two short hours later and were met by Uncle Suresh and Dev. I was surprised to see Shiv's father here. He hugged his son and me as well, his relief at seeing us alive and well obvious in the way he looked at us.

"Callie," he said as we rode back to Uncle Suresh's house, "I am so proud of you, *beti*. We were all so worried, and of course there was no way to contact you."

I smiled, feeling safe and relaxed after a long time.

"Thank you, Uncle. I couldn't have done it without Shiv."

"Dad, you have no idea about what Callie can do now," he said excitedly. "I can't wait for you all to see.

Did Mom come with you too?"

"Yes, *beta*, she is here too. Actually, we have some news."

My stomach twisted into a knot. I didn't know if I could handle bad news right now.

"What is it?" I asked.

"Callie, it's good news. Well...considering the circumstances."

I held my breath.

"We've traced your parents here to Kolkata."

The knot in my stomach loosened a little. A tiny spark of hope flared.

"Alive?"

"As far as we know, yes. They are being held by Mahisha's first lieutenants. Two brothers. They go by the names Shumbh and Nishumbh." His disgust for them was evident in the downward turn of his mouth. "They're shape-shifters and particularly cruel," he continued as I tasted bile at the thought of my parents at the mercy of these demons.

"So do we have a location?" Shiv asked, squeezing my hand. I knew he was trying to keep me calm and positive. If his dad noticed the little gesture, he didn't say anything.

"Yes, apparently they're holed up in a warehouse near Howrah station."

"Okay, so when can we go there?" I asked.

"We have to be patient and proceed with great caution. If they get spooked, they'll disappear," Dev warned. "I know how you feel. But we cannot risk losing them again."

"Mahisha knows that we have the sword," Shiv said. "That's why he had them bring your parents here. He's going to try to get it from us."

"Well, he hasn't shown himself yet. Maybe it's time for a showdown." I just wanted this to be over.

"Callie, you might just get your wish sooner than you think," Dev said.

The rest of the way home, we discussed strategy. We would scope out the area where they were being held. For all we knew, this could just be another trap to draw us out. Once we had confirmation that my parents were there and still alive, we would go in with a large enough team to make sure no demons slipped through the cracks. There was no other option and there would be no second chances.

But there was still someone else I needed to know about.

"What about Ben? Have you found out anything at all?"

Dev shook his head. "I'm sorry, Callie," he said. "I know how important he is to you. Vikram and Tara are still working on finding him. We're not going to stop trying."

I knew Dev meant well, but I couldn't take any comfort in his words. I felt a stab to my heart. There was guilt too. I had spent so much time worrying about my parents, I had barely spared a thought for Ben. We shared a bond, a special friendship, and I felt like I was abandoning him. But then my logical side urged me to focus on the two people I could rescue, and I listened to it. I would not give up on Ben. As soon as my parents were safe, I would make sure that all efforts were concentrated on finding Ben.

Thanks to Kolkata traffic, by the time we got home the sun had already set and I was ready to pass out. Aruna was overjoyed to see us, and so was Nina. After holding her son in her arms for the longest time, she turned to me.

"Callie...I don't know what to say." There were tears in her eyes and I was surprised and pleased to see that she was human after all.

"I'm just glad to be back," I said, not knowing what else to say. We ate dinner and then went up to bed. I had never appreciated a soft pillow as much as I did that night. I slept without dreams and woke up the next morning ready for battle.

The others were already gathered downstairs by the time I was dressed and ready. They caught me up over breakfast. Apparently, Uncle Suresh had received confirmation from his people in the field that my parents were indeed being held at the warehouse and that they were still alive. So our rescue mission was a go. I felt an adrenaline rush at the thought that I would see my parents very soon and that I would vanquishing some more demons at the same time. I realized I was beginning to like this. Destroying demons, of course.

Rescuing my parents or anyone else I loved...that I could live without. But I couldn't deny the rush I'd felt when I had destroyed the serpent demon and Rohini.

The next hour or so was spent getting ready for the rescue. I had never seen them all mobilize, so it was a learning experience for me. We went to the weapons room. Aruna, Shiv, Nina, Dev and I would go while Uncle Suresh would stay behind to coordinate. I watched as the others equipped themselves with various weapons: daggers, short swords, and an *urumi*. I wondered why they never used guns and bullets.

"Demons have a different physiology. Gunpowder and bullets can't really do much damage," Shiv explained when I asked him.

"But these weapons can?" I asked, still not convinced.

"They're made of *panchaloha*, and that is lethal to demons."

Panchaloha. Five metals. I dug around in my brain for a bit and remembered where I'd heard that term before. It was an alloy of five metals, gold, silver, meteoric iron, zinc and lead, used to make idols of Hindu gods and goddesses.

I made a mental note to do more research on this after my parents were back with me. Right now, we were ready to go. I had my sword, my pendant, my newfound confidence and a general badass attitude. I was good to go.

We rode in silence as the driver weaved through

the already busy streets of Kolkata. Traffic in this city had a life of its own. Huge trucks lumbered by alongside rickety carts pulled by bullocks, while men in bare feet pulled rickshaws laden with matronly women and kids. At the same time public buses drove past, filled to the brim with passengers hanging precariously from the doors. Amidst all this chaos, people, both adult and children, darted in and out, trying to get across the pothole-riddled streets. It was enough to give anybody an ulcer, but as I looked around I saw people just going about their daily business. Of course, this was normal for them. It had been for me too. Now I held on to the headrest of the seat in front of me for dear life. The irony of my situation did not escape me. Here I was, having returned from a trip during which I survived capture by hostile islanders and escaped an imploding temple, all the while fighting off terrible demons, and now I was scared of Kolkata traffic.

We rode for about an hour before the driver slowed down to turn into an alley that led to a part of town where I would never have gone to by myself. The alley opened up into a wider street lined with rundown two-storey houses. Children played outside and vendors sold everything from ice cream to glass bangles. The smell from the overflowing sewers assaulted my nostrils, and when I looked over at Shiv, I could see that he too was trying not to gag. I sat back, trying to breathe only through my mouth, and marveled at the dichotomy that was India. I was being chauffeured in a luxury car around a city where some parts of town had houses with marble foyers and others had open sewers running through them. When I had lived in Calcutta as a child I had never spared a thought to these matters. But now at seventeen, having been away for so long, I saw my city through different eyes. I realized that I still thought of it as my city; it was a part of me, much as Seattle was. I felt Shiv's hand on my arm.

"How are you holding up?" he asked.

"I'm okay, Shiv. It's just the smell, it takes some getting used to."

The driver finally stopped in front of a large group of warehouses. I glanced at my watch and realized it was only eleven o'clock in the morning, which explained why there were so many men milling about loading and unloading whatever was being stored on the premises. The other car pulled up as we were getting out, and Dev, Nina and Aruna spilled out. We got a few odd glances from the workers, but the driver said something to them and they cleared out promptly. I was glad. We didn't want any innocent people getting hurt because they were in the wrong place at the wrong time.

We split up into two groups. Shiv and I went to check out one set of the warehouse buildings, while Dev, Nina and Aruna went to another. It probably wasn't the best plan but it was efficient since we had a lot of ground to cover. We started at the back of the building first, trying to find windows or doors to look through and also to determine how many points of exit there were in case we had to make a quick getaway. But we had no such luck. The back was nothing but wall, no openings at all.

We walked all around the building looking for any clues but found nothing. We tried the next building and the one after it. All the front doors were locked. But then at the fourth building we tried, the door had a sliding latch but no lock. I slid the latch to the right and opened the door cautiously. It creaked and stuck a little, but I gave it a good pull and it opened wider. We stepped in, allowing our eyes to adjust to the darkness. This one was not empty. My heart was racing as I looked around. There were three chairs and a naked light bulb dangling from the ceiling but nothing else. I walked slowly to the chairs. Disappointment stabbed my heart and my eyes teared up. I turned to Shiv. He looked around one last time, walking along the perimeter. Just as we turned around to step out, a hand was clamped across my mouth. I tried to scream and turn around to see who it was, but before I could react something was thrown over my head and face so that I could see nothing. Someone prodded me from behind and I tried to move forward, but I was disoriented and ended up stumbling on something and falling. Again, I tried to stand up and scream, but then I felt a sharp pain on my head and everything went dark.

When I came to, I slowly opened my eyes. At first my mind was a blank, then the memory of what had happened returned and I started to sit up. That's when I realized I was lying on a bed and that my hands and feet were tied to the bedposts. I was also gagged. I almost choked when I tried to open my mouth to scream for help and inhaled fibres from whatever had been shoved into my mouth. The coughing subsided after some time, during which I felt that my lungs had caught on fire. I had to remain calm, and I had to get out of there. Had they taken Shiv too? What about the others? If not, they would be looking for me. I wriggled my hands and then my feet. It was no use — they were bound too tight. I looked around. I was in a small room, no more than eight by eight feet. Other than the bed I was on, there was also a tiny desk. The room was quite dark, but through a tiny window high up in one corner of the wall a small shaft of light managed to enter. High on the opposite wall a tiny brown house lizard made its way to a vent, disappearing through it a second later. I shivered involuntarily. I hated lizards, and even though this one was gone, I wondered what other creepy crawlies lurked in the shadows. I didn't dare to open my mouth to scream again, so I tried to loosen the bindings on my wrists and ankles, but I stopped when the skin on them was rubbed raw.

Just then the door opened. Someone entered the room and closed the door. I squinted to see better, but I couldn't make out who it was. Then the person came closer and I froze. Mr. Burke, my history teacher. *What the hell is he doing here?* My mind searched wildly for something, anything to make sense out of this. I recalled my parents' bizarre reaction to him at school. Suddenly it all began to make sense. The way they'd stormed out of there, how they warned me to stay away from him. They obviously knew that he was involved. *But how?* I waited for him to say or do something, but he just stood silently, towering over me. I would not give him the satisfaction of seeing how afraid I was at that moment, so I just stared back at him, eyes unwavering. If I could just get my hand free even the slightest bit, I was sure that I could zap him. He smirked, as though he had read my thoughts.

"So, Miss Hansen," he said. "It seems that you have run out of good fortune." His demeanor was one of supreme confidence.

I pulled at my restraints, glaring at him. My words were muffled by the rag in my mouth. He leaned back, watching me struggle, clearly deriving some twisted form of satisfaction. Without warning he reached over and pulled the rag out. I sputtered as I tried to spit out the little pieces of fibre. Then I spat at him, aiming as close as I could to his face. He slapped me hard across the face, the cracking sound of his palm making contact with my skin echoing in the room. Tears stung my eyes as I tasted blood on the inside of my cheek. Still, I would not give him the satisfaction of showing fear.

Rage shone dark in his eyes, and as I stubbornly held his gaze, he snarled, raising his hand again. I fought the urge to close my eyes at the pain I knew was coming, but it never did. Instead the door opened and another man stepped in.

"Burke...the masters have summoned you," the man said, nodding toward me. "They want you to bring her with you." He looked at me for a moment before averting his eyes and turning around to leave the room. Burke reached over and untied my legs, hauling me roughly to my feet. He held on tightly to my bound arms as he dragged me to the door and out into the dimly lit hallway. The sour smells of urine and stale sweat made me gag. We stopped abruptly in front of a door and Burke opened it. I tried to stay calm and control my breathing, as Aruna had taught me during our yoga sessions. We entered the room, which was larger than the one I was being held in, but just as bare. Two men stood by a small window at one end. They looked up when we came in and I realized they were identical. Shumbh and Nishumbh. Dev hadn't mentioned they were twins. They were both very tall, well over six feet, their skin a mottled gray. Both of their faces were riddled with scars, and combined with the vertical slits that were their eyes, it was enough to make me go cold with fear. I had no means of defending myself and no idea if Shiv and the others were even alive. I took a deep breath and looked directly at the demons.

"Masters," Burke said, bowing his head. "As I promised, here she is. The great goddess," he added mockingly.

The demon brothers walked closer to us and stopped when they were face to face with me. In such close proximity their putrid breath was nauseating. They walked around me slowly, taking in every part of me, blinking every now and then. Every time the vertical eyelids closed and opened again, I had to resist the urge to shudder. They could not know how terrified I was.

"Cut me loose," I demanded, my voice scratchy from coughing. I struggled uselessly against Burke's tight hold, eliciting smiles from the twins.

"She's feisty, this one," they said, almost in unison.

"Not like the last few." Burke smirked as one of the brothers put his hands on either side of my head. The pain came quickly, without warning, excruciating in its intensity. My screams echoed loudly through the room and just when I knew I could not bear it any longer, it stopped as abruptly as it had begun. When I opened my eyes, the tears fell freely. But I was not going to give them any satisfaction.

"Cut me loose. Let's see how well you can fight, you cowards." I spat in their faces, and this time I knew what was coming. That didn't make it hurt any less. My back arched as the pain sliced through me, leaving me gasping and weak. Then he removed his hands, but I could still feel waves pounding through me. This time it took a lot more to focus my eyes on them. My vision was hazy and I could barely speak.

I was about to say a few choice words when there was a loud crash and then yelling right outside the room, followed by a loud thud. The door burst open, and to my immense relief Shiv appeared. Aruna, Nina and Dev were right on his heels. The demons sprang into action, but even in the haze of pain, I could tell they were outnumbered. Burke shoved me against the wall and went straight for Aruna. The demon brothers went face to face with Nina and Dev, leaving Shiv free to run over to me and free my hands with his dagger.

I staggered against him, trying hard to stay upright. There was no time for words. Over Shiv's shoulder I could see that Dev was in trouble. One of the brothers had his head between his hands and I could tell from the anguish on Dev's face that he was experiencing the same pain I had felt moments ago. It didn't last long though, because in a flash Shiv was at his father's side. He drove the dagger into the demon's belly, and then there was nothing left of him except a pile of ash. A howl ripped through the room as his brother realized what had happened. In a mad rage he rushed at Dev to finish what his twin had started, but Nina was too quick for him. She plunged her *phurba* dagger into him and he joined his brother as a pile of ash. I turned away just in time to see a group of men run into the room and join in the fight. I raised my hand to use my firepower. I was able to take out two of them, which was not an easy task since the others were fighting around me and I didn't want to blow up any of them. Aruna and Shiv were fighting with two others, as were Nina and Dev. I looked around to find Burke, but he had disappeared. I took out a few more, incinerating them with the flames that shot out of my hands. As the smoke died down, I saw that the others had killed their opponents as well. Only the five of us were left.

"Burke got away," Shiv finally said. The rest of us stood silently. There was really nothing to say. But then Dev spoke up.

"At least we're rid of these two. They've been the bane of my existence for quite some time now." Nina put her arm on his and he leaned back into her. I wanted to ask what he meant exactly, but I knew I would have to wait until later.

"We have to find my parents," I said, walking slowly to the door. "And my weapons."

I was still unsure on my feet, and using the firepower had left me feeling even more drained. Shiv was by my side in an instant, supporting me as we all filed into the hallway.

TWENTY-ONE

IT WAS DESERTED, but light streamed in from a door at the end of the hallway. Above it was a red exit sign flickering in the distance. The carpet was worn and the smell of sweat and stale spices made me gag. It was an old building, by the looks of the peeling paint on the walls. There were several doors on either side of us, but there was no light or sound coming from any of them. We all opened doors as we passed them, checking for any signs that my parents may have been in there. Then we heard a shout from one of the rooms up ahead that Aruna had entered. We all rushed to it. My heartbeat quickened in anticipation, but then as I reached the doorway I realized that it was the one I was being held in earlier. I followed the others in and scanned the room. Aruna was standing in a corner, triumphantly holding my dagger. It must have been here the whole time.

"The sword's here too," Nina called out, pointing toward the bed. I got down to reach underneath, and sure enough, there was my sword. I pulled it out and sighed with relief. I knew my pendant was probably here too. They must have taken it off while I was unconscious. It would have been glowing like crazy. I checked the bed, but it was bare, no sheets or pillows. Shiv picked up the thin mattress and there, stuck in a corner of the metal frame, was my skull pendant. He picked it up and handed it to me.

"Okay, time to find your parents," Dev said as we all left the room.

We had almost reached the end of the long hallway when I noticed a faint light leaking out from under one of the doors close to the exit. I ran toward it and the others followed.

I scanned the room as soon as I entered. There was no bed here or any other furniture. But then...in a corner on the floor two figures were huddled together. My body was throbbing with more pain than I had ever felt before, but it was nothing compared to the relief and joy that coursed through me right now. My parents were here, and they were alive. But barely. I ran to them, collapsing on the floor beside them, and my heart broke. My mother's beautiful face was battered and bruised, her eyes vacant as she stared at something only she could see. My father, his handsome rugged face crisscrossed with cuts, seemed to be more lucid. His eyes showed signs of recognition when he saw my face in front of him.

I had to fight the urge to break down and I knew that I could not show any weakness. The bruises on their faces were already bluish-green, which meant that they must be at least a few days old. I shuddered at the thought of what they must have endured. I began to speak to my father gently, almost crooning. I needed him to know that they were safe now and that I would allow nothing to hurt them again. Ever. After a few tries he responded. He moved his hand slowly and put it softly over mine. It felt weightless. I looked down and saw how frail it was, the skin hanging loosely over the bones. I took it in both of mine and looked him in the eyes again.

"Daddy, it's me...Callie. You're safe now." I could barely say the words without choking on my tears.

"Callie...Callie, I'm sorry..."

"Daddy, no...you have nothing to be sorry for." I was trying desperately not to cry, but the tears started coming anyway, falling on his hand and mine.

"Your mom...I tried to stop them..." The rest of his words were lost as he broke down in sobs so hard, they wracked his whole body. The others stood back, sensing my need to have this moment with my parents. But then Dev stepped forward and spoke gently to me.

"Callie, we need to get them out of here. It's not safe." I nodded, tears still running down my face. I stood up as Shiv and Aruna helped my mom, while Nina and Dev supported my father as he rose unsteadily to his feet. We made our way out of the building to the front of the warehouse complex. It was dark outside and a little cooler than when we had arrived here this morning. The place was deserted, but farther out on the street there was the usual busy traffic. Kolkata never really slept. We went to our vehicles and carefully deposited my parents in one. I got in the back seat with them while Dev drove. Shiv, Nina and Aruna went in the other car.

After we reached the house, Uncle Suresh called his doctor to come and treat my parents' injuries. We were all checked out too, but other than a few bruises and cuts, we were fine. My dad was malnourished and had a couple of minor fractures in various stages of healing. But it was my mom who had taken the brunt of the torture. Dev and I had experienced first-hand the demon's special power of causing mental anguish, so I was convinced that if the Rakshakari hadn't come when they did, I would have been in the same state as my mother, who was almost comatose. I couldn't bear to see her like this, but I did not want to leave her side. I stroked her hair gently as she slept. Shiv came in and sat with me for a while. We didn't talk but it was comforting just to be with him. Nina came in to try and coax me into eating, but I had no appetite. I wanted to be there when she woke up, just so I could tell her that I would never let anything bad happen to her again. My dad slept for a long time then woke up and ate a little before going back to sleep again. A little bit of color returned to his face, but I still didn't want to burden him with the million questions I had rattling around in my head. I slept on the floor of their room that night, in case they woke up and needed something. I was deeply touched when Aruna spread out a mat for herself and wordlessly joined me. I was exhausted, and knowing she was with me allowed me to close my eyes for a bit and get some much-needed rest.

I woke up at the crack of dawn to see Aruna bent over my mother, wiping her face with a washcloth. I got up quickly to take over, but she just shook her head.

"Let me do this please, Callie," she said, as she tenderly dried my mother's face with a towel. "You go and be with your dad."

I squeezed her shoulder gratefully and went to sit at my father's side. He stirred as I watched him, the shadows under his eyes deepened by the dim light that streamed in through the thick curtains. His eyelids fluttered open and he smiled when he saw me.

"Callie," he said, his voice raspy and weak. "You were here all night, weren't you?"

I nodded, tears filling my eyes once again as I reached for his hand. He struggled to sit up, so I helped him.

"Callie...you must have a lot of questions," he began, but I didn't want him to worry about anything right now.

"Daddy, it's okay," I reassured him gently. "We can talk about it later."

He shook his head. "I need to tell you...I should have told you a long time ago." When I said nothing, he continued.

"I was an orphan...many years ago here in Kolkata. One day an older couple came to the orphanage and adopted me. They saw the mark on my neck." My mind was reeling with disbelief. I'd never noticed a mark like that on his neck. But then again, I never knew to look for anything like that. "They took me in and I attended the Rakshakari Academy here," he continued. "I was five years old and I began to train."

"At that age?" I couldn't imagine how he must have felt. He nodded.

"My parents were Rakshakari, of course, so when they realized that I had a power they were overjoyed."

"How old were you when you got your power? Were you scared at first?" I tried to stop myself from firing questions at him, but it was too difficult. My dad had this whole other life that I knew nothing about.

"I was seven, so yes, I was terrified the first time I went into someone's dream. I had no idea what was happening." He started to cough and his whole body shook with the effort. I immediately felt guilty. He needed to rest, and here I was pestering him. I picked up a glass of water from the nightstand and held it to his mouth. Slowly he took a few sips and then leaned back against the headboard.

"Daddy, get some rest. We can talk later," I said, stroking his hair. I looked over to my mother and realized that Aruna had left. She must have wanted to give us privacy. My mother was still asleep. My dad began to tell me more.

"So, after the initial shock, I realized I could get people to do things by going into their dreams." He smiled wryly. "It was a good thing that my parents caught on quickly, otherwise things could have gone very wrong. They immediately consulted other oneiric manipulators, who taught me how to control my powers and use them against demons instead of unsuspecting friends and teachers."

I smiled at the thought of my dad getting into trouble as a young boy. It was so crazy that he had this cool power and I had lived with him my whole life without even an inkling.

"When I got older and my power became stronger, I was able to manipulate demons into destroying each other. It didn't work on all demons. Some were more powerful than others and were able to resist me. The more powerful the demon, the more it took out of me. Sometimes it took days for me to recover. I would be weak and vulnerable. Over time, news of my power spread, and by the time I met your mother, there were many in the demon world who wanted me dead."

"Did Mom know who you were when she married you?" I tried to picture her, young and in love with a man who was destined for a higher cause.

"When we first met, I was too afraid to tell her. She sensed something different about me, but it only made her love me more. When I finally told her, she wasn't all that surprised. But then you know what Mom's like. She's always been fascinated by the strangest things."

This was true. My mother was a woman who was open to many ideas, even those that others might dismiss as fantasy. It made so much more sense to me now, why she had chosen to study mythology. As I watched my dad, he seemed to be perking up more and more as he spoke about his past. He was probably relieved to get the secrets off his chest.

"We'd been married for about a year when it happened the first time," he continued.

"What happened?"

"A demon tried to kill your mother. I came home just in time to stop him from tearing her apart. It was a Makra demon. Have you learned about them yet?"

I nodded. Mr. Perkins' lectures were still pretty fresh in my mind. Makra demons were like spiders. They had legs that attached to their victim's bodies before ripping off their limbs. I shuddered to think that my mother had come close to dying at the hands of one of them.

"Anyway, I was able to destroy it, but one thing became very clear to me. I would not continue to put your mother in danger. The thought of losing her was not something I could live with."

Even now the fear was evident on his face. I knew

exactly how he felt. The thought that I had almost lost them both was too much to bear.

"After that I decided I would leave that life behind. I had always wanted to meet my mother's family in Seattle. So my mother made the arrangements and we were on our way there to start a new life. I went to the University of Washington to get my Master's degree. I wanted to teach, but then a couple of years later my father died and we came back to take care of my mother. Soon after that you were born, and since I had left my old life behind, things seemed to be fine. There were no attacks or threats and we were happy."

Until I started having the nightmares. My father didn't actually say the words, but he didn't need to. I knew the events all too well. We sat in silence for a while.

"Why me, Daddy?" I asked, finally giving voice to something I'd been too ashamed to say to anyone until now.

He squeezed my hand and smiled, his eyes crinkling in the corners.

"I don't know, sweetheart. I used to ask myself the same question after I was adopted. I used to wonder why I couldn't just play outside like the other children. I had to learn how to fight and go to school every day with bruises. One day I just couldn't take it anymore. Some kid at school said that my parents were bad people because they beat me. I ran home crying because I was angry at the boy, angry with my parents for adopting me, angry at the world. But when I got home my mom was there and she told me I was a chosen one. That there were only a few people in the world who were worthy of such a destiny."

My eyes had filled up again, this time for the little boy who just wanted to be like everyone else.

"Callie, you too are a chosen one. You too are worthy of this destiny. You will be the one to bring down evil and restore faith in people." He took my hand in his and squeezed it. Then with a sigh he shut his eyes. I raised his hand to my lips and kissed it softly. Then I carefully put it down and stood up. Taking one last look at my sleeping mother, I quietly left the room and went downstairs. Aruna met me on the way and said she would go and watch over my parents while I took a break. I went in to the dining room and saw the others already there. They seemed relieved to see me. I was ravenous and piled my plate high with food. While we ate, Dev announced that we needed to strategize for the next attack. Now that we had vanquished Mahisha's top lieutenants it wouldn't be long before he made an appearance.

"I don't understand why he hasn't tried to kill me himself," I said between mouthfuls of scrambled egg.

"Mahisha suffered grave injuries the last time you...Kali fought against him," Dev said.

"But that was five thousand years ago. Shouldn't he have healed by now?"

"You have to remember that Mahisha received his

boon after a thousand years of penance and piety. After the atrocities he committed, the gods would never grant him anything again."

"He must have found some other way to regain his powers. The only explanation I have for his absence so far is that he is just not strong enough," Shiv said.

"So he will keep sending his minions to do his dirty work until then? And we have no way of knowing where and when that will be."

"At least your parents are back and we have the sword," Nina said.

"Ben is still out there," I said, the familiar guilt gnawing at my insides. I was so happy to have my parents back, but I couldn't bear to think what was happening to Ben or if he was even still alive.

"We'll find him, Callie," Shiv said. I appreciated their attempts to make me feel better, but I knew there was a good chance I might never see Ben again.

After breakfast, we discussed the possible locations of Mahisha and where his people might be holding Ben. I went back upstairs after a while, quite discouraged.

TWENTY-TWO

IT TOOK A few days, but slowly my mom began to regain some color and lucidity. She still didn't talk about what the demons had done to her, and having experienced just a little of it myself, I didn't want to press her for details. Things began to improve after that. She still had a long way to go, because quite often I would catch her staring off into the distance and I knew she was battling the demons in her mind. Nevertheless, she was here and I was grateful for that. My dad was getting better every day. He noticed how Shiv hovered over me, worrying about me, and that was enough for him. They began to spend a lot of time together and I went back to training with Aruna, who was slowly beginning to come out of her shell. A few days later a call came for me. It was Mr. Bhandal, the priest from the Kali temple. Shiv and I had given him our contact information in case he had some more news about my parents' research.

"Mr. Bhandal, this is Callie. How are you?" I said, really curious about this call.

There was silence at the other end. I could hear someone's labored breathing.

"Mr. Bhandal?"

"You must help me...please...they will kill me."

"Who? Mr. Bhandal, who will kill you?" I felt a familiar wave of nausea as my stomach twisted into a knot.

"They want the sword...you have to come here...alone." Then the line went dead.

My first impulse was to go to Shiv, but I caught myself in time. If I told him, there was no way he would let me out of his sight. He would have good reason not to. I knew I would be walking right into a trap. I went over all my options. One was to tell the others and go to the temple, armed and ready for battle. They would see us coming and kill the priest before we even got near. That was unacceptable. Or I could go by myself, save the priest and hopefully take out some of them in the process. I knew I was being overly confident, but I had no other choice. Obviously I was not letting anybody take the sword, so I would have to fight my way out. I sat for a while ruminating about my next step when an idea struck me. I could get the others to stay out of sight while I went in alone, and that way

308

if things went south, I would have backup. Bolstered by what I thought was a great plan, I went to seek out the Rakshakari, who were scattered all over Uncle Suresh's enormous bungalow. I should have talked to Dev or Nina first, because when Shiv heard what I had planned he went ballistic.

"Are you crazy?"

"No, Shiv, I am not crazy. Do you have a better idea?"

"Yes, I do. We all go in together and finish the son of a bitch off."

"Well, that's nice, but you're forgetting one important detail. They'll kill the priest."

That seemed to shut him up for a moment. But only for a moment.

"Okay, so that would be bad. But you know what would be worse?" He paused. He could be so dramatic. "If you got killed. Or taken."

"Are you done?"

He just looked at me.

"I know it's risky. But I am not willing to let one more person get hurt because of me."

Dev and Nina hadn't said anything yet, probably because they were stunned at Shiv's outburst.

"Shiv, calm down." Nina's stern voice had an instant reaction. Shiv sank back into his chair but glared at her defiantly.

"I like Callie's plan," she said.

"I agree," Dev said. "We can't risk them seeing us,

but of course we cannot allow Callie to go there by herself."

After our experiences on the island and then at the warehouse, I was convinced that Mahisha was still hiding out. The question was why.

"I don't think Mahisha will be any danger yet," I said. "If he had the strength he would have tried to finish me off himself instead of sending his people. There's something else going on."

"I'm inclined to agree with you, Callie," Dev said. "My theory is that Mahisha underestimated you, and now that you have the sword he is desperate."

"And that means he will get careless," Nina added.

"Okay, so I will go in there with my sword and the *gada*. I'm assuming he will have his men there to protect him."

"That's very likely," Nina said. "You will have to assess the situation. Your goal is to get the priest out safely and protect the sword."

"That's what he's really after," Dev said. "He thinks you are powerless without it."

"Is he wrong?"

I couldn't imagine what Mahisha would be like when he had his full strength, but if even the trinity couldn't destroy him, then what exactly was I going to do without the sword?

"You must not forget that when he heard about Kali he felt fear," Nina reminded me.

"It's not just the sword, my dear," Dev added.

"Kali was incredibly powerful. When she went into a rage, everyone trembled with fear."

I didn't know what to say. Right now I just wanted to save Mr. Bhandal. I was the reason he was in danger, and I would get him out of it.

"So we know Burke will be with him. Probably a few others as well."

"Yes, and once you've taken out as many as you can, we will come in," Dev said.

"I can take the priest and keep him safe," Aruna said.

"And I'll make sure that Callie's covered." Shiv had finally stopped sulking.

"Okay, so let's go," I said, leading the way to the weapons room.

We geared up quickly and made our way to the temple in two vehicles. The driver of my car stopped by the main entrance while the others stopped a bit behind me, hidden from view by a tea stall. I waited for the driver to leave before going up the steps into the temple. As I entered the inner sanctum, my eyes had to adjust to the darkness. Nobody was there. I started to go toward Mr. Bhandal's office when I heard a groan. I turned to see where it was coming from. I spied the priest propped up against a wall in a corner by the smaller statues. He was alone. My senses heightened, aware that this must be a trap. My pendant was getting warm, but that didn't surprise me. They wouldn't leave him here alone and make it so easy for me. I scanned the interior of the temple, but there was nobody else here. Cautiously, I moved closer to the priest. I wasn't sure if he was conscious, because he wasn't moving. When I reached him and bent down to touch him.

"Mr. Bhandal...it's Callie. I'm here now."

He stirred slightly and opened his eyes slowly. At first he said nothing but tried to focus his eyes on something. They fixed on something behind me. He lifted a hand weakly and pointed.

"You have the sword," he said hoarsely. "You have Kali's sword." His eyes lit up briefly and his hand fell back to his side. I nodded, trying to assess his injuries at the same time, but I couldn't see any bruises. The pendant was really hot now and glowing brightly. Something was very wrong. Then two things happened at once. Mr. Bhandal reached over my shoulder to touch the sword, which was securely strapped to my back. My pendant started to give off sparks. Mr. Bhandal was mouthing something, but before I could figure out what he was trying to say, the sparks grew stronger and Mr. Bhandal's hand jerked back as soon as his fingers made contact with the hilt. I jumped back and froze.

Mr. Bhandal began to melt. Not melt, as in from the heat, but his skin was actually melting off his bones. It was disgusting, and I could do nothing but stare at him in horror. As the skin on his face fell away it revealed a sort of skeleton but with tissue and muscle in places and bare in others. Slowly, he stood up. I gasped in horror as the figure grew taller and taller, until it towered over me. I was no longer looking at the priest but rather some kind of amorphous figure, barely human.

Although most of the face had melted off, the eyeballs were still somehow dangling in their sockets. They were looking directly at me, and I was frozen in terror. My brain was beginning to realize what my eyes refused to believe. Somewhere from the recesses of my mind, a memory surfaced. Mahisha was a shape-shifter. Even in his weakened state he had somehow morphed himself into a likeness of the priest. My pendant was burning the skin in the hollow of my neck, and I unfroze. I stepped back and reached over to draw my sword from its sheath. I raised it high above my head, ready to strike, and just then someone grabbed me from behind and wrestled me to the ground. I looked up at my attacker. It was Burke. His lips were curled in a cruel smile and he produced a dagger. As he lifted his hand above his head, I suddenly felt him being lifted off me. Then I saw Shiv's face. He had Burke by the scruff of his shirt and effortlessly flung him across the floor. The dagger he was planning to kill me with skittered along the concrete.

Shiv held out his hand to help me up. I turned to look at Mahisha, but all I saw was a shrivelled shape propped up against the wall. So that was it. The shape-shifting must have drained him of what little strength he had managed to scavenge over the years. Shiv looked at him in disbelief. My sword had fallen to the ground when Burke had attacked me. I picked it up and paused for a moment. It seemed so anti-climactic. Here was this supremely powerful demon of myth, and he didn't even have the strength to pose a danger anymore. I looked behind me. The others had followed Shiv into the temple, and they all watched now as I raised my sword, ready to finish off Mahisha once and for all.

"Move a finger and I will kill him." The voice rang out of the darkness of the temple and echoed off its walls. We all turned around. Burke stood by the statues, his arm around someone's neck. I squinted in the dim light and gasped. Burke was holding his dagger at Ben's throat.

"No...don't hurt him," I shouted, fear grabbing my insides.

"His life in exchange for my master's." I could see the insanity in Burke's eyes. He pushed the blade of his dagger against Ben's throat, and a few drops of blood slowly trickled down. Still I hesitated. I knew I would hate myself for this later. I had an opportunity to vanquish evil today. It would prevent boundless suffering; so many innocent people would live if I killed Mahisha now. But how would I live with myself? Knowing that I had sacrificed Ben. I looked at each of my friends' faces. There was nothing there to help me. It had to be my choice. Deep inside I knew I'd already decided, but I had to be sure.

I turned back to face Mahisha, who was slumped

motionlessly against the wall, his breath coming out as raspy grunts. I raised my sword...and let it fall to my side. Burke smiled in his condescending way, knowing he had won. It was almost enough to make me change my mind as he dragged Ben over to me, the blade of his dagger still precariously close to slicing the jugular vein. I held my breath as he knelt down beside his master, not letting go of Ben. He helped Mahisha up and mumbled something as he waved his hand over a spot on the wall. Suddenly the wall shimmered, as if it had liquefied. I looked on in shock as Burke released Ben, picked up Mahisha and walked right through the undulating wall. I ran to Ben, who had just crumpled to the concrete floor. He was barely conscious. I knelt down beside him and was about to help him up when Dev and Nina both cried out in unison.

"Shiv...no."

I looked back just in time to see Shiv run through the wall behind Burke and Mahisha. I jumped and ran after him, screaming the whole time, not recognizing my own voice. I was there in seconds, but it was too late. I hit a solid wall, hard, and fell to the ground. I clawed at the brick, unwilling to believe what had just happened. Nina and Dev were beside me, pushing and prodding, trying desperately to find an opening. But it was gone. The portal or whatever it was had disappeared, and we had no way of knowing how to get it to open up again.

My fingers were bloody and my face was streaked

with tears, and finally I collapsed on the floor. Nina was sobbing in Dev's arms. Aruna tried to comfort them, but there was nothing she could say or do. For any of us. Shiv was gone. I had done this. I had made a choice, and now we were all going to pay for it.

After there were no more tears left, I stood up and went to Ben. He was beginning to stir. Dev and I wordlessly helped to carry him out of the temple to the car. Aruna held Nina as she sobbed uncontrollably the entire drive home. I had no words, no thoughts. I felt like an empty shell. I knew the pain and guilt would come, and it would haunt me, but right now I felt nothing. I would take Ben home and help him recover from whatever hell he'd been through. I would take care of my parents until they were better too.

And I would find Shiv. I would do whatever it took to bring him back home. One thing I knew for certain: this time there would be no mercy for Mahisha. Nothing would sway me. I would destroy him, even if it killed me.

EPILOGUE

THE KING SAT on his throne. A servant stood at his side, ready for his next command. He trembled slightly for fear that the king's wrath would rain down upon him as it had on countless other servants who had earned his displeasure.

"Master," a voice came from the entrance to the hall. "I have brought him." As the servant watched, two men came to stand in front of the king. The one who spoke was tall, bespectacled and wore a suit. The other man was gaunt, his face covered in bruises.

The king spoke. His voice was raspy and weak, yet the servant knew that it belied the king's powers.

"Have you done as I asked?"

The gaunt man spoke, his voice barely more than a whisper.

"It is not easy, Master. She is becoming more powerful every day."

The king was not pleased. Rage contorted his face.

"Have you forgotten what I have done for you, ingrate?" His shout echoed through the hall, making the servant tremble once again.

The gaunt man bowed his head.

"I have not forgotten, Master. But I have to be careful not to arouse suspicion. Otherwise it is all over."

The king grunted. He appeared to be lost in his thoughts.

Finally he looked up.

"What is it you call yourself these days…Paul?"

The gaunt man nodded.

"Well Paul…, my patience is not endless. If you do not return soon with better news… I do not have to remind you of the consequences do I?"

"No Master." The tall one grabbed the gaunt man by the elbow and took him away. As they passed the servant, he overheard them.

"You know I'll be watching her. Tread carefully, Paul." The gaunt man said nothing as he was led away.

The servant waited with trepidation. The last time the King had been displeased, he had incinerated two of his servants just by a flick of his fingers. Now he seemed to have forgotten that he was not alone. The servant held his breath, wondering if it might be his last and waited. Then the king stood up. He was not a large man and of late he had been weak. The servant watched in horror as the skin melted away from the king's bones. Then the bones began to break and reform until an enormous creature stood where the king had been. It had the head of a bull and the torso of a man. An involuntary gasp escaped the servant's mouth just as the transformation was finishing. The demon turned its piercing gaze upon him and the last thing the servant saw was fire shooting out of its eyes.

Enjoyed the Book?

If you'd like to help an indie author, please spread the word by rating and reviewing it on Amazon.com and/or Goodreads.

Please visit realmofthegoddess.wordpress.com if you want to:

- Find out more about Callie, Shiv and the other Rakshakari
- Learn about the Hindu gods and goddesses
- Get the recipes for Callie's favorite food.

You can also follow me on:

Twitter @Sabina_Writer

Facebook: https://www.facebook.com/RealmGoddess

ABOUT THE AUTHOR

 **Sabina Khan** is the author of Realm of the Goddess, the first in a series of YA Paranormal Fantasy books based on the gods and goddesses of India. She is an educational consultant and a karaoke enthusiast.

After living in Germany, Bangladesh, Macao, Illinois and Texas, she has finally settled down in beautiful British Columbia, Canada, with her husband and three daughters, one of whom is a fur baby.

She is passionate about the empowerment of girls and women, hoping to inspire them with the strong female characters in her novel.

Follow her on:
Twitter: @Sabina_Writer

Facebook: https://www.facebook.com/RealmGoddess

Find out more at
http://realmofthegoddess.wordpress.com/